D1084749

Kipling's Imperial Boy

Kipling's Imperial Boy

Adolescence and Cultural Hybridity

Don Randall

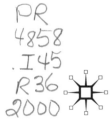

First published 2000 by
PALGRAVE
Houndmills, Basingstoke, Hampshire RG21 6XS and
175 Fifth Avenue, New York, N.Y. 10010
Companies and representatives throughout the world

PALGRAVE is the new global academic imprint of
St. Martin's Press LLC Scholarly and Reference Division and
Palgrave Publishers Ltd (formerly Macmillan Press Ltd).

ISBN 0–333–76104–9

This book is printed on paper suitable for recycling and
made from fully managed and sustained forest sources.

A catalogue record for this book is available
from the British Library.

Library of Congress Cataloging-in-Publication Data
Randall, Don, 1956–
    Kipling's imperial boy : adolescence and cultural hybridity / Don Randall.
        p. cm.
    Includes bibliographical references (p.) and index.
    ISBN 0–333–76104–9
    1. Kipling, Rudyard, 1865–1936—Views on imperialism. 2. Kipling,
Rudyard, 1865–1936—Characters—Boys. 3. Political fiction, English–
–History and criticism. 4. Multiculturalism in literature. 5. Imperialism in
literature. 6. Adolescence in literature. 7. Colonies in literature. 8. India–
–In literature. 9. Boys in literature. I. Title.

    PR4858.I45 R36 2000
    828'.809—dc21
                                                                00–041494

10   9   8   7   6   5   4   3   2   1
09 08 07 06 05 04 03 02 01 00

Printed and bound in Great Britain by
Antony Rowe Ltd, Chippenham, Wiltshire

Contents

Acknowledgements

I wish to thank and acknowledge the University of Texas Press for permission to use 'Post-Mutiny Allegories of Empire in Rudyard Kipling's *Jungle Books*' (*Texas Studies in Literature and Language* Vol. 40, No. 1, Spring 1998) as the basis for my Chapter 2. I also appreciate the permissions received from two other scholarly journals: *Victorian Review* (Vol. 24, No. 2, Winter 1998) published an earlier, shorter version of Chapter 3; an earlier version of Chapter 5 was published in *ARIEL* (Vol. 27, No. 3, July 1996). I extend the warmest thanks to the Calgary Institute for the Humanities, University of Calgary, for the postdoctoral fellowship that allowed me to develop my work for publication. Queen's University, particularly the Department of English, and the Social Sciences and Humanities Research Council of Canada have generously supported the finishing of my manuscript. For their indispensable contributions to the development this book, I thank Jo-Ann Wallace, Stephen Slemon, Patrick Brantlinger, and Juliet McMaster.

Introduction

Oh, East is East, and West is West, and never the twain shall
    meet,
Till Earth and Sky stand presently at God's great Judgment Seat;
But there is neither East nor West, Border, nor Breed, nor Birth,
When two strong men stand face to face, though they come from
    the ends of the earth!

> – Rudyard Kipling, 'The Ballad of East and West',
> *The Complete Verse* (lines 1–4)

All good people agree,
    And all good people say,
All nice people like Us, are We
    And every one else is They:
But if you cross over the sea,
    Instead of over the way,
You may end by (think of it!) looking on We
    As only a sort of They!

> – Kipling, 'We and They', *The Complete Verse* (lines 33–40)

I begin with these verse selections because they raise in a preliminary, germinal way the kinds of issues this book will explore. 'The
Ballad of East and West' begins and ends with the lines I cite,
presenting what has become, like many of Kipling's utterances, an
imperial proverb. I quote more at length than is usual to demonstrate that the assertion of irreconcilable difference dividing East
and West is immediately qualified: forthright encounter between
men, between 'two strong men', can transcend sociocultural difference. It is not enough, however, to note that Kipling here asserts
again his well-known faith in the enabling virtue of fraternal or
homosocial bonds.[1] One of the poem's strong men is, in fact, more
readily recognizable as a youth or 'boy'; he is the 'colonel's son' (9),
evidently a young subaltern in his father's service. This 'son'
receives leading information from another, 'the son of the

Ressaldar' (11), then deals successfully with the rebel colonial Kamal and becomes his 'Brother-in-Blood' (84). Finally, as pledge of reconciliation and future good faith, young officer recruits Kamal's son to the imperial Guides. Youth, as much as vigorous masculinity, is thus a key element in the poem's resolution. The differences between East and West, between the Colonel and Kamal, are reconcilable, but only by the intervention of the 'sons'. The sons of empire evidently have a special capacity for cross-cultural negotiation, which their fathers seem to lack.

In the lesser known 'We and They', a boy speaker situates himself within a familial context of Father, Mother, Sister, and Auntie, then proceeds with childish candor to muse upon questions of 'We and They' – upon questions of group identity, otherness and cross-cultural perspective. In the first four stanzas of this five-stanza piece, the speaker gains an increasing awareness of the tenuousness of group identifications; in the final stanza, cited above, he acknowledges with fear and wonder – 'think of it!' – the estrangement from one's primary group that cross-cultural encounter may provoke. Having arrived at the crucial recognition that 'They look upon We/ As only a sort of They!' (7–8), the speaker goes on to contrast the cultural habits and practices of 'We' and 'They', ending each of the poem's three middle stanzas with a perspective of 'They' upon 'We': 'We' appears, in the eye of the cultural other, 'simply disgusting' (16), then 'utterly ignorant' (24), and finally 'quite impossible' (32). Here again, as in 'The Ballad', the youthful male has a special gift, an insightfulness, but now it unsettles rather than resolves: the young officer displays practical resource and understanding, reconciling opposed groups and refashioning imperial conflict as alliance; the speaker of 'We and They' calls into question not simply group identifications but the foundational categories allowing for the articulation of cultural difference – the self and the other, the home and the world. The boy lacks the adult's easy assurance with respect to cultural difference and the tacit priorities and hierarchies that mark its encoding. His speech acknowledges that there is a *discourse* of distinctions applying to relations between 'We' and 'They'; there is a certain assembly of things that Father, Mother, Sister, Auntie, and all other 'good' and 'nice' people 'agree' upon and '*say*'. But the speaker also recognizes, at least by the end of the poem, that this discourse is susceptible to destabilizing inscriptions of vision and experience. Cross-cultural encounter provokes transformations, if not in what the 'good' and 'nice' adults say, at least in the identification of the insightful boy. The child's view ultimately undermines the perspective of the self-same or, more precisely, reveals that the notion of self-same is merely an effect of position and perspective: if one goes 'over the sea' rather than simply 'over the way', one's own 'We' may come to appear as 'only a sort of They'.

Seeking to explore more fully the linkings of youth, masculinity, and empire, *Kipling's Imperial Boy* establishes adolescent protagonists of Kipling's imperial fictions as objects of study. It examines them as literary figures whose fictional deployments articulate a Eurocentric and imperial world-view. The book also argues, however, that these imperial boys represent sites of contingency, subject positions in between opposed categories, in between formations of the subject encoded as 'European, imperial' and 'non-European, colonial'. Kipling's boy-protagonists mediate and stage the relationship between 'colonizer' and 'colonized', yet intervene in such a way as to unsettle this same binary opposition in the very moment of its articulation. Focusing specifically upon *The Jungle Books* (1894–95), *Stalky & Co.* (1899), and *Kim* (1901), my examination of the place and function of the imperial boy shows how this figure engages with, consolidates and yet calls into question, what Jenny Sharpe has called 'a Western epistemology of the subject' (*Allegories* 15).

Critical and theoretical orientations: hybridity and masculine adolescence

In *Colonial Desire*, Robert Young emphasizes that the notion of the human 'hybrid' is not new but rather an invention of nineteenth-century debate on race and race relations. He demonstrates that hybridity originally named 'a physiological phenomenon', a character of bodies and bloodlines, but that it has been 'reactivated' in the twentieth century 'to describe a cultural one' (6). Contemporary theory of the hybrid must acknowledge, in Young's view, its historical legacy, its links with the nineteenth century's vast multidimensional assembly of perspectives and controversies – concerning the relation of species and race, 'monogenesis' and 'polygenesis', 'miscegenation' and 'amalgamation', 'degeneration' or 'permanence' or 'reversion' of type, interracial repulsions and attractions, 'differing degrees of fertility', 'proximate' and 'distant' races (9–16). Young does not aim, however, to dispense with theory of hybridity by providing it with a compromised history. Historicizing the idea of hybridity and locating its genesis in nineteenth-century race theory allows him to extend Homi Bhabha's fundamentally discursive theory of hybridity and to demonstrate that racialist conceptions of the hybrid ineluctably turn upon questions of sexuality, of sexual contact and productivity. Race theories, once ordered around racial hybridization, become 'covert theories of desire' (9). But if nineteenth-century discourse of the hybrid makes interracial desire an issue, it also, still more obviously and inevitably, obliges its speakers to focus upon progeneration, upon hybrid progeny. This discourse is a way of pondering, anxiously or desirously, humanity's future and, more specifically, the futurity of nations. It asks: who are tomorrow's children? what will be the shape and character of future generations? It foresees a fearful degeneration into 'raceless chaos' (17–19) or, more optimistically, pledges a faith in progress, through 'racial amalgamation', toward a more viable heterogeneity (4, 17).

Racialist representations of the hybrid thus conceal not only a discourse of desire but also an allegory of cultural exchange. Indeed, the envisioning of hybridization exclusively in relation to race is a way of foreclosing upon the more troubled question of productive, transformative contact between cultures. It substitutes a production of bodies for a genealogy of modern cultures, provides a metonymic physiology for the transformation of codes and values that attach to the understandings of the 'subject' and the 'citizen'. Hybridity impinges upon and perturbs notions of culture and national identity, notably the idea of 'Englishness'. 'In the nineteenth century', writes Young, 'the very notion of a fixed English identity was doubtless a product of, and reaction to, the rapid change and transformation of both metropolitan and colonial societies' (3–4). 'Englishness' arose, in other words, 'to counter schisms, friction and dissent' bred by British imperial expansion (4); it is a conception of national, cultural identity that is always-already 'riven by its own alterity' (xii). And, of course, while certain nineteenth-century voices asserted the purity of English stock, others, such as Herbert

Spencer, touted the English as an example of a successful hybrid race (17).

Although Young's analysis of the genealogy of 'Englishness' allows readers to discern the ways in which hybridity can function as a key concept in the practice of postcolonial cultural critique, the focus of his argument is somewhat narrow. Gayati Spivak's 'Can the Subaltern Speak?' opens the possibility of a more broad-based account of 'Englishness', by considering the foundational concepts and categories that structure what she designates as the Western episteme. Spivak calls into question the constitution of 'Europe' as the 'Subject' of modern international and intercultural relations. Her core argument is that 'Europe' or 'the West' emerges within the space of its own cultural production as the unique, self-constituted and self-sustaining 'Subject' of the modern global community. 'Europe' comes to be understood as the agent of global history, the source of international initiatives.[2] Like Young's 'Englishness', Spivak's 'Europe' functions conceptually as an empowered cultural norm. Her 'Subject of Europe' institutes a leveling of cultural differences, their reduction to a singular difference in relation to the defining instance of 'Europe'; all non-European cultural communities are subsumed, despite their heterogeneity and diversity, as 'the Other of Europe as Self' (281). But 'Europe' remains the self-same, unmarked by its Other. Although 'Europe' shapes and informs its surrounding world, it is not reciprocally shaped and informed by that world. In this asymmetrical relation, 'the European Subject ... seeks to produce an Other that would consolidate an inside, its own subject status' (293); the European Subject thus 'presides by disavowal' (292).

In offering this epistemic critique, Spivak presents a means of moving beyond a limited understanding of modern imperialism as the manifestation of a unilateral, unidirectional project, as the process of European initiatives of violent intervention, domination, and exploitation – the process of 'the West' acting upon 'the Rest'. Her work also provides for a clearer understanding of the concept of 'Englishness', the reasons it develops and the shape it takes. Spivak's analysis is supported by her awareness that imperialism's history involves *cultural confrontations* which test and transform the nature of *both* the colonized and the colonizing cultures. 'East' and 'West' do meet, after all. The colonial 'margin' impinges upon the imperial 'metropolis'; 'Europe' is shaped in turn by the colonies it shapes. Indeed, it is precisely this fact of reciprocal transformation that is disavowed in the constitution of the sovereign 'Subject of the West' and its colonial Other. Spivak thus provides a theoretical groundwork for new initiatives of decolonizing cultural critique, first by focusing attention upon the epistemic binary opposition of self-sovereign Western Subject and subordinate Other, subsequently by emphasizing this paradigm's highly contingent formation in and by the modern European imperial project.

The concept of hybridity functions, then, as a tool that helps me measure and evaluate the impact of cross-cultural encounter within imperial representation. It provides a way of addressing what happens in the imperial 'contact zone', that space of encounter where, in Mary Louise Pratt's words, 'peoples geographically and historically separated come into contact with each other and establish on-going relations' (6). 'Transculturation', for Pratt, names the intense, typically agonistic process by which interacting cultures (and the interacting subjects of these cultures) influence and transform each other. One may also describe such a process as 'hybridization', the term Homi Bhabha uses in what has become the most influential body of work on hybridity and imperial representation. A sense of the cultural contingencies of the modern world-order clearly informs Bhabha's theorizing of the ambivalence of the discourse of imperialism. Although he discusses mimicry as an effect of this ambivalence, this splitting within the enunciation of colonial authority, his thinking is more thoroughly organized and discovers broader possibilities of critical application in relation to cultural hybridity and hybridization. Implicitly recalling Foucault, for whom power is more notably productive than repressive, Bhabha directs attention to imperial power's 'production of hybridization' as its most crucial effect. This production, he argues, is what manifests 'ambivalence' at the core of discourses of imperial authority. For this very reason a critical focus on effects of hybridization 'enables a form of subversion' and 'turns the discursive conditions of dominance into the grounds of intervention' (112). Articulations of cultural liminality or hybridity thus can enable the critic of imperial forms of culture to challenge 'colonial representation and individuation' (114), to examine and question both the discourse of imperialism and its formation of subjects.

My work strives, however, not simply to foreground the importance of hybridity as a concept but to forge a critical link between hybridity and adolescence. I want to show that, within the discourse of imperialism, conceptions of adolescence and hybridity (and responses to them) develop interdependently. As I noted earlier, nineteenth-century representations of hybridity necessarily focus on progeny, on the products of interracial unions; the hybrid, to state the case more pointedly, is first and foremost a certain kind of *child*. Racialized and sexualized hybridity thus recalls concurrently elaborated social and discursive formations of sexuality and childhood. Foucault, in the first volume of his *History of Sexuality*, highlights the nineteenth-century 'pedagogization of children's sex', observing that the child's desires and pleasures become fraught with 'individual and collective dangers' (104). The new scrutiny brought to bear upon children and their sexuality, by the state, the school, and the family, orders itself as 'a campaign for the health of the race' (146). As Ann Stoler observes, 'the strength of the nation' and more particularly of the imperial nation-state are at stake in the disciplining and education of children (143). Indeed, Stoler insists that Foucault's analysis of the disciplining of sexuality and childhood can only be sustained in close relation with European imperial projects; 'it is imperial-wide discourses that linked children's health programs to racial survival, tied increased campaigns for domestic hygiene to colonial expansion, [and] made child-rearing an imperial and class duty' (35). She also observes that 'métissage' (or hybridization) is a particularly nettled issue with respect to the child's representation within the discourses of empire: even as the child-product of white endogamy and European forms of acculturation stands as the reassuring, cherished emblem of imperial progress, so the racially or culturally hybrid child is taken to manifest the liabilities of cross-cultural contact and the shortcomings of colonial rule (46).[3] The child becomes a focal representative of the imperial enterprise, a precarious investment in the national and imperial future, an experiment that may go well or ill.

But if European childhood emerges in the nineteenth century as a site of intensified social anxieties and aspirations, adolescence does so still more specifically. Clearly enmeshed in what Foucault calls 'a new *specification of individuals*' (*History* 42–3), adolescence, the newly emphasized in-between stage of life, bears the main burden of childhood's envisioning as a time of great promise but also of uncertainty and peril. Although contemporary historians of childhood debate the precise moment of emergence of the modern idea of 'adolescence', and its distinction from the early modern 'youth', there is general agreement that the idea's institutionalization and the term's arrival as popular, current usage occur in the last decades of the nineteenth century (see Demos and Demos 632; Gillis 95, 139; Springhall 9, 14, 26). However, as Richard Phillips points out in *Mapping Men and Empire*, notions of masculine adolescence and its cultural importance are already in evidence by the mid-century. Not yet fully defined as a physiologically and psychologically specific time of life, this earlier adolescence is a less clearly delineated state of being: R. M. Ballantyne, in 1856, writes of 'that ambiguous condition that precedes early manhood' (qtd. in Phillips 56); Arnold of Rugby and Sewell of Radley College both distinguish the boy from the child and the man, the former more anxious than admiring in his recognition, the latter quite pridefully claiming this 'boy' as an English phenomenon lamentably absent in America (Musgrove 55–6).

Urbanization and industrialization have been deservedly emphasized as factors in the social production of modern adolescence (see Demos and Demos 636–8; Gillis 37ff.). First among the middle classes, one can observe the deferral of career decisions and the felt need for more extensive and exacting education that would prepare young men for the complex demands of adult social participation. The prolongation and gradual dissemination of secondary schooling, along with the increasing power and prominence of the reformed public schools, contribute significantly to the segregation and specification of adolescence. However, the powerful influence of imperial projects upon the particular forms of adolescence – how it is understood and represented – should not be underestimated. Mid-century adolescence is distinctly masculine and middle-class.[4] It is already a time of testing and experiment, a liminal time, which, as Phillips stresses, signals unmistakably its affinity with the 'liminal spaces' of imperial expansion (56ff.). Joseph Bristow, however, stresses that the late nineteenth-century burgeoning of Empire-related literature for boys – school and adventure novels, and also the ever more numerous and broadly circulated boys' papers – conferred new prestige upon boyhood and secured it as a pleasure-yielding site for imperial aspirations. Both in fiction and in fact, the late nineteenth-century public schools reveal themselves as institutions for the training of future imperial administrators (see Quigly). Boy-oriented youth movements advance steadily onto the stage of British public life during the same period, first with the various brigades, most notably the Boys' Brigade. Initially, these movements arise as a countering response to fears of increasing juvenile delinquency and the loss of promising youths to poorly paid, low-prestige forms of 'boy labor' (Springhall 26). However, the strongly militaristic and nationalistic mobilization of boys discovers its imperial mission more clearly with the crisis of the Anglo-Boer war at the century's end, which focused national attention on the poor physical condition of many of the British recruits and cast doubt upon Britain's military strength and competency. The immensely successful Scouting movement, inaugurated by the veteran hero of Mafeking and informed by ideological commitments to 'imperialism, masculine power, and racial superiority' (Macdonald 205), confirms and effectively codifies British boyhood as a foregrounded concern in negotiations of national identity and imperial status.

Although the history of modern adolescence is, as I have noted, a matter of scholarly debate, most writers concur in stressing the decisive impact of the work of American psychologist G. Stanley Hall. Hall's two-volume *Adolescence* of 1904 collects and consolidates emerging conceptions of adolescence, conferring upon them the authoritative seal of the human sciences and giving the figure of the adolescent 'a pivotal place in sociological, psychological, and literary thought' (Spacks 230); the work represents not so much a forwarding of new, groundbreaking ideas, but rather a 'culmination of views' (Springhall 29), a reshaping of 'popular belief' (Demos and Demos 636). Fundamental to Hall's thinking is the notion that individual ontogeny recapitulates phylogeny; his 'individual' is a brief and rapid 'repetition of racial history', and therefore 'the child and the race are each keys to the other' (1: viii). Like Rousseau in Book IV of *Émile* (1762), Hall argues the importance of adolescence as a time of experimentation and training. Although an ardent admirer of youthful intensity, he is responsible for establishing, more definitively and categorically, the idea of adolescence as a time of 'storm and stress', of physical and psychological turbulence, indeterminacy, and dangerous unpredictability. Adolescence is 'not only the revealer of the past but of the future, for it is dimly prophetic of that best part of history which is not yet written because it has not yet transpired' (2: 448). Yet, as Hall makes clear right at the outset, the study of this crucial phase of life also allows one to 'diagnose and measure arrest and retardation in the individual and the race' (1: viii).

Hall's writing attests to a more inclusive conception of adolescence: at least theoretically, it is transcultural and no longer gender- or class-specific. Yet there are distinct forms or experiences of adolescence. Hall effectively elides the importance of feminine adolescence, giving it much less attention and eventually submitting women to a subordinating idealization, representing them as perpetual adolescents who exhibit throughout life the virtues (and limitations) of the youthful phase (2: 624). He does not hesitate, moreover, to offer extensive reflections upon 'ethnic psychology' and the 'adolescent races', which he associates directly with the 'colonies and dependencies' under the dominion of 'a few civilized nations'. His basic premise, which is in keeping with popular ideas of his time, can be briefly rendered: 'Most savages in most respects are children, or, because of sexual maturity, more properly, adolescents of adult size' (2: 648–9). 'Race', for Hall, is not then merely a matter of 'the human race'; it entails, as with gender, a making of distinctions. Only for the male of European stock is adolescence a truly crucial time of trial and transition. If the male European adolescent carries the possibilities of the 'superanthropoid', of humanity's potentially grander future, he is also the figure in which one may read the signs of racial decline:

> The child from nine to twelve is well adjusted to his environment and proportionately developed; he represents probably an old and relatively perfected stage of race-maturity. ... At dawning adolescence this old unity and harmony with nature is broken up; the child is driven from his paradise and must enter upon a long viaticum of ascent, must conquer a higher kingdom of man for himself, break out a new sphere and evolve a more modern story to his psycho-physical nature. Because his environment is to be far more complex, the combinations are less

stable, the ascent less easy and secure; there is more danger that the youth in his upward progress ... will backslide in one or several of the many ways possible. New dangers threaten on all sides. It is the most critical stage of life, because failure to mount almost always means retrogression, degeneracy, or fall. (2: 71–72)

In discussing the general nature of adolescence, Hall evokes heady themes of racial progress and conquest, or again, degeneration, loss of vitality and power. Notwithstanding the transcultural, universalizing thrust of his writing, he clearly adheres to a fundamentally Western perspective and manifests his participation in the concerns of an imperial era. His 'adolescence' is a site of discourse where Western civilization meets savagery, where European nations discover their relation to more 'primitive' societies; it speaks of the past and future of nations and also, more generally, of the origins and destiny of the contemporary world order.

In thus highlighting the cultural significance of adolescence, particularly male adolescence, at the turn of the last century, I do not aim to set adolescence apart from more general envisionings of childhood, but rather to suggest that the newly elaborated time of life concentrates and intensifies the representation of certain key themes of childhood, most notably liminality. The adolescent is inscribed between times, already manifesting some of the power and purpose associated with the adult but still prey – indeed, all the more acutely – to childhood's uncertainties and susceptibilities. Like the child, the adolescent is a site of investment for the nation and the 'race' but, as Hall clearly suggests, a more thoroughly legible figure, one that now reveals the formerly obscure or occulted contents of the childish raw material. Hall's contribution also reveals that modern adolescence establishes links with ethnology and race theory – with the systems of ideas that circulate in discourses of the human hybrid. Modern conceptions of hybridity and of adolescence manifest a notable affinity: both are marked by uncertain status, by the instability and unpredictability of the in-between; both, moreover, are elaborated in the course of the nineteenth century and most intensely in its later decades. In both instances the dialectics of fear and desire, of forecast national and racial progress or degeneration, are powerfully evident. My purpose in this study is to focus attention on the imperial boy and to show

how this figure, as represented in Rudyard Kipling's fictions, brings ordering conceptions of masculine adolescence and hybridity together and makes them work interdependently in the formation of a distinct discourse of British imperialism. Both imperial boyhood and hybridity have been posed previously as topics for colonial cultural studies, but the possible links between them have not yet been explored. My work on one hand attests to the uniqueness of Kipling's contribution to British imperial culture; on the other hand it consistently stresses and elucidates his intense participation in that culture's more generalized evolution and transformation. It proposes the imperial boy as a principal site of sociocultural aspirations and anxieties, where envisionings of masculine adolescence and cultural hybridization are forged together as key aspects of Western imperial modernity.

The case for Kipling

The choice of Kipling as the focus of my study is variously motivated. Considering the broadest issues first, I would say that Kipling commands attention as a representative voice – arguably, *the* representative voice – of a period E. J. Hobsbawm characterizes as the 'Age of Empire', a period he considers crucial not only to the structuring of the modern world but also to 'the formation of modern thought' (4). Between 1875 and 1914, the Western imperial nations partitioned virtually the entire non-European world, restructuring it as an assembly of territories under formal or informal rule. The later nineteenth century renders more starkly the dividing lines between domination and dependence, thus consolidating the economic and political underpinnings of the modern epistemic paradigm Spivak describes. Hobsbawm emphasizes, moreover, the special importance of the 1890s, the decade of Kipling's spectacular 'entrance' upon the British cultural scene, in the formation of the new world-view:

> [T]here is no doubt that the word 'imperialism' first became part of the political and journalistic vocabulary during the 1890s in the course of arguments about colonial conquest. ... The word ... first entered politics in Britain in the 1870s, and was still regarded as a neologism at the end of that decade. It exploded

into general use in the 1890s. By 1900, when the intellectuals began to write books about it, it was, to quote one of the first of them, the British Liberal J. A. Hobson, 'on everybody's lips ... and used to denote the most powerful movement in the current politics of the western world.' In short, it was a novel term devised to describe a novel phenomenon. This evident fact is enough to dismiss one of the many schools in the tense and highly charged ideological debate about 'imperialism', namely the one which argues that it was nothing new. ... It was, at any rate, felt to be new and was discussed as a novelty. (60)

What most specifies the 1890s, and constitutes that decade's principal bequest to subsequent ones, is a generalized and intensified, emotionally and politically charged consciousness of a newly named 'imperialism'. Rudyard Kipling did much to forge, foster, and define this consciousness. As the British public – in popular, political, intellectual, and cultural circles – became more acutely and more generally aware of Britain's status as a pre-eminent imperial power, as the British Empire came to be understood in emotive and evocative terms, Kipling's reputation and popularity grew accordingly. For Benita Parry, Kipling is instrumental in the elaboration 'of England's mysterious imperialist identity and destiny' and in 'the projection of the white race as the natural rulers of a global space created and divided by imperialism' (61–2). In his work, empire becomes vividly, elaborately, intimately meaningful – a vast mirror in which metropolitan Britain, triumphantly and at times anxiously, learns to measure itself.

Notwithstanding Kipling's undeniable role as an imperial standard-bearer, the thorough evaluation of his 'representativeness' requires a sensitive appreciation of nuances. As Zohreh T. Sullivan asserts in *Narratives of Empire*, this quintessential imperial author is also 'the quintessentially divided imperial subject' (6), whose writing manifests 'the competing forces of imperial representation and domination' and 'gives voice to the full fragmentation of the colonizer's many subject positions and ambivalences' (9, 11). Kipling, then, is representative in the fullest sense: his work stages the professed hopes and disavowed fears, the obstreperous confidence and the more muted misgivings; it registers the various, often disparate and divided discourses of late nineteenth-century British imperialism. This dividedness no doubt has much to do with the fact that Kipling's work foregrounds one of the most enduring and important cultural confrontations in the history of the European empires, the confrontation between imperial Britain and India. In part through Kipling's mediation, the vicissitudes of British–Indian colonial confrontation are made to exemplify the generalized and irresolvable opposition of 'East' and 'West'. At the same time, however, Kipling registers this confrontation's transformative impact upon British thought and imagination. He provides the imaginative framework that confirms India as the core concern in the making and maintaining of Britain's status as an imperial power; he confirms, that is to say, India's importance as a key constituent of British imperial identity.[5]

Kipling's understanding of Anglo-Indian relations, one must recall at the outset, was formed after 'the Mutiny', within what I will characterize as a post-Mutiny context. The Indian rebellion of 1857 began as a multi-sited mutiny of Indian soldiers, but it became in its fuller development something much more akin to a popularly sustained, national insurrection against British rule. The Mutiny came to function as the signal event in what Eric Stokes calls an imperial 'crisis of consolidation' (*Peasant* 1), what Jenny Sharpe describes as 'a crisis of colonial authority' ('Unspeakable' 29), which provoked in turn a transformation of the attitudes and practices informing the British Raj. As Lewis Wurgaft characterizes the change, the British began to conceive of 'the gap' standing between European and Subcontinental cultures

> in absolute moral and racial terms, rather than as an aspect of intellectual or cultural progress. ... The meeting point between British and native culture had vanished. ... [T]he Anglo-Indian community became increasingly defensive, and increasingly isolated from the realities of Indian social and political life. (10–11)

Post-Mutiny isolationism takes shape as a project of detached domination: power is exercised at a certain distance, in the absence of social engagement and involvement; colonial management becomes increasingly a matter of 'scientific' knowledge-accumulation and disciplined administrative application. Positing and promulgating a social, cultural, and psychic distance separating the Briton from the menacing, alien Indian, British power becomes more watchful, more insular. Responding to the perceived threat of Indian resistance and rebellion, which the mid-century uprisings inscribed indelibly upon imperial consciousness, British imperial management exaggerates its stance of aloof authority. Summarizing the case, Edward Said writes, 'the Mutiny [is] the great symbolic event by which the two sides, Indian and British, achieved their full and conscious opposition to each other. ... The Mutiny, in short, reinforced the difference between the colonizer and the colonized' (*Culture* 147). What needs, however, to be stressed – at least in an evaluation of Kipling's understanding of British–Indian relations – is the defining impact of this 'symbolic event' upon the British: the Mutiny provided the organizing referent for a noteworthy change in the British disposition, a change that manifested itself, most notably, in the need to understand and represent British–Indian encounter in terms of opposition and difference and in this way to reassert the authority the rebellion had put into question. Kipling's work responds to the drive to assert the legitimacy of British hegemonic claims, to represent the meaning of the imperial mission in the face of contestation. Wurgaft rightly observes that Kipling forges 'a symbolic code' through which an imperial project in crisis could rediscover and redefine the sense and justification of its endeavors; 'Kipling's India' is thus not only a mythic 'construct' but also 'a compelling reality' of British imperial history (xx). Yet, both as construct and in its historical materiality and agency, Kipling's representation of British India registers and is necessarily informed by the crisis and contradiction it seeks to resolve. His texts are fraught with internal tensions, vacillations, ambivalences, which signal their pertinence as sites for a postcolonial critique of imperial ideology and its discourse.[6]

To read the complex ambivalencies of Kipling's fictions as manifestations of an imperial 'crisis of consolidation' is, however, to consider only half his 'story'. Also at issue in the analysis of Kipling's work are effects of cultural and subjective hybridization. In the process of cultural confrontation, difference and opposition must be understood not as static and absolute but rather as active, transformative forces. As S. P. Mohanty emphasizes, two cultures engaged in prolonged and intense, agonistic interaction 'can be seen as implicating and potentially redefining one another' ('Kipling's Children' 38). Reconsidered from this perspective, the conception of a 'gap' between the two cultures, between the subjects of the two cultures, reveals itself as an anxious ideological reaction against the fact of mutual 'implicatedness' and reciprocal redefinition. The 'gap', in various instances of its articulation, may mark the place of a threshold under stress, a threshold that has become, or is becoming, uncertain.[7] In the confrontation of cultures, the quest to find a 'pure' site of subjectivity, a 'pure' site for the articulation of difference, is deeply compromised, because the ever-present trace of cultural otherness reveals itself as the very condition of subjectivity.[8] Kipling's work, quite spectacularly, manifests this problem of a subjectivity constituted upon the unassimilable yet indelible trace of the other; it clearly shows, in Bart Moore-Gilbert's words, 'that imperial identity depends on subaltern culture for its self-constitution' ('Bhabhal' 123). Attempting to situate Kipling and his work within the context of post-Mutiny India is a complex but decidedly engaging undertaking, precisely because Kipling could never (try as he might) apprehend and articulate *in absolute terms* the difference and the opposition of which Said speaks. His perspective, certainly, is not 'Indian', but nor can it be described as 'metropolitan', nor even as 'Anglo-Indian' in any clear, fully coherent sense. Kipling represents a liminal subjectivity situated on the in-betweens of cultures and cultural identities involved in a process of mutual transformation. His work insistently thematizes the *limen* – the threshold that divides yet joins. If this work serves – as I think it does – in the constitution of a 'Subject of Europe' that is distinct from, set apart from, its Other, yet it also manifests the impossibility of this paradigm.[9]

Kipling's representation of the boy

Kipling's boys are very much creatures of the *limen*, figures set upon the thresholds that stand between opposing identities and worlds; these thresholds – all of them pertinent to the ideological mapping of empire – are presumed to mark the distinction between animal and human, early childhood and full adulthood, between nature and culture, barbary and civilization, between white and dark, East and West, colonizer and colonized. It is the boy's role to test, even to transgress, the borders and frontiers, not so as to destroy them, but rather the better to uphold them. Paraphrasing Baden-Powell, one could say that the Kipling boy serves to fortify the walls of empire. A figure positioned amid various cultural worlds and embodying a multivalent liminality, the hybrid adolescent acts as a 'go-between', as a mediator negotiating and ultimately inscribing the terms of ideologically pertinent distinctions.[10] By seeing and situating, he acts as an agent in the envisioning of imperial order; characterized by access and mobility, he serves to integrate and co-ordinate under a continuous *imperium* the various, dispersed sites where power intervenes.

Kipling's representations of the imperial hybrid boy command close critical scrutiny in large part because they present hybridity in cultural rather than racial terms. In this regard, they anticipate the orientations of contemporary criticism and theory. Although racialist thinking is strongly suggested by Kipling's refusal to stage a 'mixed-blood' boy protagonist, his ever-scrupulous guaranteeing of bloodlines – for example, the immediate, authoritative assertion that Kim, despite appearances, is 'white' and 'English' – serves to open the boy more fully to effects of hybridizing acculturation. Indeed, the author's fascination with childhood and adolescence seems very clearly to stem from their susceptibility to cross- or multi-cultural fashioning. An unalterable difference of species leaves the 'man-cub' free to suckle at a wolf's breast, to receive a jungle initiation from a bear, a panther, and a python; a preliminary distinction of race allows English Stalky to adopt the cultural codes of the Sikh and enables Kim to undertake a quite dizzying array of cross-cultural performances. Kipling's deep imaginative commitment to the experimentation of cultural hybridization is crucially evidenced by the fact that his fiction does not narrate liminal boyhood as a passing phase in a more extensive history of development. In keeping with the archetypal instance of J. M. Barrie's Peter Pan, Kipling's boy never 'grows up', never achieves a stable placement within a distribution of fixed, fully formed identities.[11] Kipling's enduringly liminal boys represent overdetermined sites of cultural production, where a multiplicity of meanings are maintained in complex, ultimately irresolvable interplay. Only in terms of this overdetermination does the figure discover its ideological function as an instrument of imperial power, yet this same overdetermination signals the possibility of a deconstructive critique. The boy always has the potential to destabilize the systems and structures of power he inhabits. A subject under authority, the boy is at once an agent and an object of imperial power, a site where power is deployed but also a site of resistance. Shifting amongst various subject positions, he sees and experiences his world from various, often incommensurate perspectives. Thus he represents an unstable site for British imperial identification. His own cultural identifications are divided, moreover, amongst the various communities with which he is affiliated, and these communities are differently situated within structures of imperial power. One may thus discover in the figure of the hybrid boy a linchpin constituting and assuring the strength of imperial order, but also signaling its potential weakness, its vulnerability.

Kipling's imperial boy is a staging of imperial subjectivity and agency. But the deployment of the figure does not merely reflect British imperial ideology; it intervenes both productively and disruptively in the enunciation of that ideology. The boy is a vehicle for examining, delineating, testing, in a multifaceted way, the cultural conditions of the later British Empire. Clearly, then, my critical orientation does not conform to what one might call the 'model' theory of imperial boyhood, according to which the boys represented in imperial fictions manifest certain characteristics – values, motivations, patterns of conduct – favorable to the imperial enterprise; characteristics that, in a spirit of emulation, are apprehended and adopted by the boy outside the text – the boy reader. In his introduction to *Imperialism and Juvenile Literature*, Jeffrey Richards presents a paradigmatic case for viewing empire boys as models: 'The aim of juvenile literature was clearly stated. ... It was both to entertain and to instruct, to inculcate approved value systems, to spread useful knowledge, to provide acceptable role models' (3). Without denying the value and pertinence of the 'model' theory, I want to venture beyond its bounds, initiating a critique that does not necessitate the invocation of a supposedly clear and delimited category of 'boy's literature', a literature *about* boys that is, in some unspecified yet obvious way, *for* boys. Representations of the boy do, certainly, help to define a specific subject position for young males. However, because these representations are textual and figurative, the investments they inspire, their meanings and resonances, and most importantly, the scope of their address cannot be stated and understood in simple, straight-forward ways.

The imperial boy is a signifying element that cannot be isolated or dissociated from the larger dynamic of imperialism's social effects. Around the figure of the boy and in relation to him, a variety of subject formations are structured, specified, and distrib-uted. The boy, that is, participates in a textual economy that implicates a variety of potential subjects and subject positions, a variety of possible reader-participants – a textual economy that offers a generalized address to questions of British imperial self-fashioning. To clarify by way of example, one may consider the Scout movement. It is true that, in his inaugural scouting manual, Baden-Powell proposes Kipling's boy characters as models for the scout. However, there ensues – I would say, necessarily, inevitably – a more extensive appropriation of the Kipling text: boy scout assem-blies become 'packs'; younger initiates are admitted as 'cubs'; the adult scout leader is named 'Akela'; his adult assistants are named 'Bagheera' or 'Baloo'. The Kipling boy is necessarily situated within a symbolic order of distinctions that is historically, culturally specific; however, Kipling invests the figure with the power to reor-ganize and redistribute formations of the subject, to reconfigure the symbolic order of empire.

Of course, by speaking so insistently of the imperial *boy* I intend to raise a question as to the relation between gender and empire – the very question Kipling's fictions of adolescence have always-already answered, unambiguously. These fictions participate in a generalized tendency to discursively segregate the feminine from the making and the managing of empires. Here as elsewhere, one can discern a separation of masculine and feminine spheres. Empire building, in Kipling's boy-centered narratives, is not considered a potential sphere for feminine action. Indeed, female figures, active or passive, are relatively rare. Edward Said describes *Kim* as an 'over-whelmingly male' text (*Culture* 136); this description may be extended without qualification to *The Jungle Books* and *Stalky & Co.* When female figures do appear, they intervene most typically as obstacles or causes in the enactment of masculine endeavors. The active agency of female characters – still more rare in its manifesta-tions – dependably responds and conforms to masculine instigation or need. Mother Wolf adopts and nurses the needy man-cub, bravely defends him from the formidable Shere Khan, then discreetly retires from prominence as Mowgli (very promptly) becomes the protégé of Bagheera, the pupil of Baloo. The impressive and influential Woman of Shamlegh, having provided Kim with much-needed supplies and bearers, receives in thanks an arrogant kiss, which acknowledges *but also shames* her desire for the attractive young spy. The kiss marks the woman as 'impertinently' desirous, as yet another troublesome woman; that is, the kiss codes her as obstacle (rather than agent), as an unnecessary complication in the elaboration of masculine projects. The force of feminine agency is thus elided and its effects co-opted.

Kipling's treatment of the boy, as my first chapter will demonstrate, is founded upon discourses of the child, which 'engender' this child and assign him his special role in the projects of an expanding Europe. Yet Kipling does not merely reproduce general tendencies within modern imperialism's social text. His coding of imperial action and agency in masculine terms constitutes what one might call a representative misrepresentation of late nineteenth-century imperial actuality, which is clearly, unignorably marked by women's interventions. As Napur Chaudhuri and Margaret Strobel observe in their introduction to *Western Women and Imperialism*,

> In general, theories about colonialism have stressed its 'masculine' nature, highlighting the essential components of domination, control, and structures of unequal power.... For the most part, scholarship has reinforced the common belief among imperialists that colonies were 'no place for white women'. (3)

Chaudhuri and Strobel therefore assert the importance of new scholarship that reveals 'the complex dynamic of complicity and resistance' characterizing Western women's intervention in imperial history (7). They recall the famous 'lady travelers' Mary Kingsley and Mary Hall, and the home-bound but highly influential Flora Shaw, colonial editor of the London *Times* in the 1890s. Affirming the special significance of British imperialism in India in the study of European imperial history (5), Chaudhuri and Strobel stress the prominent role of British women activists in India; also noted are women writers living in India, notably Flora Annie Steel and Annie Besant, who make use of their experience to inform 'analyses of race, class, and power' that both conform to and contest the dominant imperial ideology of their time (9). Chaudhuri and Strobel thus compellingly demonstrate British women's agency in shaping the imperial project, most notably in India, the principal sphere of Kipling's concern.

Both before and during the period of Kipling's writerly formation, Western women's agency in the elaboration of imperial ideology and actuality is undeniable. Kipling's fictions of the imperial boy thus constitute a masculinist intervention in a highly charged and immediately contemporary political arena. As Mary Poovey has amply demonstrated in her *Uneven Developments*, gender was a crucial and contested area of concern in nineteenth-century British culture. She emphasizes, however, that '[t]he system of ideas and institutions' arising around the question of gender and its representation was 'uneven both in the sense of being experienced differently by individuals who were positioned differently within the social formation (by sex, class, or race, for example) and in the sense of being articulated differently by the different institutions, discourses, and practices' (3). Thus recalling that the formation of discourses, ideologies, social institutions, and practices involves incommensurate experiences of the social which are differently articulated, Poovey goes on to assert that 'any image that is important to a culture constitutes an arena of ideological construction rather than simple consolidation' (9). The imperial boy provides, here, a key example. By articulating some of his most noteworthy contributions to imperial culture and ideology in close relation to boys at work and at play in male-dominated imperial settings, Kipling reinforces as much as reflects a masculinist bias in the envisioning of imperialism's structure, character, and mission. His boys assert, against palpable sociocultural opposition, the 'maleness' of imperial endeavor. Yet the figure of the imperial boy, which is not Kipling's exclusive property, is unquestionably an 'important image' of late nineteenth-century British imperial culture, one that commands close attention for that very reason.

Although Kipling's youthful protagonists are invariably male, they are also invariably representatives of a subjectivity that is, in other respects, troubled by indeterminacy, dividedness, undecidability. Kipling's fictions of the boy thus reflect a refiguring of Western, masculine, imperial subjectivity; they suggest a transformation of this subjectivity in response to the pressures and demands of the cross-cultural confrontations the imperial enterprise entails. These representations affirm the creative adaptability of the masculine, imperial subject, the remarkable plasticity and improvisational prowess this subject brings to the making and maintaining of a multicultural empire. Just as surely, however, they manifest a compromise of self-sovereignty and authority, an anxious, deeply unsettled awareness of the imperial subject's inescapably contingent formation. Kipling's liminal boy is a figure who counters yet confirms the fissuring of the masculine, authoritative subjectivity upon which a coherent, masculinist envisioning of the imperial project depends. As Christopher Lane argues in *The Ruling Passion*, both 'conflict' and 'oscillation' between incommensurate drives of 'desire and mastery' characterize Kipling's imperial writings. These tensions within his texts register perturbations of the delicate balance characterizing the British nation's quest for 'external security and internal control' (15), and also the imperial subject's quest for political authority and psychic self-mastery. Indeed, for Lane, the precariousness of the British imperial enterprise reveals itself not in spite but because of its professed reliance upon (and anxiety about) intensified relations between men. If the study of Kipling cannot, in and of itself, redress the gender bias of much imperial representation, it nonetheless offers an ideal occasion to analyze the imaginative and discursive structuring of masculinist empire; similarly, it allows the critic to discern and delineate the incoherencies and contradictions of such structuring.

*

To provide a cultural and historical context for my subsequent analysis of Kipling's deployments of the imperial boy, Chapter 1 presents a genealogy, outlining the sociocultural, historical processes that inform the figure, examining the articulation of childhood generally and, more particularly, the articulation of boyhood within the textual and cultural productions of an expanding Europe. Chapter 2, which focuses on *The Jungle Books*, analyzes the boy as the organizing figure in an allegorization of empire:

Mowgli's jungle history represents the history of the British in India; an imperial progress is figured as a boy's life process of growth and maturation. More specifically, the Mowgli saga articulates itself as post-Mutiny allegory, organizing itself upon various allusions to the scenes and situations of the 1857 rebellion in India, attempting – not with entire success – to resolve and assuage the imperial anxieties investing that historical event. In Chapter 3, I consider the imperial boy resituated in the context of the English school, revealing how Kipling disrupts the conception of an insular metropolitan culture by opening this 'center' to the influences and inscriptions of the imperial 'periphery', by rewriting the metropolitan world of school as a 'little empire' where schoolboys engage in territorial and discursive power games. I discover in Kipling's schoolboy an irresolvably ambivalent figure, an insurgent subaltern who takes up the practices of power, a figure in whom images of authority and subalternity come together. Chapters 4 and 5 focus on *Kim*, which I take to be Kipling's most complex engagement with the figure of the boy. Here, the hybrid adolescent engages explicitly in the practices of imperial power, exercising the gaze-of-power, mapping spaces, situating subjects, transgressing and redefining sociocultural boundaries. The reading presented in Chapter 4 is oriented by Foucauldian theory and examines Kim's role within a post-Mutiny construction of a disciplinary order of empire. Having duly noted, within the articulation of this disciplinary order, the disruptive potential of Kim's multivalent 'ethnicity', I then undertake, in Chapter 5, an analysis of the ethnographic implications of Kipling's text. This second reading reveals with particular clarity how authoritative imperial subjectivity is compromised and called into question by representations of the imperial boy.

1
The Genealogy of the Imperial Boy

Working from T. S. Eliot's analysis, in 'Tradition and the Individual Talent', of the complex relationship between past and present, between tradition and contemporaneity, Edward Said clarifies what it means to historicize a cultural critique: 'even as we must fully comprehend the pastness of the past', he reflects, 'there is no just way in which the past can be quarantined from the present. Past and present inform each other, each implies the other and ... each co-exists with the other. Neither past nor present ... has a complete meaning alone' (*Culture* 4).

Kipling's representations of imperial boyhood draw upon a richly elaborated cultural repertoire; these representations are informed by a past which they transform. To pose and subsequently to explore the question of the boy in Kipling, one must recognize that modern, Western conceptions of childhood and boyhood have a history that is implicated in the process of modern imperialism. Only in relation to this historical contextualization does it become possible and, indeed, worthwhile to consider Kipling's work as a particular textual manifestation suggesting broader, more general critical implications and applications. By examining the history of European conceptions of childhood and boyhood, by providing an account of their emergence within the social text of imperial Europe, one can begin to discover the role of 'child' and, more specifically, of 'boy' in the elaboration and deployment of 'a Western epistemology of the subject' (Sharpe, *Allegories* 15), an epistemology whose formation must be understood as an ongoing process, still susceptible to critical renegotiation. Within this process, Kipling's work represents neither a beginning nor an end, but rather a significant moment of cultural condensation in which themes and motifs of the boy come together in complex, revealing ways and signal their pertinence for postcolonial cultural critique. As Satya P. Mohanty emphasizes in his revaluation of Kipling's texts of boyhood, European imperial culture produced 'new meanings and identities, some of which in fact survive in many of our post-colonial encounters'; it established 'relations of rule, deeply ingrained habits, attitudes, even images of self and world, [which] pervade our own current social practices' ('Drawing' 313–14). Kipling's representations of the boy, which are informed by his cultural past, inform our cultural present.

My documentation of the genealogy of the imperial boy will show how childhood and boyhood are culturally invested in such a way as to allow for the coding of the boy as a privileged, prioritized representative of European childhood and, ultimately, of European imperial subjectivity. This genealogy does not aim, in the space of a chapter, to put forward a comprehensive treatment; it strives instead to outline key developments in boyhood and its represen-tation. I begin by considering the 'specialization' of childhood, which centers on the boy as a maker and marker of social distinc-tions. I then proceed to examine the centrality of childhood in modern Europe's 'civilizing process', which orients and energizes childhood's specialization, focusing attention on the child – and, in particular, on the boy – as a site of progress, as the crucial figure upon whom the production of new civil and symbolic codes depends. The pedagogy of John Locke, which advocates the trans-mission of civilized dispositions and behavior by example and imitation, is shown to be particularly instructive. I argue, moreover, that Locke's contribution lends philosophical credence to the figure of the child, offering an abundantly detailed account of the child's 'Nature' and 'Character'. Following my examination of Locke, I go on to show how and why boyhood comes to be implicated in the expansion of Europe, focusing on the emergence of the child as an organizing figure in discourses that address questions of cross-cultural encounter between 'civilized' and 'savage' worlds. Of crucial importance in this respect is the contribution of Rousseau, whose work establishes the boy as the subject-in-process of imper-ial Europe. Employing Johannes Fabian's illuminating analysis of 'allochronism' in modern discourses of culture, I go on to argue that Rousseau's particular production of the boy manifests a Eurocentric distribution of differentiated cultural and subjective temporalities. At this juncture, I confront and call into question the tropes of the 'primitive child' and the 'childlike primitive'.

I subsequently propose Edmund Burke's late eighteenth-century denunciation of boy-imperialism in India as a key manifestation of the boy's capacity to serve and yet to unsettle imperial discourse. Burke confirms the boy as a key figure of British imperial discourse, yet presents the imperial boy as a problematizing rather than an enabling element of that discourse. I therefore proceed to document the recuperation of the boy. Considering the burgeoning of adventure and school narratives both in books and in boys' magazines, I establish the imperial boy as a prominent, organizing figure within late nineteenth-century British cultural production. Having traced the progress of the boy through to Kipling's time of writing, I propose the boy as a figure that mediates an 'experience' of British imperial actions and achievements, a figure forged to enable a coherent envisioning of the relationship between British subjectivity and the British imperial project.

Ariès: the specialization of childhood

In *Centuries of Childhood*, Philippe Ariès outlines the history of 'the specialized child', a crucial development enabling the child's emergence as a specific, recognizable figure within the cultural image repertoire of modern Europe. The envisioning of childhood as a special and specifiable time of life is, Ariès argues, distinctly modern. Although he emphasizes the importance of the seventeenth century in childhood's modern evolution, he traces a specialization of European childhood that progresses steadily through the eighteenth and nineteenth centuries, becoming both more elaborate and more exacting. The child's person – his clothing, the cut of his hair – is made to reflect, ever more meticulously, his age and class. Specific playthings, games, and pastimes are relinquished by adults and enclosed within childhood's sphere. Child-focused systems of education develop, claiming more and more of the child's time and attention. The schoolboy is uniformed, sequestered from society at large and segregated from his fellows, as educational institutions take on a disciplinary and normalizing character. Both at home and at school, the child is surrounded by the various discourses that specify his being: learned voices debate as to his native innocence or depravity; manuals of etiquette dictate his behavior; prescriptions and proscriptions govern his health and hygiene.

The child's specialization has noteworthy implications with respect to issues of gender and class. If I have chosen, thus far, to specify the child as male, it is with good reason: 'boys', Ariès stresses, 'were the first specialized children' (58). In terms of dress, the difference between the boy and man of the upper classes is clearly marked, the difference between girl and woman relatively unmarked. Lower-class children of both genders are dressed in the same manner as the adults. By the late sixteenth century, many upper-class boys are going to school, whereas few girls are schooled before the late eighteenth century. The social initiation of lower-class children through apprenticeship and service continues well into the nineteenth century.

The specialization of the child is a way of making social distinctions and marking their importance – a way of making differences signify. The most important difference, the one that is most clearly and insistently marked, is that which distinguishes the upper-class boy from the man of the same class. The specialized child's dress offers, in this regard, the most revealing instance. 'Every social nuance', Ariès affirms, 'had its corresponding sign in clothing' (57). From the sixteenth century on, the upper-class boy's dress, by the very fact of its specialization, marks his difference from boys of other, lower classes. It sets him apart from men of his own class, but distinguishes him much less from lower-class men, and still less from the girls and women of his own class.

The specialization of upper-class boyhood is evidently caught up in a quite complex play of similarity and difference: the specialized boy is marked in ways that suggest his similarity (in status terms) to the girls and women of his own class, to the adults of lower classes, and his difference from boys of lower classes and from the men of his own class. The specialization of boyhood serves, most notably, to distinguish and specify a privileged boyhood and a privileged manhood. Moreover, if one considers the history of dress in relation to the development of the school, it becomes evident that the empowered adulthood of the upper-class male is not only a function of age; it is a distinction one achieves by means of an extensive and demanding process of initiation. Boyhood's specialization produces a culturally coded figure, the specialized boy, whose role it is to make and mark key social distinctions, to render visible and meaningful the specification and hierarchization of various social subjects. It is the special capacity of this boy to figure forth distinctions in social status and degrees of privilege and empowerment.[1]

Elias: the civilizing process

Ariès, in his largely phenomenological account, makes no sustained attempt to isolate the motive forces energizing the history of childhood's specialization. This specialization is, however, deeply implicated in a still more radical transformation of European culture. As Norbert Elias has shown in his two-volume *The Civilizing Process*, fifteenth-century Europe – that is, Europe in the early period of childhood's specialization – is already engaged in an increasingly intensified, far-reaching process of civilization which, in various ways, will do much to determine and define the European community's accession to its 'modernity'. 'Civilization' as cultural process and 'civility' as social value are in the process of establishing themselves as central, organizing principles of European society. National identities unified by language, law, and religion are emerging, as are the internally pacified, externally embattled, modern nation-states – most notably in England and in France, the nations that early established secure and stable frontiers. As Elias makes clear, the 'civilizing' of peoples entails a decreased reliance upon violent force, which becomes an exclusive legal prerogative of the monarch, and an increased, socially generated demand for the individual subject's internalization of social codes and etiquettes. Within the civilized nation-state, social control is an effect of the tacitly acknowledged interdependence of individuals, each of whom must conform to exacting prescriptions for drive-control and self-constraint. Elias thus anticipates the work of Michel Foucault by documenting the formation of a civilized subject, who, having been submitted to a complex play of social demands and pressures, 'assumes responsibility for the constraints of power' and 'becomes the principle of his own subjection' (Foucault, *Discipline* 202–3).

As Elias points out, questions of civility arise around the child: 'the concept of *civilité* ... owes the specific meaning adopted by society to a short treatise by Erasmus ... *De civilitate morum puerilium* (On civility in children)' (1: 53). Prominent among the productions of the sixteenth-century press were books of etiquette or 'good manners' instituted by *De civilitate* (1526) and Erasmus's earlier *Colloquia* (1516), both of which enjoyed a tremendous, pan-European vogue. For Erasmus, the child and the youth provide the foundational, focal points for the discourse of civility. As its exigencies become more exacting and complex, civility becomes a matter of specific and protracted instruction, an interrelated assembly of dispositions and behavior that must be learned in childhood and taught, in turn, to each new generation. To specify what the uncivilized child must learn is to specify what the civilized adult must know. Civilized adults become, therefore, ever more attentive to their own deportment, and exert themselves to inculcate corresponding behavior in children; 'From earliest youth the individual is trained in the constant restraint and foresight that he needs for adult functions' (Elias 2: 241). Concern with the proper formation of the young person of quality (who is most commonly figured as a young male) continues to inform the many works on civility that accompany those of Erasmus, such as Russell's *Book of Nurture*, Caxton's *Book of Curtesye*, Della Casa's *Galateo*, and Castiglione's *Courtier*, to name only a few (see Elias 1: 60–61, 79–80).

The civilizing process, as Elias perceives, must necessarily organize itself around the child. The civilized adult's susceptibility to shame and sociogenetic anxiety – a susceptibility that is, as it were, the *sine qua non* of individual civilization – 'results from the fact that the people whose superiority one fears are in accord ... with the agency of self-constraint implanted in the individual by others on whom he was dependent, who possessed power and superiority over him' (2: 292). Elias, in fact, goes so far as to affirm that 'all forms of adult inner anxieties are bound with the child's fears of others, of external powers' (2: 300). Thus, in Elias's view, 'the specific process of psychological 'growing up' in Western societies ... is nothing other than the individual civilizing process to which each young person ... is automatically subjected from earliest childhood' (1: xiii). And, more importantly perhaps, because the attainment of a high level of 'civilization' is a matter of prestige and power, children become focal points of class anxieties, aspirations, and struggles; the forming of a child reflects '[t]he continuous concern of parents whether their child will attain the standard of conduct of their own or even a higher class, whether it will maintain or increase the prestige of the family, whether it will hold its own in the competition within their own class' (2: 329–30). One may also conclude, by extension, that the child becomes a principal means of asserting, claiming, and maintaining class power.

Clearly, then, the civilizing of the child poses itself as a fraught educational problem. The school therefore, notwithstanding its growing importance, is by no means the only site where childhood is carefully watched, shaped, and corrected. The privatized, child-centered family has also an important educational function. Even before the end of the seventeenth century, the boy's education within the familial setting becomes a topic worthy of a philosopher's subtlety and seriousness: in *Some Thoughts Concerning Education*, first published in 1693, John Locke proposes various methods of educational discipline for application in the upper-class home, outlining a pedagogy 'suited to our English Gentry', which engages with the problem of forming a 'Gentleman' from a 'Gentleman's Son' (lxiii).

Locke's contribution

For Locke, the principal purpose of an education is the production or, more precisely, the reproduction of reasoned and disciplined 'Civility', which the philosopher considers the indispensable foundation of good citizenry. His methods aim to instill in the child 'Habits woven into the very Principles of his Nature' (28), an end to be attained through a 'Practice' governed by appropriate 'Example'. Observing 'how prone we all are, especially Children, to Imitation' (51), Locke argues,

> of all the Ways whereby Children are to be instructed, and their Manners formed, the plainest, easiest, and most efficacious, is, to set before their Eyes the *Examples* of those things you would have them do, or avoid; which, when pointed out to them, in the

Practice of Persons within their Knowledge ... are of more Force
to draw or deter their Imitation, than any Discourses which can
be made to them. (61)

Although the fundamentals of Locke's educational goals and
methods can be clearly discerned and simply stated, his philosophical confrontation with the child is somewhat divided in its
premises: his pedagogy is founded the famous premise that posits
the childish mind as a 'blank slate' to be inscribed by experience, 'as
white Paper, or Wax, to be moulded and fashioned as one pleases'
(187); however, his teaching repeatedly implies or asserts the existence of a specifiable childish 'Nature' to be reformed as much as
made. Locke, in his discussion, finds occasion to extol the 'Child's
Spirit' as 'easy, active, and free' (30) or to observe, disparagingly,
that 'Inadvertency, Forgetfulness, Unsteadiness, and Wandering of
Thought, are the natural Faults of Childhood' (144). Locke's child,
then, is not an empty figure but a malleable one.

The pedagogical project obliges the philosopher to characterize
childhood's estate, to submit it to a detailed descriptive account.
Not only does Locke picture the child engaged in his various life-
activities – whipping his top, playing at alphabetized dice, reciting
his lesson, socializing in various situations with adults and
peers – he also sets down an abundant catalogue of childish dispositions, susceptibilities, and inclinations, including 'Lying and
Equivocations' (24), desire for 'Esteem' and fear of 'Disgrace' (34),
'Obstinacy' and 'Rebellion' (57), love of 'Liberty' and of 'Power and
Dominion' (83), keen, virtually boundless 'Curiosity' (87), a
tendency to 'clamour' and 'complain' (88–9), 'Fool-hardiness' (94),
and 'Timorousness' (97–100). Locke also discerns almost paradoxical tensions within the childish character: he observes a disposition
toward 'Cruelty' and a delight in 'Mischief' (100–1), but also takes
note of 'Benignity and Compassion' (102); he denounces a dangerous disposition to 'sauntering' and 'trifling' (106), but finds it is
fortunately counterbalanced by a naturally 'busy Humour', a
constant need to be active and engaged (110–11). Of course, these
many and various traits or tendencies are not the exclusive property
of children. As Locke emphasizes, the child, even in his nonage, is
already a human being and therefore not *essentially* different
from the adult. He distinguishes childhood by specifying certain

recognizably human characteristics, which may or may not appear in the adult, as salient and more or less invariable in the child. A key role of Lockean education is, precisely, to determine what qualities are to endure, to what degree and in what form. Locke, moreover, freely acknowledges that each child manifests a specific configuration of childish traits, an individual 'Temper' composed of 'predominate Passions and prevailing Inclinations' (82–3). It is, above all, these 'native Propensities' that the parent or tutor must carefully observe and keep in account. Using a figure of native inscription that is curiously at odds with the notion of the blank slate, Locke anchors his argument with the assertion that the educator must read 'the Characters of [the child's] Mind ... in the first Scenes of his Life' (83).

Locke's injunction to closely observe the child culminates not only with a figuring of native inscription but, more crucially, with a theatrical metaphor, life's 'first Scenes'. This is significant because his treatment makes the child readable in figurative terms, placing the child, as it were, in a prominent role upon the stage of social life. Certainly, Locke does not, in pursuit of his educational, civilizing project, invent the modern figure of the child. Resonant evocations of childhood and the child occur in the works of earlier, widely disseminated, and highly influential writers such as Erasmus, Shakespeare and Montaigne.[2] With Locke, however, the specification and delineation of childhood and the child become tenable matters for philosophical discourse. 'Child' attains dignity as a philosophical distinction, as a figure available to, and worthy of, reasoned contemplation and analysis. Just as importantly, Locke confirms and consolidates the specular relationship between the child and the adult. The observed child reveals not only his native character but also, crucially, the progress of his reform; he reveals, that is, the degree to which his character and deportment *reflect the examples* provided by his parents, his tutor – by all those persons who make up his 'Company'. For Locke, the adult is the subject and, just as importantly, the object of a gaze. The strait ligatures of direct responsibility bind the adult to the developing child: 'You must do nothing before him, which you would not have him imitate. If any Thing escape you, which you would have pass for a Fault in him, he will be sure to shelter himself under your Example' (51). The child's education advances in so far as he comes to mirror the dispositions, behaviors, values – in short, the various civilizing examples – presented to him by civilized adults. Locke's educational philosophy thus confirms what Erasmus had earlier intuited – that the child figures forth the nature and level of the sociocultural achievement a civilizing society has attained.[3]

Civilization as achievement; cultural other as child

To speak of civilization as cultural achievement is, to a certain degree, to anticipate transformations of the conception and deployment of 'civilisation' that occur after Locke's time, in the latter half of the eighteenth century. As Elias observes, the term 'civilisation' is first derived from the earlier terms, 'civilised' and 'civility', to denote a cultural process. In publications of the 1770s, 'civilisation' first asserts itself as 'an indispensable term that is obviously generally understood' (Elias 1: 46). Although it never entirely loses its association with process and progress, its reference to 'something which is constantly in motion, constantly moving "forward"' (1: 5), by the end of the eighteenth century the term, with ever greater clarity and conviction, comes 'to epitomize the nation, to express the national self-image' (1: 49). 'Civilization' thus emerges, particularly in England and France, as the name for a pre-eminent national, sociocultural achievement. 'It expresses', writes Elias, 'the self-assurance of peoples whose national boundaries and national identity have for centuries been ... fully established ... peoples which have long expanded outside their borders and colonized beyond them' (1: 5); it characterizes, that is, the modern European, *imperial* nation-state. As an established concept, civilization henceforth 'expresses the self-consciousness of the West'; 'It sums up everything in which Western society of the last two or three centuries believes itself superior to earlier societies or "more primitive" contemporary ones' (1: 3–4). As the watchword of a specifically Western ethnocentrism, 'civilization' takes on 'a level of meaning justifying ... aspirations to national expansion and colonization' (1: 49). First deployed, in various forms and in various ways, as the exclusive property of specific dominant or ascendant groups – the courtly aristocracy, later the gentry, and later still the bourgeoisie – civilization is finally applied to the nation as a whole. Formerly informing confrontations and competitions among classes *within* the emergent nation-states, the concept of civilization now serves increasingly to distinguish European, imperial nations from other societies beyond the bounds of Europe.

Modern childhood's evolution continues throughout the period of modern colonial expansion. Just as the figure of the child focuses and organizes the class competition attending the civilizing process, so the figure takes a prominent place in the expansive, hegemonic initiatives of civilizing Europe. Indeed, even before the consolidation of the concept of civilization (as a European cultural achievement) the figure is made to serve as a sense-making device in the articulation of cultural difference. With the discovery of the Americas and the consequent pan-European awareness of the American 'primitive', modern childhood becomes more and more deeply implicated in Europe's discovery and domination of its cultural others. When Montaigne first essays the question of the primitive in his 'Of Cannibals', he makes use of the idea of the 'noble savage' (which will later allow Rousseau to establish the conceptual bond between the child and the 'savage'). Montaigne is very much concerned with comparing and contrasting the 'savage' Carib and the 'civilized' European, tending to laud the former and to disparage the latter.[4] And the idealistic rhetoric arising around the 'noble savage' has, unquestionably, its equivalent in discourse of the child. In 'Of Cannibals', Montaigne declares,

> These nations [of the New World] ... seem to me barbarous in this sense, that they have been fashioned very little by the human mind, and are still very close to their original natural-ness. The laws of nature still rule them, very little corrupted by ours. ... [I]t seems to me that what we actually see in these nations surpasses ... all the pictures in which poets have ideal-ized the golden age and all their inventions in imagining a happy state of man. ... (1.31.153)

A discourse of childhood is implicit in this passage. Montaigne's account of the New World peoples parallels a commonplace repre-sentation of the child with which it is roughly contemporary, as is evident if one considers 'The Child', the opening sketch of John Earle's *Microcosmographie* (1628):

[The child] is the best copy of Adam before he tasted of Eve or the apple. ... He is nature's fresh picture newly drawn in oil, which time, and much handling, dims and defaces. His soul is yet a white paper unscribbled with observations of the world. ... He is purely happy, because he knows no evil, nor hath made means by sin to be acquainted with misery. (qtd. in Boas 42)

When, at the end of his essay, Montaigne offers his final ironic reflection upon the Caribs' otherness – 'They don't wear breeches' – one can begin to discern the figure of the child waiting, as it were, in the wings. The difference, one recalls, between the modern, specialized boy and the European adult male is also, in part, a matter of breeches.

The child need not wait long. In 'Of Coaches', an essay composed only a few years after 'Of Cannibals', Montaigne turns again to New World reflections:

Our world has just discovered another world ... no less great, full, and well-limbed than itself, yet so new and so infantile that it is still being taught its A B C; not fifty years ago it knew neither letters, nor weights and measures, nor clothes, nor wheat, nor vines. It was still quite naked at the breast, and lived only on what its nursing mother provided. ... It was an infant world; yet we have not whipped it and subjected it to our discipline by the advantage of our natural valor and strength, nor won it over by our justice and goodness, nor subjugated it by our magnanimity. (3.6.693)

Montaigne here conceives of 'Old' (adult) and 'New' (infantile) worlds. Like the European child, the New World is being submitted (perhaps rudely and unjustly) to a process of civilizing education. Montaigne, however, orders his discourse upon a comparison of 'worlds' and does not, therefore, strike precisely upon the metaphoric link – the child is a primitive; the primitive is a child – which interests me most. The work of Montaigne clearly demonstrates, nonetheless, that when Rousseau, in his *Émile* of 1762, philosophizes upon the conceptual bond between the 'noble savage' and the 'natural' child, his contribution confirms as much as it inaugurates.

Rousseau: innovations and consolidations

Montaigne's figurative use of childhood in his representation of the Carib is by no means 'innocent', revealing as it does a noteworthy bias in European perception of cultural others. In the work of Rousseau, however, this bias discovers a fuller range of philosophical and pedagogical implications. The opening passages of *Émile* announce, 'Our wisdom is slavish prejudice, our customs consist in control, constraint, compulsion. Civilized man is born and dies a slave. ... All his life long man is imprisoned by our institutions.' As the disaffected philosopher is quick to add, 'The Caribs are better off than we are' (10). Rousseau is not the first to think and argue in terms of this civilized/savage opposition, but he *is* the first to offer an alternative educational methodology based on it. He posits the 'savage' Carib as the free and self-sufficient 'natural man', who 'lives for himself', who 'is the unit, the whole' (7). Working from this premise and using the 'savage' as his touchstone, Rousseau proffers his 'education from nature' and, in so doing, places the child, his learning experience and knowledge acquisition, in intimate relation with the cultural contexts of European imperial expansion.

It is important to note at the outset that, despite repeated invocations of the 'savage' as a principal organizing example, Rousseau's pedagogy represents an intensification rather than a relaxation of civilizing systems of restraint and control. The watchfulness required of Émile's tutor is at once more unremitting and more surreptitious than that prescribed by Locke. The tutor must demand of himself unprecedented levels of self-discipline and self-consciousness, because just as the boy is ever in his eye, he is always in the boy's. Tutor and boy are caught up together in a disciplinary process that produces subjection in the name of freedom, that binds the adult educator more closely and more subtly to his childish charge: Rousseau exhorts the tutor,

> let [the pupil] always think he is master while you are really master. There is no subjection so complete as that which preserves the forms of freedom; it is thus that the will itself is taken captive. Is not this poor child, without knowledge, strength, or wisdom, entirely at your mercy? Are you not master

of his whole environment so far as it affects him? Cannot you make of him what you please? His work and play, his pleasure and pain, are they not, unknown to him, under your control? No doubt he ought only to do what he wants, but he ought to want to do nothing but what you want him to do. He should never take a step you have not foreseen, nor utter a word you could not foretell. (84–5)

Rousseau cannot do without the disciplinary techniques developed within the civilizing process; nor can he entirely overturn or abandon the paradigms of European civility. But what the above passage enunciates most clearly is Rousseau's call for a degree of adult investment in the child's formation exceeding that which Locke's pedagogy implies. The child is now an object of minute, multifarious, seemingly unremitting scrutiny. And, what is more, this adult watchfulness aims to apprehend not only behaviors but interiority – thought, will, desire, pleasure. Rousseau's boy is very much *for* adults, a figure whose every aspect answers to adult design.

The French philosopher does not ignore the child's inevitable destiny as a 'citizen'. In the end, Émile can only be made to embody an alternative civility formulated in terms of different touchstones, notably 'nature' and the 'natural man'. However, unlike Locke, 'that wise man' whom Rousseau cites frequently (22), the French philosopher looks beyond nation and class, aiming to produce not simply a particular, national form of the 'gentleman' but 'a citizen of the world' (20). This new envisioning of the scope of citizenship tellingly signals the participation of Rousseau's pedagogy in Europe's imperial progress.

In the first two books of *Émile*, the expansive, potentially imperial energies of Rousseau's text assert themselves immediately, yet not obstreperously. Rousseau establishes that his young scholar's education is driven by need and desire, directed by curiosity. He proposes the increasing attainment of 'self-sufficiency' (a self-sufficiency he has previously ascribed to the Carib 'savage') as the educative goal; he asserts that 'freedom, not power is the greatest good' (48). Rousseau, however, follows Locke in ascribing to the child 'a natural love of power' (34), which must be properly directed and put to use. Pre-eminent, therefore, among the child's earliest apprehensions is the proper judgement and appreciation of distance – of the distance that separates the child from the objects of need, desire, curiosity, from the objects over which the child would gain a certain dominion.

In Book III, Rousseau remains true to his preceding logic. Émile, at the age of 12 or 13, begins to acquire what might properly be called 'knowledges', the first of which, significantly, is to be geography. 'Man's diverse powers', Rousseau proposes,

> are stirred by the same instinct. ... Children are first restless, then curious; and this curiosity, rightly directed, is the means of development for the age with which we are dealing.... There is a zeal for learning which has no other foundation than a wish to appear learned, and there is another which springs from man's natural curiosity about all things far or near which may affect himself.... If a man of science were left on a desert island with his books and instruments and knowing that he must spend the rest of his life there, he would scarcely trouble himself about the solar system, the laws of attraction, or the differential calculus. He might never even open a book again; but he would never rest till he had explored the furthest corner of his island, however large it might be. (130)

Having put forward this hypothetical scenario, Rousseau greatly expands its scope, and at the same moment he reintroduces the touchstone of 'savagery'. He now proposes, 'Our island is the earth'. In accord with 'the philosophy of most savage races', he then announces his intention to focus Émile's study on cosmic phenomena. Taking a moment, at this point, to anticipate and answer objections, Rousseau writes,

> What a sudden change you will say. Just now we were concerned with what touches ourselves, with our immediate environment, and all at once we are exploring the round world and leaping to the bounds of the universe. This change is the result of our growing strength and of the natural bent of the mind. While we were weak and feeble, self-preservation concentrated our attention on ourselves; now that we are strong and powerful, the desire for a wider sphere carries us beyond ourselves as far as our eyes can reach. (130)

In this way, Rousseau justifies a sudden, explosive expansion of the educational context, which is indeed startling, but not inexplicable. Already, in the mid-eighteenth century, it is evidently possible for the 'Subject of Europe' – Gayatri Spivak's formulation – to constitute a sphere of knowledge coextensive with the sphere of the Earth. Rousseau is a staunch advocate of empirical knowledge acquisition: 'Let the senses be the only guide for the first workings of reason' (131). With Magellan's sixteenth-century circumnavigation of the globe, 'the round world' to which Rousseau alludes has become an experience, an empirical reality. If Africa remains for the most part the 'dark continent' – or, better still, the blank, undifferentiated space Conrad's Marlowe will remember – yet the European presence is already established in Asia and in both American continents.

Rousseau's text, which makes frequent use of 'you' and 'we' in its address, solicits a dual identification, a dual participation, appealing to its readers as subjects of an educational project and as subjects of the European community, which is expanding and extending its knowledge and power. Europe is in the midst of forging the modern geopolitic, and, as his pedagogy reveals, Rousseau is very sensitive to his historical context. He makes clear that the Earth itself, in its entirety, has become the sphere of a knowledge *imperium.* This *imperium,* moreover, is envisioned as the inevitable (and therefore legitimate) result of 'man's natural curiosity' acting in tandem with his growing strength and power and consequent 'desire for a wider sphere'. The educational progress of the growing child can therefore provide a singularly compelling figure for the expanding domains of European knowledge and power. 'No book, but the world', Rousseau advocates (131), and his educational project therefore involves moving the child out and about, increasing in scope and in detail his grasp of the 'book' of the world. Mapping the world, both figuratively and literally, is to be the work of experience, never the substitute for experience: 'You wish to teach this child geography and you provide him with globes, spheres, and maps. What elaborate preparations! What is the use of all these symbols; why not begin by showing him the real thing so that he may at least know what you talking about?' (131) The boy learns by direct engagement with his world, by undertaking, in the manner of Robinson Crusoe, the explorations, assimilations, and appropriations that constitute the process of the 'education from nature', an education that reproduces in little Europe's imperial progress.

Rousseau's allusion to *Robinson Crusoe*, most evident in the placement of a 'man of science' on a 'desert island', is by no means haphazard. A little later, Rousseau will refer, explicitly and laudatorily, to Defoe's novel, undertaking an extensive development of the Crusoe analogy and 'mak[ing] a reality of that desert island which formerly served as an illustration' (147). *Robinson Crusoe*, one learns, will be Émile's first and, for a long while, his only book. The boy will learn by playing at being Crusoe, by identifying with him – 'Let him think he is Robinson himself' (148) – by discovering and solving problems as Crusoe does. In keeping with the Crusoe paradigm, to see the global 'island', to access its various spaces, is to know it, to appropriate it, to master it; expansion, the claiming of new dominions, is the 'natural' correlate of exploration. Rousseau, making a highly significant decision, chooses to model the adolescent between twelve and fifteen, the boy in 'the third stage of childhood' (128), upon Crusoe, in whom Martin Green locates the seminal inscription of the 'modern system hero' as colonial adventurer. Crusoe, in Green's view, provides an 'energizing myth' for modern imperialism (3 ff.), affirming the European adventurer's unique capacity to sustain himself, 'to create value', and to enact a property-oriented 'relationship of possession' in an alien wilderness (76–7). As Green notes, Defoe's hero, at least in the initiatory stages of his adventurings, is prototypically the 'young man' with whom the themes of 'empire, frontier, [and] exploration' will come to be associated (83). Significantly, however, Rousseau's early redeployment of Defoe's tale 'rejuvenates' the figure of its hero, recreating Robinson, the young man, as Émile, the boy in early adolescence. Rousseau, who follows Montaigne in positing a 'natural' analogical relation between the Carib savage and the child, thus proceeds to associate and identify the child with another quite distinct figure: the child, at a crucial stage of his development, learns to progress beyond the paradigm of noble savagery and to play the role of the adventurer, who innovatively confronts the strangeness of his world, creating value and establishing an increasing dominion over his environment. By coding the child in analogical relation first with the savage and subsequently with the colonial adventurer – the European who makes his way in alien territory – Rousseau in part creates and in part consolidates the child as an instrumental figure for emerging imperial discourses.

Just as importantly, Rousseau asserts the necessary maleness of this enterprising child. Unlike Locke, who merely ignores the case of the girl, Rousseau argues, explicitly and at length, for the girl's exclusion from the core of his discussion, thus confirming the systemic, rather than merely arbitrary, character of this exclusion. He makes no mention of 'Sophy, or Woman', until Book V, when Émile, having attained manhood, is ready to discover and pursue his need of her (321). 'Up to the age of puberty,' Rousseau affirms at the beginning of Book IV, 'children of both sexes have little to distinguish them ... girls are children and boys are children; one name is enough for creatures so closely resembling one another' (172). In the opening passages of Book V, he similarly affirms that a woman differs from a man only with respect to her sex, but then immediately emphasizes the inescapable and far-reaching implications of that one distinction. Arguing that gender differences are and should be complementary, he quickly states that 'the man should be strong and active' (as Émile has been trained to be); 'the woman should be weak and passive' (322). Similarly, the man is destined by nature to be 'free and self-controlled', the woman to be socially governed, her 'boundless passions' restrained by the feminine dispositions of 'modesty' and 'shame' (323). Not surprisingly, Rousseau's woman is not made to be 'a citizen of the world', but rather a spouse and mother, a charming companion who cares for children and accepts a general responsibility for the domestic sphere. Having described the natural character and role of woman in very conventional terms, Rousseau returns to questions of childhood and training, paradoxically discovering significant differences between boys and girls, even though he had previously characterized them as essentially similar in every way: 'Boys want movement and noise, drums, tops, toy-carts; girls prefer things which appeal to the eye – mirrors, jewellery, finery, and specially dolls. The doll is the girl's special plaything; this shows her instinctive bent towards her life's work' (330–1). Similarly, 'Little girls dislike learning to read and write' – skills which Émile, of course, duly acquires – 'but they are always ready to learn to sew' (331). One learns, among other things, that girls are usually more curious than boys and more in need of restraint, 'more docile than boys' and more in need of authority (331–2). Not self-sufficiency but dependence and uncomplaining obedience are prescribed for Sophy by nature, and these traits together make up the distinguishing character of her 'sex':

> [Sophy] is gentle and submissive. ... [S]he endures patiently the wrong-doing of others, and she is eager to atone for her own. This amiability is natural to her sex when unspoiled. Woman is made to submit to man and to endure even injustice at his hands. You will never bring young lads to this; their feelings rise in revolt against injustice; nature has not fitted them to put up with it. (359)

Sophy's potential as a human being and as an educable subject is so severely limited as to forbid her inclusion in the pedagogical regime that so clearly implicates Émile, the boy, in the thematics of adventure and empire. It is boyhood exclusively that Rousseau associates with the noble, uncorrupted, childlike Carib and with Crusoe, the European whose solitary experience upon a Caribbean island obliges him to become as a child again, to recreate and reconstitute the forms and values of his cultural heritage.

European boyhood and the time of the other

Before and even after he is invested in the trappings of the colonial adventurer, Émile is represented as 'natural man' receiving an 'education from nature'. Rousseau, throughout the duration of his pedagogical narrative, considers boyhood in imaginative relation with Europe's Other – with the European reconstruction of 'uncivilized' non-European subjectivity and with non-European places and experiences. The association of the European childhood with cultural otherness is sustained by the notion of a shared time, a time that is posited as distinct from that of European adulthood. What distinguishes the child from the cultural other is the former's capacity to progress, to access, with time and maturation, European adult subjectivity and to participate in European initiatives and projects. Implicit in Rousseau's philosophical maneuver is a deployment of distinct temporalities, which are coded culturally and geographically.

In *Time and the Other*, Johannes Fabian documents a post-

Enlightenment 'secularization of Time' (11), which allows the secular conception of 'natural history' to supersede Christian history and its providential teleology.[5] During the eighteenth century, time's secularization gives way in turn to its spatialization; 'it is naturalized-spatialized Time which gives meaning ... to the distribution of humanity in space' (25). The globe is now conceived as a composite of distinct temporal spaces. Europe comes to represent history's here and now, and distant 'other places' become, in various ways and to varying degrees, its there and then. A new conception and practice of travel, Fabian finds, most clearly manifests the temporal distance marking the distinction between Europe and its others. By the later eighteenth century, travel to distant places, to strange cultures 'was to become (at least potentially) every man's source of "philosophical," secular knowledge'. But most crucially, philosophical travel, '*travel as science*' (6), comes to be understood as time travel; 'The philosophical traveller, sailing to the ends of the earth, is in fact travelling in time; he is exploring the past' (7). In the experience of non-European cultures, the traveler seeks and 'finds' manifestations of Europe's past; he perceives relatively 'primitive' social formations that serve to confirm Europe's singular, exemplary modernity. In the figure of the cultural other, similarly, the philosophical traveler may confront and contemplate the image of a former self, a past self inhabiting a past time and place. As Fabian notes, 'Primitive being essentially a temporal concept, is a category, not an object, of Western thought' (18). It is, moreover, a temporal concept that invokes the child; it comprehends the child and calls him into relation with the cultural other. As Montaigne's essaying of New World questions already indicates, philosophical travelers (even those of the 'armchair' variety) are disposed to discover in 'primitive' societies the 'childhood' of Europe.[6]

   Fabian, in developing his argument, both acknowledges and contests the analogy that links the child and the primitive. Challenging the 'taxonomic innocence' of the analogy – the position, as argued by Lévi-Strauss, that '[a]ll we do in calling primitives infantile is class perceived similarities' – Fabian asks,

   Are we to accept [Lévi-Strauss's] contention that in our own society relations between adults and children merely reflect different degrees of 'extension' of knowledge? Are we to overlook that adult-child relations are also, and sometimes primarily, fraught with barely disguised attitudes of power and practices of repression and abuse? Even worse, are we to forget that talk about the childlike nature of the primitive has never been just a neutral classificatory act, but a powerful rhetorical figure and motive, informing colonial practice in every aspect from religious indoctrination to labor laws and the granting of basic political rights? ... Moreover, what could be clearer evidence of temporal distancing than placing the Now of the primitive in the Then of the Western adult? (63)

These rhetorical questions clearly suggest that the studious and insistent infantilization of the primitive enacts and legitimizes a practice of domination. The question, then, is not so much how to perceive and understand the primitive, but rather how this primitive is to be managed, controlled, ruled. The former concern is in the service of the latter. Within an epistemological economy that comprehends 'difference as *distance*' (Fabian 16), as distance in space *and time*, the 'primitive' other is made to occupy an 'other time' – a cultural past, already known, already ordered, a time over which the European adult has already established his (putative) dominion. By situating cultural others the more clearly and securely within a different time, the figure of the child lends support to European discourses of domination, facilitating the psychic and symbolic management of cross-cultural encounter.

Fabian objects to the politics of the construct 'childlike primitive' and points up the lack of intellectual rigor in its deployment, yet leaves its fundamental logic unquestioned. 'The reasoning', he states,

is as follows: We do have a valid point after all when we observe that the primitives appear to think like (our) children. Calling the primitive childlike is to 'generalize' him as someone with whom we share a common transcultural basis. Analogies between socialization into a culture and learning a language supposedly demonstrate this. (62)

Fabian questions the validity of such premises – specifically, their capacity to function as cornerstones in the elaboration of a theory of culture. He does not debate with the implicit, apparently a priori assumption that the child can function, within such reasoning, as a stable term. The implicit, foundational logic – we can understand primitive strangeness in terms of the familiar child – needs, however, to be questioned. 'Child' is also a conceptual construct engendered and 'othered' by an action of 'temporal distancing', by the epistemological and discursive technique Fabian calls 'allochronism' or 'the denial of coevalness' (33). Neither the child, when considered as primitive, nor the cultural other, when considered as childlike, is allowed to occupy the same temporal frame as the civilized and enlightened European adult. The child, like the primitive, lives a different time. And, if this is so, can the child be so securely situated and deployed within the sphere of Western power and knowledge?

Fabian's analysis fails to take account of the possibility of a 'return of the repressed' operating within emerging discourses of culture and cultural difference. Considering the disruptive effects occasioned by the experience of such a 'return', Freud posits 'the uncanny' as 'something repressed which *recurs*', affirming that 'this uncanny is in reality nothing new or alien but something which is familiar and old-established in the mind and which has become alienated from it only through a process of repression' (634). As Jack Zipes has said, commenting upon Freud, 'the uncanny or unfamiliar (*unheimlich*) brings us in closer touch with the familiar (*heimlich*) because it touches on emotional disturbances and returns us to repressed phases in our evolution' (173). Now, if one conceives the association of the figures of the child and the primitive in terms of the Freudian economy of the familiar and the uncanny, it becomes clear that while the concept 'child' may serve to familiarize the more troubling concept 'primitive', this 'primitive' may serve equally well to defamiliarize 'child'.

During the formative period of Western modernity, the imperial nations of Europe are expanding and attempting to dominate various, newly encountered societies; Europe's expanding nations are also occupied with scrutinizing and striving to domesticate children. In both cases, one must speak of process and struggle rather than of *fait accompli*. Elias points out that the modern European nation-state is both externally embattled and internally pacified. Yet, as he emphasizes, internal pacification, which is crucial to the definition and expansion of the state's hegemonic frontiers, is never to be understood as entire and complete. Deeply implicated in the negotiation of internal pacification is the figure of the child, as my earlier discussion has shown. The child is not always-already a specified subject of early modern, European societies. On the contrary, the child represents a subject-in-process, a focal concern of social projects of civilization and subjection. To establish an economy of association and substitution, of metonymy and metaphor, between the child and the 'primitive' cultural other is in fact to bring one unmastered, one un- or under-subjected element, into confrontation with another. Similarly perturbatory in its discursive effects is the tendency to associate childhood, and notably adolescence, with the spaces and contexts of cultural alterity. The association of the child with the cultural other may serve to compound rather than to simplify the epistemological complexities attending both imperial expansion and internal pacification – two distinct yet henceforth intimately inter-linked projects of domination.[7]

What needs to be stressed, then, is a certain degree of uncertainty and instability in this analogical relation, which must be renegotiated, at least to some small degree, in each instance of its application. As Fabian stresses, the 'childlike native' is an ideological and discursive construct replete with political implications. The same must be said of that 'little heathen', the child. One must recognize, however, that the modern discourse of the child, as exemplified by Rousseau, does not produce an *absolute* equivalence between the child and the 'primitive' cultural other. The child's relation with the other is envisioned and articulated as one of compelling similarity *and significant difference*. It is therefore noteworthy that Rousseau's Émile is made to develop beyond the state of noble savagery in which he first gains awareness of himself and his world, to progress toward a prescribed state of European adulthood. As I pointed out earlier, Rousseau in no way relaxes the demands for the painstaking practice of observation and discipline by which the civilizing process seeks to remake the child in the image of the adult. The developing child thus stands between the European adult and the 'primitive' cultural other. The child is a bi-focal figure, a little Janus who looks in two different directions, backward to what he has been (and, to a certain degree, still is) and forward to what he will become. Considering Fabian's critical intervention, one can say, more precisely, that the figure of the child represents a gap of uncertainty between two distinct temporalities, between the time of the European subject and the time of the other. Three interdependent figures – the child, the 'primitive' other, and the European adult – are thus brought into play, with the child sustaining a precarious balance between the other two. The figure of the child renders the encounter of Europe with its others meaningful in Eurocentric terms: both the child and the other are apprehended in subordinate relation to the privileged and defining case of European adulthood. Yet, by the mediation of the figure of the child the European subject is implicated, brought into psychic and symbolic relation with cultural otherness.

Burke's imperial boys

To repatriate, at this point, the figure of the boy, to resituate him within the specifically British sociocultural context of the later eighteenth century, provides the possibility of discovering all the more clearly and plainly the figure's intimate involvement with projects of imperial expansion. This recontextualization can also serve to confirm the generalized currency and resonance of the boy and, on the other hand, the unstable, unsettling signifying effects the figure's deployment may entail.

In *The Rhetoric of English India*, Sara Suleri has located noteworthy inscriptions of the boy as an organizing figure in Edmund Burke's late eighteenth-century articulation of an imperial crisis of conscience. Burke, unlike Rousseau, is concerned with India, not with the New World, and clearly recognizes that Indian culture cannot be assembled and ordered under the aegis of the 'primitive'. When brought into confrontation with India, Burke's boy asserts his potential for strangeness, manifesting an estrangement of the British imperial project from itself, from its own actions and ideals, and also from the Other it seeks to fashion for itself and dominate. Burke's discourse introduces the boy to India, the crucial cultural referent of Kipling's narratives of imperial adolescence, but deploys the figure to register disruption of the British imperial enterprise, to question rather than to affirm.

Addressing the House of Commons in 1783, Burke denounces the abuses and failures of the East India Company, interrogating, more generally, the Company's adequacy as the governing body of a vast, culturally complex Eastern empire. India presents 'many orders and classes of men ... infinitely diversified by manners, by religion, by hereditary employment, through all their possible combinations'. Burke undertakes to 'map' the object of his concern, both geographically and culturally. He invokes India's vastness and diversity, but places the object of contemplation almost beyond the ken of both reason and imagination, in this way redoubling the complexity attending the question of just and appropriate colonial rule. Submitted to the analysis of the most distinguished eighteenth-century theoretician of the sublime, India emerges, in Sara Suleri's words, as 'the age's leading moral example of the sublime' (28). And as Burke proceeds to characterize British–Indian relations, his rhetoric counterpoints the Indian sublime by implicitly introducing the figure of the child: the speaker scrupulously avers that India, for the metropolitan observer, is 'a very remote object [seen] *through a very false and cloudy medium*' (390, emphasis added). Burke's metropolitan observer takes shape, figuratively, in relation to the Pauline child, whose predicament it is to see the world 'through a glass darkly'. The implicit biblical allusion would seem to suggest that a sense of Britain's 'youthful' inadequacy haunts the more general form of Burke's meditations upon British–Indian relations; the ascription of childishness is not to be limited to the 'boys' of British India, who quickly become the focus of Burke's denunciation.

As Burke proceeds with a more frontal attack upon Company administration, he organizes his rhetoric, very explicitly, around the figure of the boy:

> The natives scarcely know what it is to see the grey head of an Englishman. Young men (boys almost) govern there, without society, and without sympathy with the natives. ... Animated with all the avarice of age, and all the impetuosity of youth, they roll in one after another; wave after wave; ... an endless, hopeless prospect of new flights of birds of prey and passage, with appetites continually renewing. ...
>
> There is nothing in the boys we send to India worse than the boys whom we are whipping at school, or that we see trailing a

pike, or bending over a desk at home. But as English youth in India drink the intoxicating draught of authority and dominion before their heads are able to bear it, and as they are full grown in fortune long before they are ripe in principle, neither nature nor reason have any opportunity to exert themselves for remedy of the excesses of their premature power. (402–3)

Clearly, these schoolboyish delinquents, drunk on a premature accession to power and wealth, are *reprehensibly* young; there is no virtue in their youthfulness, which stands in sharp contrast to India's venerable antiquity. Burke, moreover, remains true to his initial version of the English imperial boy. He offers first an ample account of misdeeds, then returns to the figure of the boy to sum up his case against Company rule, professing himself

stupefied by the desperate boldness of a few obscure young men, who having obtained, by ways which they could not comprehend, a power of which they saw neither the purposes nor the limits, tossed about, subverted, and tore to pieces, as if it were in the gambols of a boyish unluckiness and malice, the most established rights, and the most ancient and most revered institutions, of ages and nations. (427)

In his effort to stage and denounce the inadequacy and irresponsibility of the British colonizer in India, Burke limns the figure of the wanton boy. What he would require, to give a more precise name to the topic of his concern, is a discourse of adolescence. Burke's rhetoric vacillates back and forth between the 'young man' and the 'boy', unable to settle upon the precise figure he needs, which is the boy *as adolescent*, the precariously indeterminate boy who is more than 'child' but still something less than 'man'. The problem, of course, is that a discourse of adolescence is not available *yet*; as C. John Sommerville notes, it is only during the course of the nineteenth century that childhood is 'extended into something called adolescence' (179), an intermediate time of trouble and uncertainty closely associated with 'stress', 'delinquency', and 'antisocial behavior' (Sommerville 198–208). Burke's speech nonetheless evokes the character of fractious adolescence with fair exactitude: imperial Britain's representatives in the East are abundantly energetic yet irresponsibly impetuous, lacking in self-knowledge, unreflectingly driven by passion and appetite; comprehending neither 'the purposes nor the limits' of their increasing stature and strength, the Company youths isolate themselves ('without society ... without sympathy') and set themselves disruptively at odds with their social environment ('toss[ing] about, subvert[ing] and [tearing] to pieces' the social forms that would seek to restrain them). As Suleri maintains, one of Burke's 'most significant recognitions ... concerns the adolescence of the colonizing mind' (32).

Suleri duly notes that Burke's discourse has as its setting the crucible of British legal and governmental power. Once presented in the House of Commons, Burke's 'figures of speech' may be said to enjoy a kind of 'spontaneous legitimation' (Suleri 28). And after Burke, Suleri observes, 'The youthfulness of colonialism, its availability to the mythmaking of adolescent adventure, remains a central figure in the rhetoric of English India' (32). She duly notes, however, that Burke's dismayed denunciation differs sharply, in content and in tone, from the representations of adolescent imperialism and imperial adolescence that will follow upon it:

> When Burke indicts the colonial project as 'the desperate boldness of a few obscure young men,' he dismantles, a century before its time, the prevailing colonial stereotype of Anglo-Indian narrative. ... The adolescence which registers with Burke as an ethical and epistemological vacuity will be recuperated in the era of the Raj as a source of national pride and self-congratulation. (33)

Unlike Rousseau, who perceives the relation between boyhood and cultural alterity as one of natural affinity, Burke responds with dismay and astonishment to the boy-imperialist's intervention in India. The British boy-imperialist, far from being 'right at home' in India, is entirely and reprehensibly out of place. Yet, while Burke ignores or rejects the child–native analogy in his analysis of cross-cultural, imperial relations, his intervention nonetheless implicates British imperial subjectivity in themes of adolescence. He also establishes the imperial boy as a core concern of the British imperial mission and, more particularly, of the imperial mission in India, the colony that will be of salient importance in Kipling's fictions. Burke contributes significantly to the formation of the imperial boy, but leaves the figure much in need of moral recuperation. Burke's discourse is indeed proleptic, as Suleri suggests, in that it critiques an imperial figure that is not yet fully formed – a figure, moreover, that will be formed, in part, in response to Burke.

James Mill and Thomas Babington Macaulay, Suleri suggests, are among the first to significantly reshape the anxious envisioning of British–Indian colonial encounter which is Burke's legacy. Whereas Burke, in representing India, had striven to evoke sublime complexity, Mill, in his *History of India* (1817), disparages a subcontinent that has failed to progress beyond the forms of its antiquity. Macaulay, to further the anglicizing project proposed in his 1835 Minute on Indian Education' (*Selected Writings*) famously propounds the superior value of a few select works in English over the entire archive of classical Indian literatures. He assumes, in Suleri's words, 'the fundamental "irrationality" of all the productions of Indian culture' (34). Even in his essay on Warren Hastings, which is in the main a generous appraisal, Macaulay questions Hastings's status as a 'virtuous ruler' on the basis of his commitment to the study of South Asian arts and sciences; Hastings's fault is that he did not help '[t]o make the young natives of Bengal familiar with Milton and Adam Smith, to substitute the geography, astronomy, and surgery of Europe for the dotages the Brahminical superstition' (*Critical and Historical Essays* 615). Like Mill, then, Macaulay thus indirectly enables an envisioning of British intervention as needfully enterprising and potentially regenerative. And in his popular essay on Clive, Macaulay repeatedly records Clive's age alongside his actions; he fashions an imaginative link between Clive's remarkable achievements and his youth, thus providing a kind of prototype for the narration of British imperialism as a matter of youthful endeavour. Without addressing himself to questions of 'adolescent' imperialism, Macaulay helps to create the possibility of an imperial discourse that represents its 'youthfulness', not as malignantly absurd, but rather as salutary. One should add, however, that Burke's representation of the delinquent boyishness of the imperial venture is susceptible to recuperative configuration in large part because it flies in the face of a new cultural trend C. John Sommerville characterizes as 'the glorification of the child' (120 ff.), which begins to manifest itself in the eighteenth century and is consolidated, in large part, by nine-teenth-century literatures of the child. And certainly, to speak of a specifically *imperial* ideal of childhood and, more particularly, of boyhood requires one to focus upon popular fiction. Suleri, in the course of her discussion, briefly acknowledges the special impor-tance of 'the popular fiction of the late nineteenth and early twentieth century' in the cultural process that reworks the seminal contribution of Burke (32). The rehearsing of the paradigms of British imperialism's glorious 'youthfulness' occurs most obviously and insistently in the arena that will come to be known as the 'boys' book'.

Boyhood and imperial literature

Jeffrey Richards, in his introduction to *Imperialism and Juvenile Literature*, locates in the latter half of the nineteenth century 'the creation of a genre – the boy's adventure tale' (3). Yet even before the mid-century this new genre begins to take shape. 'Marryat,' writes Richards, 'observing how his adult novel *Mr. Midshipman Easy* (1836) had obtained wide popularity with boys, turned his energies to writing books specifically for boys, notably *Masterman Ready* (1841) and *The Children of the New Forest* (1847)' (3). (*Masterman Ready* is especially noteworthy in that, following the example of Rousseau, it reworks the Crusoe narrative as a vehicle for boys' instruction.) Captain Marryat's seafaring, frequently militaris-tic fictions, with their diverse, far-flung settings, help to set the standard for a host of popular and prolific writers of imperial adven-tures for boys, including W. H. G. Kingston and R. M. Ballantyne (who produced between them nearly 300 novel-length adventures for boys), W. Gordon Stables, G. A. Henty, and Mayne Reid. The list of the more distinguished, influential, and widely read practitioners of the imperial adventure tale in the period after 1850 would include Charles Kingsley, H. Rider Haggard, R. L. Stevenson, and of course Rudyard Kipling, all of whom may be credited with produc-ing 'classics' of the genre. Typically entailing cross-cultural encounter (generally of a violent nature) in India, Africa, the Americas, and the Pacific Rim, the adventure tales consolidate the imaginative linkage between youthful, enterprising masculinity and the contact zones of empire.[8]

Also in the second half of the nineteenth century, another important juvenile literary genre appears – the school story for boys. In 1857, Thomas Hughes publishes *Tom Brown's Schooldays*, a tremendously successful, much-imitated work that presents the English public school as the principal setting for the ethical and psychological training of future administrators of the Empire. Significantly, Hughes sets his story in England, at Rugby, yet proudly names his fiction's larger context as 'our' British Empire. Hughes sets in motion a recoding of the school in imperial terms. As Joseph Bristow puts the case, 'the mid-1850s established the beginning of a new type of public-school ideology, one connected with war, honour, and, above all, doing well on the playing field' (57). For Hughes and for the school-tale writers who follow his lead (the most notable among these being the popular and very productive Talbot Baines Reed), the school is an imperial training-ground: rugby matches are battles, where honour is won or lost; cricket matches provide training in esprit de corps.

In 'A New Grub Street for Boys', Patrick Dunae observes that the nineteenth century's final decades 'witnessed a dramatic growth in popular literature for boys', and he discovers in this burgeoning body of literature 'a potent agent in promoting imperial enthusiasms'. Accounting for this specific transformation of the literary marketplace, he emphasizes three key factors: 'the Victorian discovery of adolescence, technological advances, and educational reforms' (13). The later Victorians, Dunae argues, sharpen the distinction between the girl and the boy, and between the child and the adolescent. 'From about the 1860s', he writes, 'literature was produced specifically for adolescent readers. About the same time, the literature also became sex-segregated.' And, as he stresses, boys' literature quickly establishes itself as 'the most important sector of the youth publishing industry'.[9] On the topic of technological innovations, Dunae draws particular attention to the development, also in the 1860s, of the Hoe cylinder press, which 'dramatically increased the speed of printing and paved the way for mass circulation periodicals'. He similarly emphasizes the importance of Forster's Education Act of 1870, which, within ten years, 'created over one million new places in the schools of Britain' (14). The expectation of 'a vast new market' of youthful readers 'prompted the [publishing] industry to focus on the youth market for the first time' (14–15). Along with the boy's book, another relatively new cultural phenomenon, the boys' magazine, becomes an increasingly unignorable presence in the British cultural scene. The new initiatives in the publishing industry reflect, moreover, the popular fervours that signal the advent of the 'New Imperialism'. Advocacy of Britain's imperial mission is ever more frankly stated in the pages of the new magazines, where school and adventure tales, along with geographical and historical accounts of the growing Empire, figure prominently.

Evaluating the various pertinent developments in late nineteenth-century British culture, Bristow writes, 'Imperialism made the boy into an aggrandized subject ... with the future of the world lying upon his shoulders' (19). Called upon to identify with his nation's imperial prestige,

> the boy was idealizing a quality he himself enshrined. Empire and boyhood ... were mutually supportive. Everywhere the nation's young hero encountered texts and illustrations that made him the subject of his reading. Here the boy was both the reader and the focus of what he read. (41)

British popular culture thus manifests, as Bristow, Richards, and Dunae all emphasize, an unprecedented capacity to shape young minds and to inspire in them appropriately imperial values and aspirations. Yet the cultural scenario Bristow describes has implications that extend beyond the circumscribed space of boyhood to the national culture as a whole. During the period in question, the imperial boy clearly emerges as a key figure preoccupying and giving expression to a national consciousness, a British sense of self, a shared, national envisioning of imperial aspiration and destiny. The youthful heroes of the new adventure literature, although commonly young men, are frequently adolescents – adolescent heroes such as Ralph Rover, Jack Martin, and Peterkin Gay of Ballantyne's *The Coral Island*, Dick Humphries and Tom Jackson of Henty's *The Young Colonists*. The principal characters of school fictions are invariably adolescents. These abundant representations of empire-affirming boyhood command the attention not only of boys, but of publishers, writers, critics, parents, teachers – briefly, the growing segment of the adult population that reads, writes, publishes, distributes, praises, condones, or deplores these same representations. British imperial culture richly invests the boy, but also implicates itself in the figure it creates.

Richards, Dunae, and Bristow characterize the boys' magazine as a fiercely contested discursive space. Probably the single most significant event in British culture's battle for the boy is the appearance in 1879 of 'one of the most influential and long-lived boys' magazines, *The Boy's Own Paper*, in which the empire was promoted as the ideal vehicle for the spread of Christian civilization' (Richards 5). Published by the Religious Tract Society, *BOP*'s explicitly stated agenda is to counter the supposedly nefarious influence of the enormously popular 'penny dreadfuls' or 'bloods', which Dunae characterizes as 'cheap, rumbustious publications that featured the quixotic exploits of highwaymen, pirates, and boy brigands' (22). Drawing upon its substantial financial resources, *BOP* employed the talents of such as Henty, Reed, Stables, and Kingston to produce venturesome but appreciably virtuous imperial heroes who might displace, in the minds of the nation's youth, Tom Wildrake, Jack Harkaway – the whole crew of self-serving, devil-may-care delinquents populating the 'dreadfuls'.

Debate over boys' literature generally and over the 'dreadfuls' in particular is significantly inflected by questions of class. Tom Brown, the prototype of the school hero, is of the English gentry. Similarly, the vast majority of adventure heroes manifesting the youthful form of robust, gamely 'Christian manliness' have their provenance in the middle or upper classes. 'Dreadful' heroes, despite their frequent usurpation of the forms of the rogue aristocrat, are generally charismatic youths of undistinguished or unspecified class origins who, having chosen adventurous criminality over dutiful laboriousness, gallantly flout the law and gracefully elude the incompetent pursuit of its representatives. As Bristow notes, the 'dreadfuls' generally target 'a working-class readership' with which they enjoy an 'enduring popularity' (31). And it is their influence upon the laboring classes that their critics fear and denounce. The principal rival publication, the *BOP*, proposes to remain 'sound and healthy in tone' (qtd. in Bristow 39), advocates patriotism and duty, and provides both 'useful knowledge' and stimulating yet right-minded entertainment. Although the success of its bid for boy readers is indisputable, it is by no means entire.

The 'dreadfuls' continue to haunt boy's literature: first, by their unabated popularity and salient presence in the marketplace; secondly, and perhaps more crucially, by their unacknowledged yet seemingly unavoidable influence upon the saner and sager publications that arise in reaction against them. *Boy's Own Paper* or *Boys of England*, for all that their material is informed by 'key middle-class values' (Bristow 33), cannot do without fictions of action and adventure similar to those offered by their predecessors and competitors, the 'dreadfuls'. Stating the case more succinctly, Bristow writes, 'Violence had to be taken away from the recently named hooligan and restyled for the respectable boy' (47).

This 'respectable boy', however, reveals a certain affiliation with the 'blood' hero: although he is patriotic and responds to duty's call, the *BOP* boy is, in Bristow's words, 'aggressive, competitive, and yet gentlemanly' (41), a representative of 'a new kind of militaristic masculinity' energized by 'a distinctive imperial spirit' (47). Despite the necessity of marking and maintaining its class divisions, an aggressively expansive, imperial nation clearly must demand something other than 'sweetness and light' from its youth. Summarizing the curious progress of British popular culture in 'Penny Dreadfuls: Late Nineteenth-Century Boys' Literature and Crime', Dunae observes that the literature that 'one generation of critics had denounced as "blood and thunder" came, in a slightly altered form, to be regarded by the next generation as wholesome and patriotic' (150). The battle for the boy thus arrives, by the end of the nineteenth century, at its peculiar resolution: empire and the imperial boy emerge as the victors in a discursive struggle organized around disparate forms of class consciousness. This imperial boy, moreover, is now established as a familiar, current figure within a variety of class locations, as a figure that effectively calls upon a broad-based national consciousness.

The adolescent imperial protagonist, representing in Kipling's time a newly energized element in the British cultural scene, is yet a curiously overdetermined figure fraught with anxious aspirations susceptible to a variety of incommensurate and incompatible representations. Indeed, what most distinguishes the new boy is the excessive burden of societal investments he must bear. Taking shape amid class conflict and in the forge of emergent imperial meanings and values, the boy is a figure emblazoned with the mora ideals of his society's dominant classes, but one who may also appear in guise of the delinquent or the renegade; a potential representative of imperialism's noble mission of disinterested Christian service, yet a manifestation of a newer, aggressive, and opportunistic imperial mood. Even the ideal boy, as outlined in the pages of 'respectable' boys' popular literature in the last decades of the nineteenth century, resembles not only the 'blood' protagonist but, still more closely, the boy-imperialist Burke had denounced a century before. Certainly, the new boy, unlike Burke's, has been made to understand something of his imperial responsibilities. Indeed, in Bristow's view, popular discourses of the boy conspire to make imperial Britain's 'new generation of young men feel that they [are] the central social actors of their day' (48). What has occurred is a reorganization and rearticulation, in close relation with the demands of energetic imperial expansion, of the pre-existing myths and ideals of childhood that assign the child a place and role within the social dynamic. Established in this process as the key figure is the adolescent boy, a principal site of sociocultural aspirations and anxieties, where the double wager of social evolution at home and the imperial mission abroad is played out.

This imperial boy thus possesses a resonance extending well beyond the literary, fictional realm that constitutes the principal site of his formation. R. S. S. Baden-Powell, writing just after the turn of the century, situates the adolescent boy, specifically the 'scout', at the very center of imperial questions:

> From this little island of Great Britain have sprung colonies all over the world, Australia, New Zealand, South Africa, India, Canada.
>
> Almost every race, every kind of man, black, white, or yellow, have furnished subjects of King Edward VII.
>
> This vast Empire did not grow of itself out of nothing; it was made by your forefathers by dint of hard work and hard fighting. People say that we have no patriotism nowadays, and that our Empire will fall to pieces like the great Roman Empire did. ... I am not so sure about that. I am sure that if you boys will keep the good of your country in your eyes above everything else she will go all right. But if you don't do this there is very great danger, because we have many enemies abroad. ... (28–30)

Baden-Powell imagines the British island as a prodigiously genera
tive dam, a mother country that gives birth to colonies. Thes
colonies, as if born pregnant, dutifully 'furnish' subjects for th
British king. Responsibility for the 'mother' country and her abur
dant progeny passes by natural succession from the hard-working
hard-fighting 'forefathers' to the new generation of boys. Th
Empire is presented as the filial, familial duty that falls upon th
duly designated heirs apparent.

The boy and British imperial self-fashioning

The figure of the imperial boy needs to be understood as providin
the occasion for a fuller, more richly invested imagining of Britain
imperial status. Despite its vastness, complexity, and diversity, th
British Empire is presented to British subjects as appropriabl
Through cultural mediation the Empire at large becomes a matter c
public and also private interest, a national yet also a person;
possession. British subjects, even those who never venture beyon
the bounds of little England, can thus be made to understand an
appreciate their status as imperial subjects, a status that
confirmed and sustained not only by the grand spectacle c
frequent, fully public manifestations, but also by a multiplicity c
everyday experiences. Through the abundance and ubiquity of it
representation, 'the Empire' effectively becomes a key locus whei
British subjectivity shapes itself.

Popular literature representing both boyhood and empire partic
pates in the popularization of imperial actuality. The books be;
colorfully illustrated covers, as do the magazines. The magazine
invariably, and the books very commonly, include illustrated page:
Moreover, this literature conspires with other mediating vehicles
picture postcards, commemorative collectibles, music hall perfo;
mances, theatrical panoramas, and, of course, the 'grez
exhibitions' – to make the Empire imaginatively accessibl
Kipling's work very clearly invites readers to pleasurably envisio
foregrounded boy characters, to identify with Mowgli, in the India
jungle amongst his wolves; with Stalky, in maneuvers both ;
school and on the Indian frontier; and with Kim, jubilantly astrid
the Zam-Zammah gun or avidly observing the bustle of India
Grand Trunk Road. One sees and experiences the Empire in tander

with the boy. The figure of the imperial boy (typically imaged on the cover of the publication that narrates his exploits) is offered as an emblematic protagonist orienting and mediating various experiences of empire. Visual and literary representations combine to make the individual Briton's relationship with 'the Empire' seem intimate, immediate, intensely meaningful. Offering a detailed, pleasurable, and affirmative envisioning of the British Empire is an important function of the fictional literature of the boy.

Fictions of the imperial boy participate in the ordering and constitution of the British subject's apprehension of the relationship between self and world, self and other. The boy instigates and facilitates processes of identification binding that subject to the imperial project of the nation. The figure represents a significant contribution to what Satya P. Mohanty calls the British imperial 'project of self-fashioning' ('Drawing' 328), the forging of an image of selfhood in relation to which imperial aspirations and values can be affirmatively enunciated. As Said, following Foucault, makes clear both in *Orientalism* and in his more recent *Culture and Imperialism*, imperial discourses actualize power, especially when the power that is professed correlates with other established structures and practices of political, economic, and sociocultural domination. Notwithstanding this power-productive materiality of discourse, its sense-making role must be stressed: representations of empire and the boy are, first and foremost, enabling fictions bearing the promise – perhaps the false promise – of a coherent relation between the British imperial subject and the history and actuality of British imperialism.

In speaking of the boy as a *figure*, I propose him as a culturally generated site of investment and identification positioned within that larger configuration, 'the Empire'. My analysis of structures of investment and identification in Kipling's narratives therefore will evidence quite frequently a Lacanian orientation, employing, most crucially, the concepts of the Imaginary and the Symbolic. In his essay on 'the mirror stage', Lacan outlines the first of these, emphasizing the specular economy of self-recognition the Imaginary entails. The Imaginary mode of experience institutes identification, the self-defining 'transformation that takes place in the subject when he assumes an image'. However, despite its foundational role in 'the functions of libidinal normalization', Imaginary identification orders the subject's 'reality' in relation with a fictional and alienated self-image: it 'situates the agency of the ego, before its social determination, in a fictional direction'; it 'symbolizes the mental permanence of the *I*, at the same time as it prefigures its alienating destination' (2–3). These dynamic tensions informing Imaginary identification make of it an enduring psychic and experiential orientation. The mirror image or *imago* ultimately provides the basis for 'heteromorphic identification' and intimately links itself to 'the signification of space for the living organism' (3). It becomes 'the function of the *imago* ... to establish a relation between the organism and its reality' and to inscribe its peculiarity upon the entire 'anatomy of phantasy' (4–5). The Imaginary mode of experience and the movements of identification it entails continue therefore to orient much of the individual's being-in-the-world.

It is, however, in the initiation to the Symbolic order of language that Lacan locates the definitive emergence of the fully human subject. Eventually there must occur 'the deflection of the specular *I* into the social *I*' (5), the restructuring of the *I* in 'socially elaborated situations' and its 'normalization' through processes of 'cultural mediation' (5–6). Language is the structuring apparatus that constitutes the child as a social being susceptible and responsive to social demands and constraints. The acquisition of speech, however, redoubles the self-alienation already evident in the mirror stage, obliging the child-subject to identify in the locus of the Other, to take place in relation to systems of meaning that are not of his own making. In 'The Function and Field of Speech and Language in Psychoanalysis' (*Écrits*), the lecture in which the notion of the Symbolic first takes shape, Lacan asserts that, for the human subject, 'It is the world of words that creates the world of things'. Intersubjective symbolic exchange does not merely mediate but rather structures and defines the human reality: 'Man speaks .. but it is because the symbol has made him man' (65). Employing the Saussurean distinction between *langue* (the system of language) and *parole* (the act of speech), Lacan emphasizes how *langue* circumscribes and constrains each enactment of *parole*, thus portraying 'man' not as an autonomous speaking being but as a subjected being constituted by social symbolic networks, regimented by the array of language systems whose imperatives precede and far exceed all merely individual initiatives. The Symbolic is thus the order in which the subject must discover and assume a place. It is to be understood as a self-sustaining and self-referring system that confronts the individual speaking subject and recruits her or him to its service.

Although both constitute, for the subject, enduring orders of experience, the relationship between the Imaginary and the Symbolic is neither complementary nor commensurable. The Imaginary and Symbolic must be understood as competing orders that orient and organize subjectivity in distinct ways. Both orders, moreover, are unavoidably at odds with the Real, which, in Lacanian theory, resists and disrupts both orders of experience. A criticism oriented by Lacanian notions of the Imaginary and the Symbolic must therefore remain aware of the tensions with which the triad of the Imaginary, the Symbolic, and the Real are fraught.

As my subsequent chapters will manifest, Kipling's boy serves to specify and distribute imperial and colonial subjects, to imaginatively dominate and order various spaces of empire. Kipling's fictions establish – as the preceding tradition of adventure and school literature begins to do – the boy as the principal, indeed representative protagonist in the 'story' of British imperialism. My scholarship will strive to illuminate something of the relationship between Kipling's fictions and imperial history and to show how these fictions allude to and stage real practices of domination. However, a principal concern throughout will be to show how these fictions, by the mediation of the boy, strive, not always successfully, to produce coherent, attractive Imaginary and Symbolic envisionings of the British imperial enterprise; to show how the boy facilitates, yet also at times perturbs, the identifications of British imperial subjects with that enterprise. Kipling's boy images an imperial 'ego-ideal', an appealing *imago* for the imperial subject. Yet Kipling, in offering such ego-centered gratification, does not forswear the struggle to represent the British imperial project as symbolically coherent, as the intersubjective undertaking of a community informed and sustained by shared codes and meanings. My next chapter, which considers the function of Kipling's boy in the allegorization of empire, will establish clearly and in detail the figure's dual role as Imaginary hero and as mediator of a Symbolic ordering of 'the Empire'.

2
The Jungle Books: Post-Mutiny Allegories of Empire

In *Rule of Darkness: British Literature and Imperialism, 1830–1914*, Patrick Brantlinger highlights the special status of the Indian Mutiny in the British Empire's cultural legacy. Briefly documenting post-Mutiny literary production, he observes: 'at least fifty [Mutiny novels] were written before 1900, and at least thirty more before World War II. There was also a deluge of eyewitness accounts, journal articles, histories, poems and plays dealing with the 1857–58 rebellion.' Brantlinger concurs with Hilda Gregg, who first affirmed, in 1897, the Mutiny event's unparalleled capacity to capture the British imperial imagination. He also remarks that Gregg, more impressed with the quantity than the quality of Mutiny fictions, regretted that Rudyard Kipling (in 1897 a young writer at the zenith of celebrity) had not made his contribution. Duly attentive to the inflammatory xenophobia of much Mutiny-inspired writing,[1] Brantlinger suggests, 'Perhaps Kipling intuitively avoided a subject that so tempted other writers to bar the doors against imaginative sympathy' (199).

Unlike so many of his predecessors and contemporaries – Meadows Taylor, G. A. Henty, Flora Annie Steel, among others – Kipling never produced what one might properly call 'a Mutiny tale'. Given, however, Kipling's status as the popularly acclaimed 'bard' of the Indian Empire, his maintaining an unremitting silence upon the topic of the Mutiny would be very strange indeed. A Brantlinger asserts at the outset, 'No episode of British imperial history raised public excitement to a higher pitch' (199). Making an abundantly documented case, he establishes the 1857 revolt as an emotionally charged, key referent of later nineteenth-century imperial myth-making and ideology. To accept, then, the main thrust of Brantlinger's argument is to recognize that the Mutiny constitutes, for Kipling, an unavoidable topic. The question is not if but rather where and how he addressed it.[2]

In this chapter, I will strive to show how British imperial history and, more particularly, Mutiny history inform Kipling's fictions, and also how these fictions rework imperial history. As James Morris affirms in *Heaven's Command*, 'the emotions of the Mutiny found their echoes all over the British Empire, permanently affecting its attitudes, and leaving scars and superstitions that were never quite healed or exorcised' (246). Kipling's engagement with the emotionally fraught issues of the Mutiny topic is, for the most part, oblique, allusive, and allegorical. Post-Mutiny allegories – that is, narrative sequences organized upon allusive evocations of Mutiny scenes, situations, and events – occur most notably where one might expect them least, in the best-loved and most widely known of Kipling's narratives of the boy, that is, in the Mowgli tales of *The Jungle Books*. This working-through of a major moment of imperial crisis in a fantastic boy-narrative demonstrates clearly that such narrative is not only for boys; fictions of the imperial boy, as I have suggested, address a much broader public and take up issues of general social import. Kipling's jungle saga, as I will argue, presents an allegorical, empire-affirming restaging of the history of British India, a restaging that is ordered upon yet unsettled by its inscription of the Mutiny crisis.[3]

Historical crisis and folkloric triumph

To consider Kipling as a post-Mutiny imperial allegorist requires that one place his fictions in relation with Mutiny history and, more particularly, with the British story of that history. In *Allegories of Empire*, Jenny Sharpe considers the complex intertextual relation between the stories and histories of empire, advocating a historically informed reading of literary texts, but cautioning against 'treating "fact" and "fiction" as repetitions of each other'. Following upon initiatives of Pierre Macherey's *The Theory of Literary Production*, Sharpe proposes a critical orientation that strives to discover 'the absent text of history in the margins of literature, as its unconscious or "unsaid"'. In Sharpe's view, 'History, forming the conditions of existence of the literary imagination, places limits and restrictions on what can be represented at any one moment. Fiction is granted license to imagine events as they might have happened or in a way that history has failed to record' (21). Insofar as fictions may be said to represent 'possible worlds rather than probable ones', critical analysis may take as its task 'to show how [literary works] stage social contradictions and strive to resolve them' (21–2). Taking, then, the Indian Rebellion of 1857 as the 'absent text' of Kipling's fictions of the jungle-boy, my analysis will strive to show how the history informs the fictions, and how the fictions reconstrue and reshape the history.

'Popular cognizance of the modern history of the Indian subcontinent', writes Eric Stokes in *The Peasant Armed*, 'is limited appropriately to three episodes dignified by the names of "Clive", "the Mutiny", and "Gandhi". For these unerringly epitomize its three decisive historical phases – the colonial onset, the crisis of consolidation, and the colonial defeat and withdrawal.' Thus naming 'the Mutiny' as the signal moment and organizing referent of a British imperial 'crisis of consolidation', Stokes also acknowledges the prevalent if potentially perturbatory influence of 'popular cognizance' or 'the folk memory' upon the historical analysis and evaluation of 'the Mutiny'. The 1857 insurrection takes shape as 'a period-piece' that 'still holds Western attention because of the intimate, human scale on which the action was conducted'; it evokes 'the picture-book world with which the later Victorian age peopled its imagination and named its streets and public houses' (1). For Stokes, the very vividness and abundance of Mutiny lore poses an acute problem, even for the assiduous historiographer: 'That the past should remain charged with emotion is the precondition of the historian's activity, but such emotion almost imprisons him within the framework of its own lines of interpretation' (4).[4]

To confront the Mutiny as history is to recognize, first and foremost, that the uprisings of 1857–58 offered a deeply disruptive, multifaceted challenge to British claims to colonial authority, a complex, multiply articulated calling into question of the reign of 'justice' and 'efficiency'. Curiously, from the mid-nineteenth century forward, the Indian rebellion has been represented as 'mutiny', as a military revolt against a constituted, ostensibly legitimate authority. Certainly, the sepoys did rebel against their British officers. However, the military insurrection rapidly acquired a more than military character. As Indian nationalist historian Sashi Bhusan Chaudhuri first emphasized, the rebellion's overall development consistently evidenced non-military, populist and regional aspects, which are effectively effaced by the name of 'Mutiny'. Stokes, in his study, speaks of a 'Mutiny Rebellion', subdividing his topic into zones of military mutiny or of civil rebellion and submitting the revolt to a scrupulously regionalized analysis. He stresses, moreover, that, among nineteenth-century British interpreters, 'The nature of the 1857 uprising aroused fierce controversy from the outset'. The name of 'Mutiny' reflects a reassuring official perspective: 'The official British explanation was that the Bengal Native Army alone had mutinied and that any civil disturbances were the natural by-products of the breakdown of law and order' (*Peasant* 4). Other sources perceived, however, 'a formidable civil rebellion' or even 'a national insurrection' evidencing 'premeditated design' and, for some, 'a Mohomedan conspiracy' (5–7). Yet another interpretation, more securely grounded in historical data, propounded a 'peasant revolt' energized by disruptive British interventions in pre-existing local systems of property (9–12). This 'predominantly economic interpretation', Stokes observes, 'is far from modern. Like most other theories of the revolt, it was one originally advanced by contemporaries' (11). It obtained, moreover, a significant degree of purchase in powerful circles, among post-Mutiny policy-makers.

Clearly, what British imperial interpretations grapple with – affirming or disavowing, to varying degrees and in different ways – is the possibility that 'the Mutiny' constituted a broadly based popular insurrection, a generalized, if variously articulated, disaffection with and resistance to British rule – a view, as Stokes notes, that was not without its proponents in the post-Mutiny debate. During the 1857 revolt, India asserted itself as a multifarious socio-cultural territory, which assembled various classes, castes, regional groups, and communities having various relationships with British colonial power. The insurrection, as history, therefore tended to resist British attempts to submit it to an all-encompassing interpretation, to generalize upon an event that appeared so spectacularly plural in its motives and its enactments. If it revealed anything with clarity, it was a troubling precariousness of British power.

Still more curious, therefore, than its naming is the fact that this so-called 'Mutiny' ultimately takes shape in the late Victorian popular imagination not so much as crisis but rather as triumph. First for journalists and subsequently for poets, novelists, historians, it becomes the object of an oft-repeated, obsessive return. As Brantlinger's richly detailed and evocative treatment reveals, in innumerable retellings the 1857 revolt finds the forms of the grand narrative, with its sites of tragedy ('the Well at Cawnpore'), its great actions ('the Relief of Lucknow'), its heroes and martyrs (Lawrence, Havelock) and its villains (Bahadur Shah, Nana Sahib). It becomes, to use the famous phrase of Anglo-Indian historian Charles Crosthwaite, 'the epic of the race' (qtd. in Morris, *Heaven's Command* 243). The celebratory assertion of ultimate victory thus subsumes and elides the discourse of crisis. Transformed by its passage into popular discourse, the historical event is recuperated for imperial ideology and acquires, moreover, the status of folklore. The Indian Mutiny becomes, as both Stokes and Brantlinger suggest, a constitutive element of the British Empire's story of itself – the very stuff imperial dreams are made on. Kipling, therefore, is able to rewrite the Mutiny story and, at the same time, the story of British India in allegorical form, as imperial fable. His allusive and evocative jungle fictions register imperial fear and desire, aspiration and doubt, drawing upon and contributing to a shared sociogenetic image-repertoire that emerges in response to the Mutiny crisis.[5]

This chapter, then, will not strive to contribute to historiography of the 1857 rebellion nor to claim for Kipling any status as a historiographer. It will, however, demonstrate that Kipling fictionally re-stages the Mutiny story and in so doing consorts with what Ranajit Guha calls 'the prose of counter-insurgency', that is, the British 'historiography' that strives to assimilate Indian anti-colonial insurrection 'to the transcendental Destiny of the British Empire' (74). This writing of Indian history, like Kipling's rewriting of it, implicitly or explicitly 'celebrate[s] a continuity – that of British power in India'. It 'serve[s] admirably to register the [insurgent] event as a datum in the life-story of the Empire' (71). Kipling, as I will show, renders the imperial 'life-story' affirmatively yet allegorically. In his tales of the feral boy who becomes, gradually but inevitably, the 'Master of the Jungle', Kipling produces a fictional 'prose of counter-insurgency', which attempts to resolve the enduring anxieties and tensions informing the history and discourse of British imperialism in India.

My analysis of the Mowgli saga seeks to demonstrate, first, that Mowgli's *Bildung* – the narration and figuring forth of his individual formation – is an empire-affirming allegorization of the history of British India and, secondly, that this allegorization is organized upon and ultimately disrupted by the Mutiny moment. I begin by considering the triumphant representation of imperial consolidation in the tale of Mowgli's early manhood, 'In the Rukh', which stages Mowgli's enabling identification with the British Empire and establishes his status as an imperial hero. Turning subsequently to the tales of boyhood, my argument identifies the adolescent Mowgli as an imperial proxy, as a protagonist who represents the British imperial mission in the absence of the British colonizer. I then examine the structuring of Mowgli's world as an Indological India constituted upon and deeply informed by Western, imperial 'knowledge' of India. Moving on to a close examination of the jungle-boy's narrative progress, I isolate and analyze the unsettling, allegorical inscriptions of the Mutiny upon Kipling's tales.

Identification with(in) the Empire

An oddity in the publication history of the Mowgli saga makes it a narrative that discovers its resolution in advance of its elaboration, a drama that is preceded by its epilogue. 'In the Rukh', published in *Many Inventions* in 1893, a year before the appearance of the first of the two *Jungle Books*, provides the comedic, empire-affirming dénouement of an as yet untold story: Mowgli, in the fullness of his youthful manhood, takes a wife and embarks upon a career of imperial service with the Department of Woods and Forests. His two principal actions are intimately intertwined, each being contingent upon the other: by accepting an imperial career under Forest Officer Gisborne, Mowgli assures himself of the status and income necessary to claim a wife; by taking a wife, he confirms his stable placement within the human community and hence his candidacy for imperial service. Mowgli espouses, at one and the same time, humanity and the Empire.[6]

In 1894, readers of Kipling can open *The Jungle Book* with the reassuring foreknowledge that the ambivalences marking Mowgli's

drives, sympathies, and identifications, will move toward an appropriately imperial resolution: the feral child among the wolves will
ultimately pursue his human destiny in the service of the Empire.
He has been chosen, moreover, to play an important role within the
imaginative economy of the British imperial project. As the text of
'In the Rukh' announces in a moment of epiphanic revelation,
Mowgli is to be a hero of the imperial Imaginary. Having tracked
Mowgli through the woods, Gisborne, accompanied by the wood-
demon's reluctant father-in-law-to-be, comes upon a wondrous
pageant:

> There was the breathing of a flute in the rukh, as it might have
> been the song of some wandering wood-god. ... The path ended
> in a little semicircular glade walled partly by high grass and
> partly by trees. In the centre, upon a fallen trunk, his back to the
> watchers and his arm round the neck of Abdul Gafur's daughter,
> sat Mowgli, newly crowned with flowers, playing upon a rude
> bamboo flute, to whose music four huge wolves danced solemnly
> on their hind legs. ('Appendix A' of *The Jungle Books* 345)

This sylvan flautist, this demi-god who commands the natural
world, associates himself with Orpheus or Pan or, as Gisborne's
German colleague, Muller, observes, with 'Adam in der Garden'
(344). The *rukh* is presented in this key scene as an enchanted glade,
as a little world constructed upon Mowgli's personal and individual
scale, a world where everything is fitted to him – within his reach,
available to his grasp. As the young man states his case, 'The jungle
is my house' (346), and the wolf-brethren 'my eyes and feet' (347).
Mowgli's lupine *imago*-figures have not, here, the potentially threat-
ening, confrontational aspect that they, along with the other jungle
denizens, frequently reveal in the tales of the hero's boyhood. The
ego has tamed its images, which now dance in ceremonial obei-
sance to the music of a sovereign will. Mowgli enjoys, in other
words, what one might describe, in Lacanian terms, as an ideal
Imaginary relation with the jungle world: he is able to apprehend it
in specular relation to himself, as a self-affirming system of simili-
tudes and equivalencies organized around his own body and
selfhood.[7] He therefore provides the possibility of a personal, intimate envisioning of an alien world. Certainly, there is truth in

Muller's lament, 'I shall nefer know der inwardness of der *rukh*' (344). And Gisborne, the other imperial alien, might also voice such a lament were he not granted a vision of that mysterious inwardness. To appreciative British eyes, Mowgli offers a glimpse of a 'real' India, of a 'natural and essential' India residing beyond the confounding veil of culture.

It is curious, yet strangely apt, that Mowgli, still the most famous of Kipling's adolescent heroes, should be a feral child. The Mowgli saga draws upon existing knowledge of feral children, plays upon the European public's fascination with them. But, of course, Kipling's interest in the wild child is mythic rather than sociological and anthropological. Objects of public and scientific curiosity since the seventeenth century, feral children in Europe, as C. John Sommerville remarks, had been quite extensively documented by Linnaeus and others. Victor of Aveyron, a wild boy captured in 1798 (at the estimated age of 11) and placed under the care and supervision of French physician Jean Itard, provides the most famous, most fully detailed case. Victor, under Nature's tutelage, acquires neither physical grace nor heightened sensibility and intelligence. He is, when first apprehended, 'a surly, snapping beast' – amoral, emotionally and intellectually stunted, sensorially deranged (Sommerville 134). 'The crowds that turned out to watch Victor', Sommerville pertinently notes, 'expected that in a few months he would have picked up enough of the language to offer some striking observations on his life in the wilds' (135). In this respect, Victor frustrates most acutely the cultural desire he provokes, responding in significant ways to socialization, *but never learning to speak*. Kipling chooses against the historical feral child, electing instead his Mowgli, who gratifies, allegorically, the desire the factual and historical Victor disappoints; who brings a voice, provides a view, into the silence and secrecy of an alien world – the colonial 'wilds'.

This offering of a privileged view into the secret world of the Other is not, of course, the full extent of the jungle-youth's largess. Mowgli in his enchanted glade also presents an ideal image of imperial authority. 'To be above yet to belong', writes John McClure, 'to be obeyed as a god and loved as a brother, this is Kipling's dream for an imperial ruler, a dream that Mowgli achieves' (60). And if Mowgli's power and knowledge must remain in large part mysterious, yet they are pledged to imperial service rather than to subversion and resistance: 'I have eaten Gisborne's bread,' Mowgli affirms, 'and presently I shall be in his service, and my brothers will be his servants' (347).

'Mowgli's paradise', ascertains John McBratney, 'is not a creation independent of imperial politics but a coextensive product of it' (289). That Mowgli is not simply an Imaginary hero but a remarkably serviceable *imperial* hero is most saliently marked by Kipling's tale's subtle deployment and manipulation of the two modes of psychic identification, which Slavoj Žižek, working from Lacanian psychoanalytic theory, has characterized as 'imaginary' and 'symbolic' identification. Emphasizing the crucial role of the gaze in processes of identification, Žižek explains,

> imaginary identification is identification with the image in which we appear likeable to ourselves, with the image representing 'what we would like to be', and symbolic identification, identification with the very place *from where* we are being observed, *from where* we look at ourselves so that we appear to ourselves likeable, worthy of love. (105)

The clear and thorough apprehension of the significance of the enchanted glade experience requires, then, the recognition that it is (and must be) *observed*. The glade is not a site of free-standing, 'private' experience, but rather the setting of a pageant, whose presentation within the narrative is contingent upon the advent of a spectator, Gisborne. As Žižek stresses, 'imaginary identification is always identification on behalf of a certain gaze in the Other. So ... apropos of every "playing a role", the question to ask is: for whom is the subject enacting this role? Which gaze is considered when the subject identifies himself with a certain image?' (106) Gisborne's status as the appropriate spectator is confirmed, of course, by the presence of an inappropriate candidate, Abdul Gafur, whose terror and abject incomprehension contrast sharply with the ranger's appreciative wonderment and thus signal the colonial subaltern's effective exclusion from the economy of ideal imperial identifications. While the fulfillment of Mowgli's Imaginary identification is contained within the glade (in the figures of the dancing wolves who 'reflect' the jungle-master's sovereign status), his Symbolic identification is to be located in the figure of Gisborne, who provides the imperial presence and the imperial perspective. It is only in the eye of empire that the lupine sovereign of the jungle can fully appreciate his own charms. And of course, one should note that Mowgli repays Gisborne in the same coin, by offering himself, first, as a pleasing image-object for imperial sovereignty. Subsequently, by returning the gaze – 'Mowgli turning with his three retainers faced Gisborne as the Forest Officer came forward' (347) – the young jungle-lord provides the site of Symbolic identification, the perspective from which Gisborne (as the wondrous Mowgli's acknowledged master) appears agreeable to himself, worthy of esteem.

For both Gisborne and Mowgli, symbolic identification constitutes the empire-affirming nature of their encounter. 'It is', writes Žižek, 'the symbolic identification (the point from which we are observed) which dominates and determines the image' (108), which shapes and gives a fully social meaning to Imaginary identification. Both Gisborne and Mowgli locate symbolic identification in a representative of empire: Gisborne apprehends himself from the perspective of the Master of the Jungle; Mowgli from the perspective of the British imperial officer. Each character recognizes and accepts 'a certain "mandate", ... a certain place in the intersubjective symbolic network' (Žižek 110): Mowgli (together with the 'retainers' of his little empire) is pledged to service in the British empire; Gisborne is confirmed as a duly empowered, responsible representative of British imperial authority. A finely balanced economy of complementary identification securely situates individual Imaginary gratification and self-fashioning within the defining Symbolic context of the British Empire. But more crucially (for the analysis of the Mowgli saga that follows), the seminal scene in the *rukh* announces a mutually sustaining Imaginary and Symbolic relation between Gisborne and Mowgli, between an imperial subject whose characterization is marked by historical referentiality – there is, in British India, a Department of Woods and Forests; there are Forest Officers – and an entirely mythic, liminal boy. In 'In the Rukh', the first and the last of the Mowgli tales, the narrative point of origin and of resolution, imperial subjectivity is produced in contingent relation with the myth-figure of the boy, who represents, in ideal terms, the British Empire and who is represented at the same time from the perspective of the Empire.

The liminal boy as imperial proxy

Whereas Gisborne and Muller are prominent in 'In the Rukh', the Mowgli tales of *The Jungle Books* contain not one European character. The English are a matter of rare allusion, a distant, vaguely understood presence that never intrudes upon the little world of jungle and village. Imperialism, however, is always-already there in the Indian scene even in the absence of the imperialist; it is, as the preceding analysis of 'In the Rukh' has shown, inscribed in advance as the beginning and the end of the narrative progress. The Mowgli saga, as it is detailed in *The Jungle Books*, allegorizes an imperialist world-view in the absence of British colonizers, inscribing and 'naturalizing' imperial codes and values without immediate recourse to imperial intervention.

Crucial to this work of allegorization is the liminal boy (situated upon the in-betweens of the animal and the human, of nature and culture) who serves as an imperial proxy. Mowgli's jungle history repeats, in ideal form, the history of the British presence in India. In 'Mowgli's Brothers', a weak yet 'bold' newcomer pushes his brethren-to-be aside to reach the she-wolf's nurturing teat and gradually establishes himself in jungle society. Following upon 'Mowgli's Brothers', 'Kaa's Hunting' clearly reveals that Mowgli receives an education in which imperial codes are re-envisioned as jungle laws: under Baloo, 'the Teacher of the Law', Mowgli learns more and different lessons than the young wolves do, receiving instruction in 'the Master Words of the Jungle', which allow him to move freely and safely in jungle spaces controlled by potentially hostile jungle peoples (23). By the end of the third tale, '"Tiger! Tiger!"', one can see that the boy has succeeded in reorganizing the jungle world around himself and has emerged as its new master. An imperial progress is thus figured as an extraordinary *Bildung*, as a jungle-boy's life process of growth and maturation. The imperial thrust of Mowgli's jungle formation is most clearly in evidence, however, as the boy establishes relations with the specifically Indian world of the village. Employing quite sophisticated techniques of strategy and 'intelligence', Mowgli, aided by his jungle allies, uses village bullocks to destroy his arch-enemy, Shere Khan. And when the jungle-boy moves against the village in 'Letting in the Jungle', his mastery of techniques of surveillance and infiltration is indisputably the key to his success. An insider/outsider in both the jungle world and the village world, liminal Mowgli is different from and superior to all other characters (animal or human) he encounters: he has always a mysterious supplementary power – the mystique of 'Man' or the uncanny jungle knowledge. Native-born, yet set apart, Mowgli is different, undeniably special. Caught between two opposing worlds, divided in his identifications and his affiliations, he can be read as a fabulous, idealized analogue of the sociocultural in-betweenness of an India-born Englishman (like Rudyard Kipling). With greater certainty, however, one can discover in Mowgli, the hybrid adolescent, an allegorical representative of a youthful, vigorous British imperial project and a figuring of Kipling's ideal imperial subject, a subject capable of negotiating – not without hardship but with ultimate success – the antithetical demands of domination and assimilation.

The allegorization of imperial space: the jungle and the village

Reading Mowgli as a protagonist of imperial allegory demands, of course, a reading of his world as allegorical fictional space. I would need to demonstrate, moreover, that Mowgli's progress toward the mastery of his world does not simply represent an archetypal, generalizable *Bildung* within a generalizable, more or less transcultural microcosm. At the literal level, the Mowgli saga is set in India, in an Indian jungle and in an Indian village. However, allegorically too, India, or rather the 'India' articulated by Western Indology, is the principal referent of Mowgli's little world. Imperialism, the 'absent presence' of the Mowgli tales of *The Jungle Books*, is thus inscribed, conceptually and tropologically, in relation to biased European knowledge systems that reconstruct India as the Western world's dominated Other.

  In *Imagining India*, a revaluative, deconstructive study of Western Indology, Ronald Inden documents the development and consolidation, particularly during the nineteenth century, of the notion of Hinduism as the religion that expresses and effectively embodies the 'Mind of India' (85 ff.). To understand Hinduism is, for the Indologist, 'to grasp the mind of the entire [Indian] civilization' (86). Hinduism and, by extension, Indian civilization are made to represent the negation of conceptions of rational order bestowed upon Western thinkers by the Enlightenment. The Enlightenment's 'principles of order', Inden recalls, are 'mutual exclusion, unity, centredness, determinacy, and uniformity'. Entirely antithetical to these principles, the Hinduism of Indology 'does not consist of a system of opposed but interdependent parts, but a wild tangle of overlapping and merely juxtaposed pieces. It is uncentred ... , unstable ... , and lacking in uniformity ...' (88). What Hinduism entirely lacks is Western 'world-ordering rationality'. Not surprisingly, therefore, 'the most widely used metaphor' in Indological accounts of Hinduism 'is that of Hinduism as a jungle' (86).

Kipling's use of jungle as the principal setting of his tales is not to be read, then, as the elimination of specific cultural traces, but rather as the specification of cultural reference: Kipling's Indian jungle is not simply a culturally unmarked 'World'; it is India as jungle. Like the 'jungle' of Indian civilization, Kipling's jungle manifests, in its nurturing adoption of the alien man-cub, a remarkable capacity 'to absorb and include, ... to tolerate inconsistencies' (Inden 88). Significantly, however, Mowgli's jungle home is not entirely lacking in world-ordering rationality: for all that it is a world of predation, where brute force is often the final arbiter, Kipling's jungle includes a 'Jungle Law' quite distinct from what one would ordinarily understand as 'the law of the jungle'. If, as one learns in 'How Fear Came', the Jungle Law is mythic and archaic in its origins, it is nonetheless eminently pragmatic in its applications. As the narrator informs the reader, as Mowgli learns from Baloo, this Law orders and codifies all the eventualities of jungle life. Although it is not the work of reason, it is rationalizable.

Although on first consideration the inscription of the Law would seem to place Kipling's jungle world at odds with the Indologist's 'jungle', the presence of Law – and, by implication, of world-ordering rationality – actually confirms the allegorical jungle's affiliation with Indological discourse more clearly and decisively than its absence might do. As Inden makes clear, Indology's 'jungle' is disorderly, but, for the duly informed, analytically adept Western specialist, not beyond reasoned comprehension. The 'Hinduism' that reveals 'no apparent order' is nonetheless posited as 'knowable' (86). This 'jungle' is 'after all, a part of the orderly world in which the jungle officer of the Indian mind, the Indologist, wishes to live'

(87).[8] Indeed, world-ordering rationality is precisely what Western systems of analysis and interpretation bring to the study of Indian civilization, just as Western legal and administrative intervention (supposedly) brings that same rationality to Indian cultural and political actuality. Indologists, observes Inden, 'do not constitute an order out of the jungle, for it is inherently disorderly, but they can, it would seem, introduce a certain degree of rationality to it' (86). Even so, Kipling writes a jungle that knows disorder – for example, the interregnum that follows upon the fall of Akela – but also provides his jungle with an inscription of rational organization.

Significantly, the 'rationalizing' of the jungle is energized by an alien element. As Hathi relates in 'How Fear Came', the formation of the Law is instigated by the advent of an alien, Man, who sets in motion a chain of events that produces first Fear and subsequently, in response to that Fear, the Law. In a somewhat similar way, the much later advent of a man-cub provokes a massive mobilization of the Law: Mowgli's reception is attended by a quite complex process of 'litigation'; his initiation to the Law requires one full- and two part-time instructors; his mastering of the jungle ultimately entails his unique privilege of taking the Law into his own hands. Kipling's writing of the Law in the Indian jungle thus conforms quite closely to what Inden puts forward as Indology's central tenet – that world-ordering rationality must be imposed on India by an external agency. Kipling's jungle is an Indologically informed invention that sets the stage for the jungle-boy's allegorical reconfiguration of British imperial history in India. In keeping with his status as a protagonist who negotiates, allegorically, an imperial 'crisis of consolidation' (Stokes), Mowgli's role is not to initiate but to confirm the jungle's colonization – a role he fulfills very prettily in 'In the Rukh'.

As I noted earlier, Mowgli's world includes a secondary space, an Indian village. The village, quite clearly, is of lesser importance in the articulation of the boy-protagonist's life-story. The jungle-boy is never allowed to discover a securely defined place within the village's social structure, and, more importantly, the village is clearly represented as subordinate to the jungle, the defining space in Kipling's fictive world. As is made clear when the jungle is 'let in' upon it, the village is, in the last instance, a differentiated space *within* the jungle world, a space the jungle has the power to 'de-differentiate' and reclaim. It is noteworthy, moreover, that Kipling's portrayal of the relationship between jungle and village reverses the expected distribution of the terms of contrast: in the jungle, there is law; whereas, the village, a place of folkloric 'tall tales' and super-stition, is ultimately lawless – like the Monkey People's anarchic community, which provides (as Mowgli duly notes) the jungle analogue of village society. Kipling envisions his village as an insular, tenuously differentiated space within an encompassing, ultimately dominant order, the jungle, even as the Indian village is envisioned by the Raj as an insular, representatively Indian, social structure encompassed by, and securely contained within, the British colonial administration.

Kipling's village, like his jungle, manifests a close affiliation with British Indological discourse. As Inden argues, the Indian village, an object of British survey and classification throughout the nine-teenth century, becomes, like India's 'jungle'-mind, another 'pillar of ... imperial constructs of India' (132). As the 'living essence of the ancient' (131), the village-construct enables Indological discourse to contrast the 'archaic' (as represented by the Indian village) with the 'modern' (as represented, of course, by British imperial government):

> [T]he constitution of India as a land of villages was ... due to the efforts of the British to deconstitute the Indian state. As they were composing their discourses on India's villages, they were displacing a complex polity with an 'ancient' India. ... The essence of the ancient was the division of societies into self-contained, inwardly turned communities consisting of co-operative communal agents. The essence of the modern was the unification of societies consisting of outwardly turned, competitive individuals. Just as the modern succeeded the ancient in time, so the modern would dominate the ancient in space. (132)

Kipling's Mowgli tales first displace Indian sociopolitical structures on to the relatively simple, yet ostensibly representative village, then submit this same village to very literal extinction. Even a cursory consideration of Kipling's jungle-boy reveals that he is clearly (if somewhat surprisingly) imbued with the spirit of modernity: starkly an 'individual', he is an 'outwardly turned' character who competitively seeks dominion over others, a character whose thrust will inevitably set him at odds with the 'inwardly turned', organic and exclusive community of the village. Mowgli's relationship with the Indian 'archaic', as manifested by the village and, in a different way, by Shere Khan, is intransigently aggressive, a relationship that is only to be resolved by the extremity of violence. Kipling's village figures forth an 'ancient' Indian social structure posited and defined by an imperial knowledge system and pledged to destruction by the irresistible 'modern' force of imperial power. The village is not simply 'the social world' any more than the jungle is simply 'the natural world'; both these fictive spaces represent highly specific Indological and imperial constructs for the imaginative ordering of colonial India.

The Mowgli saga as post-mutiny allegory

Notwithstanding the quite assiduous organization of his allegorical world, Mowgli's rise to prominence and power within his microcosmic Indian empire does not proceed without noteworthy instances of trial and contestation. It is in such instances that the shadowy and fearful presence of the Mutiny can be discerned. Despite Mowgli's liminal placement between worlds, which signals his potential capacity to negotiate cultural difference, the narration of his allegorical *Bildung* allows no place for an India that resists. The boy invariably resolves adversarial confrontations by violence and, in a singularly important, defining instance, by the effacement of inimical Indian otherness.

   The earliest and also the most obdurate adversary Mowgli must confront is Shere Khan. The tiger shares his name with a sixteenth-century Afghan chieftain, who invaded the subcontinent and for a short time unseated the Moguls. As Percival Spear observes, Sher Khan (also known as Sher Shah) is commonly credited with being 'the virtual founder of the future Mughal empire on the ground that he provided the essential administrative framework' (28). The tiger's name thus associates him with the conquest and consolidation of empires, and more particularly with the Mogul dynasties. Significantly, Kipling's Shere Khan is old and lame, yet very dangerous – a rogue tiger, a cattle-killer, a man-hunter. Both in relation to the wolf pack and in relation to the human society of the village, he is an outsider – almost an 'alien', very much an outlaw.[9] Mowgli, another outsider, but one who becomes an initiate and a representative of the law, stalks and kills the tiger and by this richly symbolic action establishes himself unmistakably as an *imperial* protagonist.

As Sujit Mukherjee emphasizes in 'Tigers in Fiction: An Aspect of the Colonial Encounter', the tiger and the tiger-slayer are significant figures in British imperial mythologies. The myth-tiger of imperial imaginings purportedly has its origins in the north and is frequently envisioned as a 'white tiger'. A pale invader from the north, this tiger 'is clearly reminiscent of the fair-complexioned Indo-Aryan or Caucasian tribes who are believed to have entered from the north and conquered India several thousand years before the British did' (Mukherjee 11). The tiger-hunt thus takes shape as a contest between conquerors, one modern and one archaic. By his victory over the tiger, the British tiger-slayer implicitly lays claim to imperial authority, as the tiger's successor. Similarly, the killing of the tiger refigures the British conquest of India as a kind of return, as the re-enactment of an earlier 'white' conquest.[10]

Mowgli, by overcoming Shere Khan, stands in the place of the British imperial adventurer and restages the British consolidation of empire in India. This jungle-child (youthful and energetic, yet duly schooled in the codes of the Law) is the alien liberator whose final victory signals the establishment of just rule in the place of an ostensibly corrupt and decrepit Mogul dynasty. As the rebel Sepoys of 1857 looked to Bahadur Shah for leadership, so, during a troubled period of interregnum within the Seeonee pack, restless young wolves rally around Shere Khan and turn against Mowgli. Just as the British, in 1858, put an end to the symbolic kingship of Bahadur Shah, so Mowgli puts an end to the lame tiger's pretensions to power. As the British, after 1858, articulated 'a new imperial order ... through Mogul emblems of power' (Sharpe, *Allegories* 4), so Mowgli uses the tiger's splendid skin to symbolize his accession to the role of Master of the Jungle. The story of Mowgli's ultimately victorious struggle against Shere Khan thus mirrors key features of Mutiny history and of the British reconstitution of that history, recapitulating a British 'triumph' in the midst of treachery and adversity.

The death of Shere Khan, however, cannot be taken to announce the definitive consolidation of Mowgli's imperial progress, because, as Mukherjee remarks, the myth-tiger is never definitively dead:

> Particularly when we recall the nature and range of human qualities attributed to the tiger by Anglo-Indian writers of fact as well as fiction – memory, cunning, vengefulness, to mention only three – we shall realize that the tiger represented some enduring spirit of India that the British felt they had failed to subjugate. No matter how many successful campaigns the British had waged, how many decisive battles they had won, how many cantonments they had founded to guard settlements, some basic fear of India continued to haunt British Indian life and imagination. Therefore the tiger had to be shot again and again. (12)

One can begin, at this point, to appreciate the full resonance of Kipling's allusion (in his title, '"Tiger! Tiger!"') to William Blake's tiger of 'fearful symmetry', eternally burning 'in the forests of the night'. The Mowgli saga, evidently, must be considered as an optimistic yet anxious discourse, as a narrative that assuages yet also revives the nagging doubts and fears troubling post-Mutiny British India. The new conqueror *dis*places rather than *re*places his predecessor (as is tellingly signaled by the retaining of the tiger's pelt). The menacing tiger asserts the 'undying' resistance with which the old order confronts the new, the resistance of 'archaic' India to imperial innovation. Not surprisingly, therefore, the imperial hero who defeats the tiger immediately faces renewed resistance – this time from the very village he has saved from the ravaging 'Khan'.

Already in '"Tiger! Tiger!"' the tiger-vanquisher's heroic achievement goes unrecognized and unappreciated by those it presumably benefits most: Mowgli becomes the object of the villagers' superstitious fear and loathing and is cast out from their society. However, it is in the sequel tale, 'Letting in the Jungle', that the narrative organizes itself around themes of treachery and violence, punishment and revenge, and emerges most clearly as post-Mutiny allegory. To effectively read 'Letting in the Jungle' as a post-Mutiny allegory requires a focusing of attention upon the production of a certain thematics of femininity within the tale. Mowgli's revenge upon his enemies is inspired not so much by violence against himself as by violence against his mother: upon seeing Messua's blood, Mowgli ominously declares, 'There is a price to pay.'

As Gayatri Spivak has observed, 'To mark the moment when not only a civil but a good society is born out of domestic confusion, singular events that break the letter of the law to instill its spirit are often invoked. The protection of women by men often provides such an event' (298). In the course of the Mutiny crisis, British women were captured and killed, most notably at Delhi and Cawnpore (Kanpur). In response to these events, the British press circulated lurid and richly detailed if unsubstantiated rumors of rape and sadistic torture. British counter-insurgency, in its effort to restore order and assert the 'rightness' and necessity of British authority, took the form of punishments whose barbarous extremity was justified by the invocation of a moral imperative, the protection of women. As Jenny Sharpe argues in 'The Unspeakable Limits of Rape: Colonial Violence and Counter-Insurgency',

> During the 1857 uprisings, a crisis in colonial authority was managed through the circulation of 'the English Lady' as a sign for the moral influence of colonialism. A colonial discourse on rebellious Sepoys raping, torturing, and mutilating English women inscribed the native's savagery onto the objectified body of English women, even as it screened the colonizer's brutal suppression of the uprisings. (29)

Messua's role in Kipling's story parallels that of the Englishwoman in inflammatory Mutiny narratives: the violence done to her justifies the most extreme reprisals. Messua too is produced as an object, as a body whose function is to serve as a focus for violence, as the body that must be violated if the narrative is to move forward. Mowgli 'protects' his abused and endangered mother by instigating a suspension of Jungle Law and unleashing the jungle's savage, 'primordial' forces upon an offending village. Messua provokes the action by providing an image of outraged virtue and kindness.

Just as importantly, Messua serves as the site of a *displaced* violence, which must, if she were absent, expend its full force upon Mowgli himself. As Sharpe points out, the public narratives of the events of 1857–58 rarely produced the broken bodies of English *men*. To have acknowledged this much more pervasive reality of the Indian uprisings would have been

> [to deny] British power at the precise moment it needed rein-
> forcing.... Once an English man has been struck down, then
> anything is possible; in death his mortality is revealed and sover-
> eign status brought low. A focus on the slaughter of defenseless
> women and children displaces attention away from the image of
> English men dying at the hands of native insurgents.
> ('Unspeakable Limits' 34)

Clearly, the symbolic importance of the 'English man' resides in his being the representative of constituted imperial order and author-ity. In a like manner, authority and order in Kipling's allegorical empire (the little world composed of lawful jungle and ultimately lawless Indian village) are centred upon the figure of Mowgli, the Master of the Jungle. In '"Tiger! Tiger!"' Mowgli does, in one brief moment, fall victim to village violence: a cast stone bloodies the boy's mouth. Mowgli's being bound, beaten, and imprisoned by the villagers, however, would entirely undermine his charismatic authority and dispel the illusion of his heroic invulnerability. This much more humiliating treatment, which would constitute not a provocation but a defeat, is therefore displaced upon Messua.

Of course, 'Letting in the Jungle' does present a male victim, a rather significant one – Messua's husband, Mowgli's human father. Kipling's dismissive rendering of this fellow-sufferer, however, serves to confirm 'violated woman' as the site of narrative focus. As Mowgli secretly enters the hut where his mother and father are being held – captives awaiting torture and death – the articulation of Kipling's text deftly shifts attention away from the *male* victim onto the injured and outraged *female*, carefully constituting the abuse of the woman as the violence that signifies:

> Messua was half wild with pain and fear (she had been beaten
> and stoned all the morning), and Mowgli put his hand over her
> mouth just in time to stop a scream. Her husband was only
> bewildered and angry, and sat picking dust and things out of his
> torn beard.
>   'I knew – I knew he would come', Messua sobbed at last. 'Now

do I *know* that he is my son!' and she hugged Mowgli to her heart. Up to that time Mowgli had been perfectly steady, but now he began to tremble all over, and that surprised him immensely.

'Why are these thongs? Why have they tied thee?' he asked, after a pause.

'To be put to death for making a son of thee – what else?' said the man sullenly, 'Look! I bleed.'

Messua said nothing, but it was at *her* wounds [Kipling's emphasis] that Mowgli looked, and they heard him grit his teeth when he saw the blood.

'Whose work is this?' said he. 'There is a price to pay.' (193)

The passage names Messua, but not 'her husband'. Although 'the man' cries out for attention – 'Look! I bleed' – he receives none. Conforming to the pattern of Mutiny reprisals, Mowgli's revenge concentrates upon and shapes itself around the staging of violated femininity.

It would be worthwhile, at this juncture, to consider the answer to Mowgli's question, 'Whose work is this?' His father answers, 'The work of all the village' (193). The crime to be punished is the action not of specific individuals but of an entire community. Here, Kipling's narrative arrives at the core of the contradictory logic characterizing British response to the 1857 rebellion. On the one hand, the insurrection is constructed as a 'mutiny', as a thwarting of authority that has a specific and delimited context – the military hierarchy. But, on the other hand, the uprisings are taken as a manifestation of the 'truth' of Indian 'character', of deep-seated traits of Indian culture. The ascription of responsibility and guilt is generalized: to be Indian is to be guilty. Reprisals therefore enjoy the very broadest scope: not only rebel sepoys but chance-encountered peasants can be given over to summary execution; whole villages can be razed; estates and temples can be vandalized and looted (see Morris, *Heaven's Command* 243–46). The barbarity of the avenger's justice surpasses the savagery that is ascribed to the insurgent.

In Kipling's tale, the village functions as the *representative* Indian social unity, and this village now stands unambiguously accused. The tale moves, not surprisingly, toward the logic of Mutiny retribution. Admittedly, treachery and outrage are not punished by a bloody revenge. The villagers are spared, but their village is utterly destroyed, effaced. Kipling thus restages one specific strategy of British counter-insurgency, and his choice is quite significant: Mowgli spares the villagers' lives, but destroys all traces of their shared existence as a community, all the material manifestations of their society and culture. Certainly, Mowgli's revenge does stop short of the British excesses of 1857–58, but in evaluating this fact, one should recall that Messua is saved from violent death, whereas the women captured at Delhi and Cawnpore were not. While this tale is clearly marked as a post-Mutiny allegory, it stops short of invoking 'unspeakable' acts of rape and mutilation. Although the villagers' will to commit atrocities *is* suggested – 'Let us see if hot coins will make them confess!' (199) – Mowgli's heroism pre-empts enactment. Kipling's tale, however, does not really turn away from the logic of British reprisals; it confirms and reinforces that logic. If one considers the relation of the crime to the punishment, one can detect the influence of the extreme emotional responses Mutiny scenes can evoke. Messua, an innocent woman, is bound and beaten; her son, to avenge the abuse, eradicates an entire village.

Interestingly, Mowgli's revenge takes shape as a sort of abandonment: the jungle is 'let in' upon the offending village. The archaic and chaotic forces, which Mowgli had symbolically mastered by killing the tiger-outlaw, are unleashed, allowed to return. Not jungle law but a kind of primordial jungle madness takes possession of the village, negating, indeed effacing, all vestiges of sociocultural order: 'by the end of the Rains', writes Kipling, concluding his tale, 'there was the roaring Jungle in full blast on the spot that had been under the plough not six months before' (210). Kipling thus portrays, allegorically, the fate of a rebellious India. There would be no need of active punishment. India might simply be left to itself, abandoned to the misrule and disorder that supposedly preceded the establishment of British government.[11] And indeed, even at the literal level of the story, British government – although distant and but dimly comprehended – represents the sole possibility of order and justice: it is to 'the English' at Khanhiwara that the fugitive victims of brutality must fly.

But in the last analysis, of course, Mowgli is far from passive in the destruction of the village; he does not merely 'unleash' the jungle's destructive forces, he commands and directs them. In

'Letting in the Jungle', as in '"Tiger! Tiger!"', the resolution of conflict requires a decisive act of violence. The liminal boy, who would seem to bear the promise of new possibilities for the negotiation of agonistic colonial encounter, does not in fact provide alternatives that differ significantly from those of 1857–58. 'In the Rukh' stages, as I have shown, the liminal boy's capacity to experience seamless union with the spaces and societies of the colonial 'wilds'; it reconfigures the imperial project as a masterful participation in the world of the colonial Other. Another sort of masterful participation is evident in Kipling's Indologically informed constitution of the protagonist's allegorical world. Nonetheless, Mowgli's world includes elements that offer an intransigent resistance to the process of imperial domination, assimilation, and incorporation represented in his *Bildung*. As Edward Said has argued in his analysis of Kipling's *Kim*, the liminal boy can be made to serve as an enabling figure in the representation of a putative 'absence of conflict' in imperial affairs (*Culture* 140–1). Yet situated in the imaginative context of Mutiny lore, where imperial terror and conflict are ineluctably inscribed, the liminal boy proves unwilling or unable to manage difference and forge a passage between opposing worlds. To employ Anne McClintock's recent formulations concerning imperial representations, one may say that Mowgli progresses, ever more clearly, through a 'poetics of ambivalence' to a 'politics of violence' (28). The wolf-boy ultimately follows upon the actions of his less gifted predecessors, resolving terror and conflict as British forces did during the mid-century crisis.

The intractable problem of post-mutiny imperial allegory

To conclude this discussion, I will briefly step outside the Mowgli saga, but remain within *The Jungle Books*. Examined in relation with 'Letting in the Jungle' (the tale that immediately precedes it), 'The Undertakers' appears to present an interesting turn in Kipling's narrative strategy. The former tale allegorically invokes and revives the actions and emotions of the Mutiny story. 'The Undertakers', which contains explicit allusions to Mutiny events, attempts to bring the Mutiny narrative definitively to a close, or at least to assert the possibility of closure. In this tale, the forces of colonia disorder are embodied – most compellingly if not exclusively – in a gigantic crocodile, 'the Mugger of Mugger-Ghaut', a monster that grows fat upon Mutiny corpses. When, however, the mugger stalks a refugee-boat and tries to carry off a British boy, the boy's mother – in the heroic style of 'the Judith of Cawnpore' (see Sharpe, *Allegories* 69–73; Brantlinger 295n) – rewards the overly intrepid mugger with several shots from her revolver.[12] The boy thus saved grows to manhood, becomes an engineer – the very man in charge of the building of a railway bridge at Mugger-Ghaut. Upon completing the bridge, the engineer shoots and kills the crocodile, ending his fearful reign over the village that bears his name.

It is the successful building of the bridge that announces the end of uncanny Indian monster, the mugger that gorges himself upon Mutiny horrors. The mugger's death seems almost a necessary effect of the triumphant manifestation of British technological and administrative know-how. The bridge manifests new possibilities for communication and exchange in the erstwhile divided spaces of empire. And in lieu of a liminal Mowgli, this story offers a different sort of hero, a boy who is saved from the grim menace of the Mutiny, spared to become a bridge-builder. This imperial protagonist is evidently secure in his British cultural identity but possessed nonetheless of the capacity to negotiate cultural difference in the divided, agonistic spaces of empire. His answer to the problems of the Eastern Empire is technical rather than intuitive – the engineering (physical and social) of modernization. And yet the bridge and the bridge-builder, being nothing more than new manifestations of an ongoing imperialist project, bring no really new potentiality to post-Mutiny allegory. The British–Indian colonial confrontation resolves itself once again in favour of the imperialist and by means of extreme violence: the mugger, like the tiger before him, must be shot. As if by the blast of 'a small cannon (the biggest sort of elephant-rifle is not very different from some artillery)' (232), the Mutiny crocodile is blown apart, 'literally broken into three pieces' (233). The mugger's grisly end recalls the brutal execution of rebel sepoys, many of whom 'were lashed to the muzzles of guns and blown to pieces' (Morris, *Heaven's Command* 245). Thus, the closure of the Mutiny story, which 'The Undertakers' seems intent to announce, is really only another return to that story, one more return to a story for which no *imperial* resolution is possible.[13]

Recalling Foucault's assertion that discourse is 'a violence we do to things', Stephen Slemon defines colonial discourse as 'that system of signifying practices whose work it is to *produce and naturalize* the hierarchical power structures of the imperial enterprise, and to mobilize those power structures in the management of both colonial and neo-colonial cross-cultural relationships' (6). Considering the example of imperial allegory, Slemon goes on to suggest that the discourse of colonialism strives to recuperate its Other 'by reference to [the colonizer's] own systems of cultural recognition' (7). Following from Slemon's argument, I would suggest that, at least for colonial discourse in Kipling's historical moment, the mid-century Indian rebellion stands as an instance of the irreclaimable; the Mutiny, that is, manifests itself as British imperialism's limit-text – the social, historical 'text' that can neither be circumvented nor made to serve. Although Kipling's jungle allegories confirm the validity and viability of the British imperial mission, they acknowledge and revive post-Mutiny doubts and fears, reasserting their presence and pertinence, giving them a renewed shape and substance. Although the Mutiny history is a constitutive element in the empire's story of itself, its evocation also invariably interrupts that story by inscribing the agency of intransigent opposition, by speaking, albeit partially and indirectly, the story of the rebel. Imperial 'systems of cultural recognition' can provide no secure and stable placement for such agency, for such a story – hence the fearsome tiger that must be shot again and again or the hideously uncanny, *unrecognizable* crocodile that must be blown to bits. As Guha observes, in the prose of counter-insurgency 'the rebel has no place ... as the subject of rebellion'; empire-affirming historiography does not, cannot, 'illuminate the consciousness which is called insurgency' (71). Significantly, however, in the Mowgli tales of *The Jungle Books* the place of the intransigent, resistant element is not simply empty. It is designated and then voided by violence, submitted, in psychoanalytic terms, to an action of disavowal. Although Kipling's post-Mutiny imperial allegories represent utopian potentialities of imperial subjectivity, agency, and experience, the enactment of domination ultimately requires a violent self-assertion, a violent disavowal of the agency of the colonial Indian subjects. Allegorical empire, like the historical empire upon which it is predicated, is sustained by a violence that never

achieves its final act; it recalls that 'Colonization begins and perpet-
uates itself through acts of violence', which become the necessary,
indispensable events of imperialism's 'agonistic narrative of desire'
(Young 173, 174). One cannot put an end to the Mutiny story, one
can only return to it – again and again.

Kipling's repeated inscription of violence, as the seemingly
inevitable final arbiter of imperial order, tears the fabric of his imperial allegory, revealing that the structure and meaning of social,
cultural, and political relations within the Empire are not constituted in advance, as reiterable features of given social 'reality', as
stable points of reference for the process of allegorical reframing
and restaging. The aggressive initiatives marking Mowgli's boyhood
progress, his combative response to intransigent configurations of
resistance, repeat, albeit in a different way, the enabling exclusion
of Abdul Gafur from the magic moment in which the imperial
subject attains clear, coherent recognition of itself. Such initiatives
confirm the necessary exteriority of 'In the Rukh' in relation to the
narrative of Mowgli's boyhood: it is only in an idyllic narrative of
utopian fulfillment – situated outside and beyond, both 'before' and
'after', the agonistic context of Mowgli's *Bildung* – that imperial
subjectivity can be constituted within a stable, self-sustaining
economy of recognition and identification.

The narrative of the jungle-boy has then, at its core, acts of
violence that acknowledge an India that resists, acts of violence
that compensate for imperial power's less than entire control over
its cultural and geographical domains. *The Jungle Books*, however,
does not present Kipling's final exploration of imperial boyhood,
nor are his later works mere recapitulations of the treatment found
here. Indeed, the later works manifest a will to write violence out
of the narration of imperial enterprise. As my next chapter will
show, *Stalky & Co.*, appearing a few years after *The Jungle Books*,
culminates with an envisioning of a pacified India, where violence
is a matter of the 'frontier', where the sphere of consolidated British
power is represented synecdochically by a Sikh community that
happily subscribes to British rule. The schoolboy-turned-officer ultimately situates himself in a remarkably secure Indian setting. In
Kim of 1901, the imaginative pairing of boyhood adventure with
pacified colonial space is more thoroughly established. The Kipling
who composes *Kim* has not resolved the problems entailed by the

imperial adolescent's divided identifications, but he has managed to imagine successful imperial endeavor as a matter of political science – seriously pondered and rigorously applied. Sustained by the complex, extensive apparatus of social control which is the Great Game, Kim can explore, more thoroughly than Mowgli, his role as a culturally hybrid mediator of imperial power; he can serve in the fictive articulation of an empire that has to do with collaboration more than conflict.

3
Stalky & Co.: Resituating the Empire and the Imperial Boy

In 'The Contents and Discontents of Kipling's Imperialism', Benita Parry ascribes to Kipling an unflagging 'lifelong devotion to dominant beliefs and values' (52), asserting that 'Kipling's writings moved empire from the margins of English fiction to its centre without interrogating the official metropolitan culture' (51). While Parry is able to make a quite compelling case by concentrating upon Kipling's 'Indian' writings, her article makes no mention at all of *Stalky & Co.*, which explores imperial issues within the context of the 'home front'. As I observed in the preceding chapter, British imperial authority is a discreet, albeit crucial presence in the Mowgli stories of *The Jungle Books*. These tales render the imperial intervention Indologically and allegorically, thus eluding any direct and detailed examination of the motives, methods, and effects of British imperialism in India. It is as if imperial values are inscribed in nature, already there in advance of any particular imperialist force or faction. However, this naturalizing of imperialist drive and desire does not necessarily serve, in all cases, the 'dominant beliefs and values' of British imperial culture. Ideologies, one must recall, articulate themselves within an agonistic social and discursive context, each competing against others. While it may be true, as Althusser affirms, that 'Ideology has no history' (159ff.), yet ideologies, in the plurality of their actuality, have histories, which are fraught with tensions arising from conflict and contradiction in the social arena. And indeed, as this chapter will show, the school stories of *Stalky & Co.* register noteworthy cultural developments in England, interrogating 'official metropolitan culture', challenging and to some degree redefining established understandings of its nature and its meaning.[1]

One may say, moreover, that in the school series one begins to see more clearly the capacity of the figure of the boy to make a difference, to inscribe a distinct envisioning of imperial enterprise, to put forward a sense of new possibilities for imperial action. Mowgli's allegorical progress, as I have argued, conforms in large part to historical patterns of imperial violence, notwithstanding the extraordinary, unique attributes that invest the child of the jungle; whereas in Stalky one can clearly perceive a tendency to 'go against the grain', to play the imperial game in notably unconventional ways. Certainly, Mowgli's jungle and Stalky's school are peculiarly similar, as if the first is a prototype for the second. Despite significant differences in the overall handling of the boy protagonists, their boyhood worlds make very similar demands upon them. But one must recognize that when Kipling transports imperial imaginings from a mythic, exotic Indian jungle to the familiar setting of the British boys' school, he remakes a supposedly stable metropolitan setting as yet another imperial 'combat zone', as yet another site of power struggles and violence.[2]

Adopting a critical stance quite distinct from Parry's, I argue that Kipling's empire, as presented in *Stalky & Co.*, is not divided between a stable, metropolitan centre and a changeful periphery, but is rather one great, intimately interconnected assembly, a relatively seamless whole. His envisioning of empire reflects – indeed heralds – a new 'emergent global logic' of modern European imperialism (Wegner 132), a breaking down of center/periphery thinking in favour of a more continuously applied, globalized view. The most crucial point in this chapter, however, is that Kipling's perspective upon imperial globalization troubles conventional imperial inscriptions of borders and barriers between races and cultures – the very borders and barriers that serve as cornerstones of racist and Eurocentric imperial ideology.

The school as imperial space

As Isabel Quigly affirms, *Stalky & Co.* 'is the only school story ... in which life at school is shown as *directly* parallel with life in the Empire; ... no book went as far as *Stalky & Co.* in making exact comparisons' (116). Here, I think, is a principal innovation that sets *Stalky & Co.* apart from its predecessors, such as Thomas Hughes's *Tom Brown's Schooldays* (1857). The organizing sociocultural referent of Hughes's novel is 'the whole empire on which the sun never sets', and his beloved Browns are the indispensable protectors of 'that empire's stability' (5). As Ian Watson has argued, the novel can and should be read as a key text furthering the mid-century English gentry's bid for dominance in the administration of the British Empire. Yet Hughes's seminal school story serves to establish the public school as an insular, class-specific 'little world', which must be understood, first and foremost, on its own terms. On one hand, it is the structural specificity of the Rugby public-school world that enables it to serve the Empire: school experience inscribes attitudes, values, codes of conduct that, ostensibly, can be transported to the distant and distinct contexts of the Empire. On the other hand, Hughes's Rugby is an 'enclosed world', as Robert Dingley argues, and its very insularity may signal its inadequacy as a 'privileged discursive space' for an expanding empire (9, 10). Kipling, however, as Martin Green asserts, 'sets boyhood in an imaginative context radically unlike *Tom Brown's Schooldays....* Kipling's heroes set themselves positively against traditional images of school piety and training' (274). The school of *Stalky* is not an insular world susceptible to internal, self-referential definition; it is a carefully delineated microcosm of the British Empire. Recalling his school experience in *Something of Myself*, Kipling stresses that the United Services College 'was in the nature of a company promoted by poor officers and the like for the cheap education of their sons.... It was largely a caste-school – some seventy-five per cent of us had been born outside England'; many 'hoped to follow their fathers in the Army' (16). Understandably, then, Kipling's fictive school not only reflects the larger world of empire but is fully permeable to the practical and material, ethical, and cultural influences of the imperial enterprise. The school is not merely a training ground; it *is* imperial space, a 'combat zone' characterized by factional conflicts and territorial struggles.

Even a brief consideration of a few of the Stalky stories reveals that school conflicts develop and resolve themselves as do imperial conflicts; the same concerns are in evidence, and similar factors determine success or failure. The story 'Stalky' recounts one confrontation of '[t]hree years' skirmishing', pitting the tactical abilities of the wayward schoolboy Stalky against the 'natives' of Devonshire, 'a hard and unsympathetic peasantry' (17). Imperial language and practice are very much in evidence, as emphasis is placed upon such matters as the proper deployment of 'pickets' and the full knowledge of 'the lie of the country' (13, 14). 'In Ambush' draws the schoolmasters into a similar imperial game, as boys and masters compete for control of various out-of-bounds spaces. In 'An Unsavoury Interlude', Beetle undertakes a close study of architecture to discover the optimal strategic placement of a dead cat, which has been recruited to 'stink out' enemy houses. 'The Moral Reformers' provides yet another example of the underlying coherence of the Stalky series: playing upon their adversaries' taste for cruelty, Stalky and company lure two upper-form bullies into their study and, exploiting the territorial advantage thus gained, submit them to a humiliating session of taunting and torture. In the final tale of the series, 'Slaves of the Lamp, Part II', Stalky, now an imperial officer in India, overcomes renegade colonial tribesmen, using the same tried-and-true delinquent tactics that made for successful school maneuvers.

What Kipling puts forward, then, is an imperialist rendering of a time-honored philosophical adage – 'Everything is in everything'. The Empire, in its various manifestations, is here in the school, just as the school, represented by its graduates, is out there in the Empire. As an early reviewer, Robert Buchanan, revealingly laments, Stalky, M'Turk, and Beetle 'are leagued for purposes of offence and defence against their comrades ... they join in no honest play or manly sports, they lounge about, they drink, they smoke, they curse and swear, not like boys at all, but like hideous little men' (785) Within the school context, Stalky and company reproduce, with fair precision, Kipling's earlier trio of imperial ne'er-do-wells, Mulvaney and company of *Plain Tales from the Hills* (1888) and *Soldiers Three* (1890). Indeed, Robert Moss, in his study of Kipling's fictions of adolescence, examines the early soldier tales before moving on to the works explicitly concerned with adolescence. Whether or not one considers them 'hideous', Kipling's schoolboys and his imperial soldiers are remarkably alike. His boys are sons and heirs of the Empire, and their school world is presented, not so surprisingly, as valid, viable space for imperial endeavor.

The poetics and politics of space

The opening of 'In Ambush', the first story of the 1899 collection, immediately establishes the importance of space and initiates, in relation to space, a reworking of the school world and the figure of the schoolboy: 'In summer all right-minded boys built huts in the furze-hill behind the College – little lairs whittled out of the heart of the prickly bushes, full of stumps, odd root-ends, and spikes, but, since they were strictly forbidden, palaces of delight' (29). This early mention of 'right-minded boys' initiates an ongoing, increasingly corrosive parody of 'Eric-ism', the sentimental, idealistic envision-ing of the schoolboy commonly associated with the school novels of F. W. Farrar. In Kipling's text, the right-minded boys are those who thwart authority and its rules in pursuit of their own pleasure. Indeed, indulgence in the realm of the 'forbidden' is acknowledged as a principal source of 'delight'. Moreover, forbidden pleasures associate themselves very closely with forbidden space. As one learns, Kipling's key threesome, Stalky, M'Turk, and Beetle, have forged for themselves a private, personal space out of bounds long before attaining such a space – a study – within the school. Not at all a matter of occasional and sporadic lapse, being out of bounds is, for these boys, characteristic.[3] Just as clearly, to establish oneself out of bounds is to take up empire-building on a small scale: oppor-tunistic and industrious, the boys venture out to discover and appropriate alien space as their own, submitting untamed, virgin land – the 'furze-hill' – to the rule of domestication and utility. Yet if 'right-minded' (that is, delinquent) boys appear in the guise of little imperialists, they also appear as little savages: their 'palaces of delight' are decidedly primitive structures, 'huts' or 'little lairs', barely more hospitable than the original landscape; not radical reconstructions, not decisive transformations of that landscape, but mere modifications 'full of stumps, odd root-ends, and spikes'. Evidently, the wild space of the furze, which will later be character-ized, not so surprisingly, as 'jungle' (33), imposes itself on the boys as much as they impose themselves on it. The characters dominate space but, at the same time, discover themselves in creative relation with it; space impacts upon character in such a way as to create indeterminacies and ambivalences in the coding of identities – are the boys in the furze little imperialists or little savages or both at once?[4] 'In Ambush' thus wastes no time in showing that the subversion of the conventional codes informing fictions of the school and the schoolboy will occur simultaneously with the production of alternative, delinquent codes. The contents of such familiar topics as 'character' and the public-school ethos are being rewritten; the process and the purpose of schooling implicitly subjected to revaluation.

Throughout the several texts of *Stalky & Co.*, Kipling subverts the school as a stable, conventionalized textual domain, a symbolically coherent world ordered and hierarchized under authority. Notably, the nickname, which stands in for and thus effectively effaces the 'proper name', applies to schoolmasters as well as boys. In 'In Ambush' alone, the stalky trio refer to their housemaster and principal adversary, Prout, by a variety of unauthorized names, beginning with 'Hoofer' (in recognition of the master's remarkably large feet) and moving through such playful derivations as 'Heffy', 'Heffles', 'Hoophats', and 'Hefflelinga'. Language practice thus signals and enacts a leveling of school hierarchy. At least from the boys' perspective, boy and master confront each other as adversaries, certainly, but also more or less as equals. The school, as becomes increasingly clear, is divided into competing camps, all of them engaged in the struggle to obtain or retain degrees of dominance. And of paramount importance in this struggle are the control and manipulation of spatial relations, the perceiving and the playing of spatial advantages. In situations oriented in terms of competition for space, the subversion of conventional discursive codes of school fictions is most fully in evidence.

'In Ambush' initiates the struggle for spatial dominance as Prout, assisted by the Sergeant, 'take[s] the field', leaving the tell-tale 'track of his pugs' writ large upon the floor of the lair (29). 'Pugs', derived 'from the Hindustani word "pag", the track of an animal' (298n.) marks the first step of Prout's degeneration, which is more specifically rendered when Stalky discovers the offending prints: 'Crusoe at the sight of the foot-print', one learns, 'did not act more swiftly than Stalky' (29). Prout, who had 'taken the field' invested with the dubious dignity of a military adversary, is placed in association first with brute beasts and then with Defoe's Carib cannibals. He i rhetorically repositioned as a savage intruder, one whose tactica sophistication, moreover, is very much open to question. Th master's discovery of the out-of-bounds haven is figured, straight-forwardly, as a moment of colonial encounter that carries the implied potential for aggression and hostility. And when the Sergeant allies himself with Prout, the boys characterize their new opponent as 'a giddy Chingangook' (39), thus providing him with a place within the pre-established figurative economy.

To counter Prout's initiative, Stalky makes perverse use of school codes, enlisting himself and his cohorts with the school's Natural History Society, a club whose members are granted a relatively free exploration of the school environs. The threesome then sets out on an authorized search for new smoking grounds and finds an agree-able locale upon the private estate of Dabney, a retired colonel. Here again, the interlinkage of language practice and territorial maneu-ver is evident, as M'Turk, 'viceroy of four thousand naked acres, only son of a three-hundred-year-old house', slips into the dialect of the Irish gentry and winningly addresses the Colonel 'as one gentle-man to another': 'It was the landed man speaking to his equal – deep calling to deep – and the old gentleman acknowledged the cry' (35). The erstwhile trespassers are granted occasional access to the estate, which therefore falls within their bounds as 'lawful Bug-hunters'. Thus established in a position that is 'legally unassailable', the boys prepare for the nonetheless inevitable assault of school authorities, by exploring the wilds of the estate 'with the stealth of Red Indians and the accuracy of burglars' (41), and by winning the sympathies of Dabney's keeper, with whom Stalky familiarly converses in 'the broad Devon that [is] the boy's *langue de guerre*' (42). Stalky and company are now 'in ambush', ready to 'entrap the alien at the proper time' (46). Allowing themselves to be followed by their too ardent overseers, the boys lure the Sergeant, Prout, and King (who by now has joined the fray) onto the estate.

The climactic moment of the narrative intrigue registers victory (and a corresponding defeat) by bringing to fulfillment a series of discursive and spatial maneuvers. Speaking in a Devonshire accent, Stalky excites the keeper's suspicions (by suggesting that the noisy out as yet unseen trespassers must be 'poachers simly') and thus ensures that the enemy threesome will be brought before Dabney. Although the absurd poaching charge is quite promptly dropped, Dabney alludes repeatedly to his numerous forbidding 'notice-boards' and stands firm on the charge of trespassing. Prout, who has yet to learn that language is a weapon to be deployed with due attention to time and place, defends himself by recourse to a conventional formula of the school code: 'I stand *in loco parentis*' (44). The phrase '*in loco parentis*' in itself invokes the power of place and raises a question, at least potentially, about standing in a place that is not one's own. The enunciation of '*in loco parentis*' in an out-of-bounds context is the prelude to a fall, which is not long in coming. Dabney responds with a question, parodically posed in schoolish Latin: '"*Quis custodiet ipsos custodes*?" If the masters trespass, how can we blame the boys?' (45) The answer to Dabney's Latin question is obvious enough (though perhaps not to him): the overseers, the guardians, are watched, are controlled, by their wards – by the boys (who are indeed observing the scene surreptitiously). Dabney's second question, moreover, invests the word 'trespass' with the fullness of its moral and legal implications. Who, indeed, may be said to transgress and offend in a fictive world in which everyone, patently, is playing the same game, in which boys and masters engage in a struggle to dominate and control various spaces, to win and exercise power over the opposing faction? Both sides concoct strategies, undertake initiatives and counter-initiatives, attempt (with greater or lesser skill and success) to discover and develop strategic advantages. Maintaining a moral distinction between authority and delinquency becomes decidedly difficult when the operative characteristics of the one are remarkably similar to those of the other. In fact, it is only too clear that authority and, by implication, power are entirely situational and contextual, subject to fluctuation as conditions and positions change. School conflicts develop and resolve themselves as do martial, imperial conflicts; the same factors determine success or failure. As the Sergeant, a veteran of the Indian Mutiny,[5] correctly concludes, 'I might ha' known when they led me on so that they 'eld the inner line of communications' (52). In the world of school and in the Empire, the same rules of thumb apply.

The savaging of metropolitan culture

To appreciate the cultural impact of *Stalky & Co.*, and also to form a primary sense of its participation in an 'emergent global logic', require a return to Kipling's own time of writing and, specifically to contemporary critical response his work provoked. Robert Buchanan's 'The Voice of "The Hooligan"' clearly registers the disruptive power of the new in Kipling's school series. Publishing in 1899, shortly after the first appearance of the Stalky stories in book form, Buchanan denounces 'the restless and uninstructed Hooliganism of [his] time' (777), of which Kipling and his work are both symptomatic and representative. Kipling, for Buchanan, gives voice to 'The Hooligan' or, more precisely, to 'Hooligan Imperialism' (776) – the aggressive, opportunistic, and pragmatic spirit of 1890s imperialism. Against 'Kiplingism' or 'Hooligan Imperialism' Buchanan affirms his enduring faith in the earlier established (and more idealistic) ideology of the civilizing mission. This 'nobler Imperialism' is clearly informed by the centrist view of empire: it is actualized 'in the federation of Great Britain and her colonies, and in the slow and sure spread of what is best and purest in [British] Civilization' (788).

While Buchanan damns with scant praise the 'Indian' stories (including *The Jungle Books*) and frankly deplores the *Barrack-Room Ballads* (1892), he singles out *Stalky & Co.* as the text in which 'the inmost springs of [Kipling's] inspiration' are definitively 'laid bare'.[6] The logic orienting this decision to foreground the Stalky series deserves some attention. According to Buchanan, 'there is nothing which so clearly and absolutely represents the nature of a grown man's intelligence as the manner in which he contemplates, looking backward, the feelings and aspirations of youthful days'. Employing Goethe, Dickens, and Thackeray as his examples, Buchanan posits the figure of the boy as being both projective and reflective: upon the literary representative of his former self the writer projects the key values and most essential character of his mature self; in so doing, he reflects most clearly and incontestably the character of this mature self. 'In Goethe's reminiscences of his childhood', for example, the writer's 'eager intelligence, the vision, the curiosity, are all there, in every thought and act of an extraordinary child' (774). In the case of Hooligan Kipling, the degraded adult writer is, once again, clearly delineated in his loosely autobiographical portrayals of the English schoolboy. But, given that 'Kiplingism' clearly names a cultural (rather than merely individual) phenomenon, Buchanan's logic must be extended and generalized beyond the singular case: in its representations of boyhood a national culture writes its character most tellingly. This tacit assumption, which invests and energizes much boy-oriented imperial myth-making, would seem to stand at the core of the fear and revulsion Buchanan brings to his evaluation of Kipling's school tales.

Buchanan's Kipling is made to personify 'all that is most retrograde and savage' in contemporary British society (777), and this character is most in evidence, according to Buchanan, in Kipling's portrayal of the schoolboy and the school world. So what is it exactly that Buchanan finds new and irksome in contemporary British culture and in Kipling's school fictions? Certainly, the orienting terms 'Hooligan' and 'Hooliganism' deserve some attention. These terms evoke images of corrupt, misguided, insubordinate, urban youth, together with a notion of delinquent confederacy: according to *The Oxford English Dictionary* (1989), a hooligan is 'a young street rough, a member of a street gang'. An inflection of Irishness is immediately audible: 'Hooligan' slurringly recalls such common Irish names as Hoolahan or Finnegan. And, indeed, the *OED* article under 'hooligan' (a word that first appears in print in 1898), notes that several sources 'attribute it to a misunderstanding or perversion of *Hooley* or *Hooley's gang*' – 'hooley' being an Irish word for 'a noisy party, a spree'. One learns, moreover, that 'The name *Hooligan* figured in a music-hall song of the eighteen-nineties, which described the doings of a rowdy Irish family, and a comic Irish character of the name appeared in a series of adventures in *Funny Folks*'. Establishing its significance within the context of the English, but more specifically, the London press – the *Daily News, Daily Telegraph, Daily Graphic, Westminster Gazette, Pall Mall Magazine* (see *OED* citations) – 'Hooligan' is an English word that implicitly ascribes Irish identity and agency to an English, urban and metropolitan, social problem. It names and condemns the Irish *in England* and, more precisely, the displaced, disenfranchised Irish in the slums of London's East End. In the coinage of 'hooligan', a new word at Buchanan's time of writing certain key metropolitan issues – modern youth, urban criminality civil disorder and unrest – are reorganized in relation to an implicit questioning of the Irish presence in England.

To evoke the Irish, the people of the oldest, the nearest, and, in the context of the later nineteenth century, the most obviously refractory of Britain's colonial possessions, is almost of necessity to evoke the broader reality of empire. The widespread contemporary 'Hooliganism' of which Buchanan complains is of 'Irish' and, speaking at once more broadly and more to the point, of *colonial* extraction – an assertion that can be verified by examining Buchanan's discourse of 'savagery'. The key words 'savage' and 'savagery' recur resoundingly throughout Buchanan's vituperative critique: *Stalky & Co.* is a 'savage caricature' (774), and as such it is entirely in keeping with the 'horrible savagery' manifested in certain of Kipling's other works and with the 'savage animalism' of an increasingly barbarous England (779, 783). 'Savage' and 'savagery' are, of course, terms of description that are generally associated with the cultures of the colonial periphery – a metonymic link they can scarcely elude. These terms name the obstacle facing the European civilizing mission 'out there' in the Empire at large; they specify a European perspective upon the history and, in many cases, the actuality of non-European societies. Yet it is not Europe's peripheries, nor the civilizing mission abroad, but rather the present state of civilization in England generally and in London in particular that is the focus of Buchanan's concern. His is a discourse about contemporary 'man' in 'the great civic centers' of Europe (775), which strives to denounce and also to account for metropolitan England's 'present wild orgy of militant savagery' (789). Buchanan's advocacy of cultural purity, progress, and civilization is thus undermined – one may say contaminated – by the repeated inscription of terms that effectively remap the centre in terms of the periphery. The rhetorical and metonymic processes of his article situate 'savagery' *in England*, in the cultural site of the civilizing initiative; the distant, alien 'savage' thus returns home.[7] As Buchanan's comparison of the *Stalky* schoolboys to 'the savages of the London slums' clearly indicates (786), the new and the dreadful in Kipling and in contemporary British culture is *metropolitan* 'savagery', which also goes by the name of 'Hooliganism'. Kipling's writerly crime resides in his failure to respect and uphold – or perhaps restore – the sociocultural barrier that is supposed to divide the metropolitan center from the colonial margin. His British schoolboys are very frequently represented as thinking and behaving like 'savage' colonial subjects; his school world is thoroughly infused by inputs and influences from the Empire's wild frontiers.

The logic of imperial globalization

Kipling's particular writing of the schoolboy and his world, and the offence Buchanan takes at it, have everything to do with the clash of competing visions of what empire is and how it works. Kipling's is a globalized perspective of the sort best exemplified, in non-fiction prose, by J. A. Hobson's *Imperialism: A Study* of 1902. Hobson argues against the grain of the center/periphery paradigm of European imperialism; he reasons in terms of a global system continuously applied in a diversity of sites. As Phillip Wegner stresses, 'Hobson breaks with an older ethical critique that focused primarily on conditions at the imperial periphery, and argues that economic and political conditions at both the core and the periphery can only be understood when the two are treated as an inseparable whole' (133). Published three years before the Hobson book, *Stalky & Co.* applies this logic of 'an inseparable whole', focusing upon familiar, palpable, 'everyday' formations of subjectivity, society, and culture; it reshapes the school, a key site of the Empire's sociocultural core, in the image of the colonial periphery and in so doing subjects the public school and the figure of the schoolboy to a process of revaluation and transformation.

One must acknowledge, however, that Kipling's globalized view is compromised by an elision of questions of cultural difference. In this, Kipling differs most notably from the anti-imperialist Hobson. The multiplicity and diversity of colonized cultures are core concerns in Hobson's analysis of globalized imperialism, which foregrounds, right from the start, the impediments that 'reluctant and unassimilable peoples' pose for unbridled imperialist expansion (6). Focusing in detail upon recent imperial initiatives in Africa, India, and China, Hobson denounces, among other things, the opportunistic confiscation of land and the concomitant production of the 'system of indentured labour' (275), the deliberate under-mining of local industries, the multifaceted derangement and destabilization of local forms of social and economic organization, and the general scorn and ignorance characterizing imperialist encounter with the cultures of the colonized. He concludes his study by naming expansionist imperialism as 'the supreme danger of modern national states' (360), as the principal obstruction to enlightened internationalism, 'on the one hand setting nations on their armed defence and stifling the amicable approaches between them, on the other debilitating larger nations through excessive corpulence and indigestion' (362). In sharp contrast with Hobson's analysis, Kipling's *Stalky & Co.* presents an avid *bricolage* of the signs of the far-flung Empire, but the writing entails no 'thick' engagement with questions of colonial cultural alterity. The question becomes, in Thomas Richards's terms, 'what it means to think the fictive thought of imperial control' (2) – and what it means to represent this thinking in relation to a multifarious, global empire. Kipling therefore ascribes to his schoolboys 'the stealth of Red Indians' (41), represents their antic maneuvers in relation to situations of the Indian Mutiny of 1857, and imports for their use colonial 'artefacts' from Africa and the East. Each of these fictive maneuvers is 'a means for representing the vast and various Empire as a closely ordered whole' (Richards 13). And, as is unmistakably evident when an ever-triumphant Stalky arrives on the Indian frontier, to represent the Empire in this way is to secure, at least imaginatively and symbolically, its control and maintenance.

Kipling's articulation of empire thus differs significantly from Hobson's in its envisioning of cross-cultural encounter and exchange. Yet it is precisely through its elision of fraught negotiations of cultural difference that Kipling's globalized view perturbs conventional, centrist notions of British imperial authority and subjectivity. Centrist ideology, as evidenced in Buchanan, requires the segregation or insulation of the British home culture and its representatives from the influences of the colonial periphery. Such insulation enables the constitution of 'England' as the self-sovereign source of imperial authority and initiative, as the ordering pinnacle of a carefully structured hierarchy of nations, races, and cultures. Kipling's version of imperial globalization, however, tends to compromise the ideological borders and barriers that are established to separate, distinguish, and hierarchize the various races and cultures of the British Empire.

Inhabiting the imaginary empire

As I have indicated, Kipling's globalized perspective is most evident in his creation of a specular relation between the school world and the Empire at large. This relation of mutual mirroring is most clearly rendered in 'Slaves of the Lamp', a story in two parts. Each part, although complete in itself, verifies and consolidates the representations of the other. Stalky, the roguish schoolboy of 'Part I', elucidates, and is elucidated by, Stalky, the unconventional imperial commander of 'Part II'. Similarly, Stalky's two worlds, the school and the Indian Empire, are rendered as analogous manifestations of the one all-encompassing imperial world to which both pertain.

In 'Slaves of the Lamp, Part I', the schoolboy is decked out in the forms of the colonial subject. Stalky and company, now part of 'the "Aladdin" company', rehearse an Orientalist pantomime, wear pseudo-Arabian costumes, and answer to character names taken from the 'Arabian Nights'. The libretto they work with, moreover, has been 'rewritten and filled with local allusions' (54) and thus represents the school world in intimate relation with Orientalist fantasy; it plays, without any too rigorous regard for precision, upon 'a kind of free-floating mythology of the Orient' and attempts in its small-scale way 'to *stage* the Orient and Europe together in some coherent way' (Said, *Orientalism* 53, 61).

Significantly, Stalky, the Slave of the Lamp, remains in costume throughout the duration of the maneuver he and his cohorts eventually undertake against housemaster King. Also noteworthy is the trio's call-to-arms – 'King! War!' – which resonates with themes of colonial insurgency. Moreover, the boys initiate their offensive by pounding on 'a small West-African war-drum' (60) – here is an instance of the schoolboy savagery Buchanan so despises. The maneuver that follows anticipates quite precisely the pattern of the future initiatives of Stalky's imperial career – as recounted in 'Slaves, Part II'. In this second story, a reunion of alumni brings together the former players of an Orientalist pageant, who now pursue careers in the Eastern Empire: erstwhile Aladdins and Abanazars appear now as captains of Native Infantry, as functionaries of the Indian Political Service and the Telegraph Department. A 'Burmese gong', reminiscent of the earlier African war-drum, aptly heralds the serving of 'a dinner from the Arabian Nights'. The conversation, like the libretto of the earlier pantomime, proves to be a promiscuous mixture of the local and the far-flung, of school reminiscences and the news of empire – 'a cheerful babel of matters personal, provincial, and imperial, pieces of old call-over lists, and new policies' (280).

Stalky, ever busy with the affairs of empire, is the only absent member of the original 'Aladdin' company. He is prominently present, however, as the organizing topic of the dinner's imperial discussions. Formerly a schoolboy mischief-maker in Orientalist garb, Stalky remains true to this earlier incarnation, figuring now as the unconventional commander of a Sikh detachment, one who lives on familiar terms with his men, speaking their tongue, adopting their forms of dress and deportment, eating, sleeping, even praying with them. 'Stalky', one speaker avers, '*is* a Sikh' (283). This is a noteworthy progression: what was formerly a coincidental performative identification, a schoolboy's portrayal of an Oriental lamp-genie, is now presented as a thoroughgoing cross-cultural identification.

The mirror effects of the two 'Slaves' stories both raise and address an important question about the imaging and narration of imperial affairs in a time of unprecedented expansion. 'The shift from a regional to a global model of imperialism', Wegner remarks, 'produces its own cognitive dilemmas – for how does any one individual grasp and finally represent this new situation?' (135) The resolution of this question, for Kipling as for Stalky, involves reading the inscription of the whole in each of its parts, the inscription of the global reality of empire in each of its regional or local manifestations. As Wegner rightly avers, neither 'the global empire's massive structure' nor its 'pervasive hegemonic force' can be grasped from a single perspective; both lie 'beyond the cognitive horizons of any individual agent' (136–8). What is required, then, is the forging of a subjectivity capable of effectively inhabiting in turn each of the Empire's various spaces. One must see the similarities and continuities that (ostensibly) reside beneath the surface of differences, read each new, unfamiliar space or situation as an analogue of a familiar one, and apply pre-established modes of perception and action. Faced with an empire whose expansive, Symbolic dimensions (as a global, political and economic, cultural and discursive system) are beyond the ken of any individual, one shifts perspective from the macrological to the micrological, from the macrocosmic to the microcosmic; one adopts, in other words, an Imaginary orientation. The global Empire must be subdivided into manageable 'little worlds' that the individual can conceivably apprehend and organize on his own terms, in close relation with the personal perspectives and initiatives of one's 'selfhood'; one moves from life in the little world of school to life with a frontier regiment in one small corner of the Empire. For charismatic Stalky, the management of Indian colonial affairs seems to come as readily as the earlier cunning and adept manipulation of school intrigues. He shares with Mowgli a capacity to master the Empire at the level of the microcosm.

Stalky, like Mowgli before him, is schooled, moreover, to take up a heroic role within the imperial Imaginary. This becomes most clear when the middle-aged M'Turk offers the final vision of Stalky in India, a vision that strikingly resembles Gisborne's enchanted glimpse of Mowgli in 'In the Rukh'. In the final passages of 'Slaves of the Lamp, Part II', one finds a very similar iconographic tableau, which seats the garlanded hero, becalmed and bemused by the full-ness of his pleasure and power, in the center of the charmed circle of the Imaginary order: 'I was in camp in the Jullunder doab,' M'Turk relates, 'and stumbled slap on Stalky in a Sikh village; sitting on the one chair of state with half the population grovellin' before him, a dozen Sikh babies on his knees, an old harridan clappin' him on the shoulder, and a garland o' flowers round his neck. 'Told me he was recruitin'' (296). In keeping with his informal apotheosis, Stalky has been inadvertently renamed for the Muslim holy book: slightly but significantly deformed in the mouths of the Sikhs, 'Corkran Sahib' becomes 'Koran Sahib'. Stalky thus takes shape as a version of the Word made flesh – not a Sikh version, perhaps, but one that is local and distinctly non-European in its associations. The British officer becomes for his Sikhs a less remote, more recog-nisable manifestation of imperial authority.[8]

Stalky's apotheosis distinguishes itself from Mowgli's, however, by the inclusion within its economy of historically referential colo-nial Indian subjects. The moment of magical, mutual recognition binding together Mowgli and Gisborne occurs in the presence of the wolf-'retainers', but only upon the withdrawal of both Abdul Gafur and his daughter, Mowgli's bride; whereas Stalky's moment of glory occurs in the midst of 'his' Sikhs. The Sikhs, however, func-tion (like the wolf-brethren) exclusively as objects of Imaginary identification – 'Stalky *is* a Sikh' – and not as the collective site of Symbolic identification. Stalky, in whom the imperial officer and the liminal boy come together, finds his point of Symbolic identification in the admiring gaze of M'Turk, schoolfellow and fellow representative of empire. Stalky appears 'likeable' to himself, worthy of esteem, not so much in the eyes of his Sikhs, but more in the eyes of M'Turk, who marvels at the sight of Stalky among 'his' Sikhs. It is through M'Turk that the scene discovers its imperial content, as is made clear when Stalky addresses to him the crucial aside – that he is engaged in 'recruitin'' – and when M'Turk, just as crucially, recounts his vision of Stalky-among-the-Sikhs to an assembly of British servants of empire. But the inclusion of colonial Indian subjects in the economy of identification is only partial: the Sikhs are not there to see (an action entailing a certain degree of autonomy and agency) but to be seen, to be the 'scene' of a staging of the imperial hero.

Racialized distinctions and cross-cultural negotiations

What is most striking, I find, in Stalky's last scene is its entirely resolved, pacified quality. The utter absence of antagonism, of disparate and divided interests, contrasts sharply with Hobson's representation of the pronounced cross-cultural antagonism that marks the imperial progress. And this absence is also at odds with the general rule of Kipling's own text. Having established the school as a site of ongoing imperial conflict, Kipling shifts the scene of the action only to find that in the Indian Empire, there is ultimately no conflict: among his Sikhs, Stalky enjoys an uncontested mastery (something his own masters at school never enjoyed); the subjects under authority, the colonized and regimented Sikhs, do not resist, do not strive to assert themselves in opposition to constituted authority and its representatives. Plucky *British* boys are, it would seem, significantly different from *Indian* colonials. Kipling, at the crucial moment of resolution, draws a colonial 'color line', to employ S. P. Mohanty's useful notion; he delineates a markedly racialized view of imperial subjectivity and agency.[9] But, in so doing he inscribes a contradiction: the schoolboy's wily insubordination, which is consistently imaged in relation with the colonial world and the colonial subject, becomes finally the very feature that distinguishes the enduringly boyish British officer from the Indian colonials of his entourage. Moreover, this peculiarly contradictory 'color line' is drawn upon very unsteady ground: the schoolboy turned imperial officer is no longer readily recognizable as 'British'; 'Stalky *is* a Sikh.' Implicitly, Stalky dominates Indian colonials by first establishing a marked degree of sociocultural commonality with them. Stalky's special authority, like that of the lupine Mowgli among his wolves, depends in large part upon his being first among brothers. As I have suggested, to experience the global Empire as an assembly of manageable little worlds, one must thoroughly and effectively *inhabit* each new world in turn.

The final scenes of 'Slaves, Part II' thus raise, quite pointedly, a question of cultural hybridization, a question which, in Hobson, receives very scant address.[10] Stalky's final presentation offers him as a hybrid figure formed within the contingent negotiations of cross-cultural confrontation. Admittedly, the figure of Stalky is unmarked by the complex ambivalencies of cultural identification that characterize the eponymous protagonist of Kipling's *Kim* – a text that will appear two years later, in 1901. Yet the final story of *Stalky & Co.* clearly implies that Sikh culture has, at least partially, written itself upon Stalky. It thus fulfils a preceding textual process that writes the signs of colonial subjectivity upon the British schoolboy, and in this way registers – even as it disavows – the agency of the cultural other in the production of the hybridized imperial subject. As Homi Bhabha affirms, to locate and to read the hybrid signs produced by cross-cultural colonial confrontations is to undermine 'the binary opposition of racial and cultural groups' (207). Despite its attempt to essentialize cultural difference, *Stalky & Co.* ultimately confirms the breakdown of imperialism's center/ periphery paradigm of global relations. Stalky is not an essentially British, metropolitan figure but rather one that suggestively reflects processes of hybridization in the contact zones of empire – in the British boys' school (which Kipling clearly envisions as a type of contact zone) and in the frontier regions of India. To borrow the evaluation Bhabha applies to the case of Conrad, Kipling '(be)sets the boundary between the colony and the metropolis' (213).

Both Kipling's school and his Indian Empire necessarily register effects of cultural hybridization. Undermining the distinctions dividing the center from the periphery, Kipling generalizes the imperial reality to include the world of school and in so doing splits the identity of the schoolboy, making of him a little imperialist and a little savage, an agent and a subject of imperial authority. To mend or 'suture' the split identity of the imperial schoolboy, Kipling must produce the boy as a hybridized imperial subject. His schoolboy imperialist therefore emerges not as the unified subject of a self-sovereign British metropolitan culture, but rather as a site of unsettling resemblance, as a figure produced by the mutually transformative confrontations of British and non-European cultures. Clearly, *Stalky & Co.* manifests what Parry finds to be a general (if often more implicit) characteristic of Kipling's fiction: his work, in her view, turns upon 'the construction of an identity that is dependent on the conquest of another's self' (51). Yet, at the same time, the construction of an imperial identity, in Stalky's world, is not simply a unilateral conquest but also a cross-cultural negotiation, a transformation of self in response to an other.

Considered in broader relation with Kipling's *œuvre*, the final imaging of Stalky looks backward to Strickland of *Plain Tales from the Hills* and forward to Kim. Stalky enacts Strickland's orienting theory that the European master 'should try to know as much about the natives as the natives themselves' (*Plain Tales* 24). Yet Stalky's passage across cultural barriers is more than simply strategic. Stalky in India is represented as one who has discovered a place *between* cultures, a place of intercultural *confluence*, as is suggested by his final location 'in the Jullunder *doab*' – a *doab* being 'a tongue of land between two rivers' (*Stalky* 325 n.). Yet his 'becoming' a Sikh apparently provokes no 'identity crisis'; whereas the troubled interrogation of identity is, of course, a salient aspect of the more thoroughly imagined hybridity of Kim. Stalky, in this respect, is like Strickland, who represents 'a successful acclimatization', a partial and strategic cross-cultural identification that enables the British colonizer 'to know and control the native Other' (Arata 23, 27). Stalky, however, significantly distinguishes himself from Strickland (and announces the advent of Kim) in that his capacity for cultural cross-dressing manifests an enduringly boyish liminality: Strickland's powers of cross-cultural disguise, acquired in his maturity, are the result of a disciplined (if at times outlandish) process of research; Stalky, at least in part, learns a new culture as the child Kim does, by initiation. This initiatory aspect is most clearly confirmed by the evidence of cross-cultural ties of affection and trust, as when, in a telling moment, Stalky is imaged encamped and asleep, snuggling upon the breast of his Sikh adjutant, Rutton

Singh. Bonds of affectionate cross-cultural identification, so crucial to the representation of Kim, are never manifested by Strickland.

Stalky and Kim thus reveal Kipling's recognition of and imaginative response to the egregious flaw in British imperial management of India – the all but entire absence, in Hobson's words, 'of real, familiar, social intercourse' between British imperial representatives and their Indian subjects (301). Kipling's creation of Stalky thus manifests something more than 'the observer's sharp eye', but does not yet give full expression to what Mark Kinkead-Weekes describes as 'the dramatist's longing to get into the skin of many "others"' (217). Only in *Kim* does Kipling thoroughly envision an imperial subject whose complex hybridity enables him to access and represent the cultural diversity of the Indian Empire and, at the same time, a sophisticated system of imperial domination (almost) capable of harnessing the particular powers of such a subject.

Yet one must recall, with Thomas Richards, that in Kipling one discovers 'the British Empire not as it was but as it was imagined' (8). Stalky, particularly as represented in the 'Slaves' stories, is best understood as a fetish-image of imperial representation – if one accords with Anne McClintock's recent revisionist treatment of the Freudian fetish. Theorized beyond its too strait association with the family drama and the primal scene, the 'fetish', for McClintock, 'stands at the cross-roads of psychoanalysis and social history' (184). It 'marks a crisis in social meaning as the embodiment of an impossible resolution', a 'displacement' of 'social contradictions' henceforth embodied by the fetish object (184, 202). Indeed, it is '[b]y displacing power onto the fetish, then manipulating the fetish, [that] the individual gains symbolic control over what might otherwise be terrifying ambiguities' (184). As a figure of fetishistic investment, Stalky, like the later Kim, embodies and stages the contradictions that inhere in Kipling's imperial imagination: the figure acknowledges and represents the inevitable and necessary hybridization of an imperial culture of global proportions, yet safeguards and retains the supposedly unique talents and prerogatives of British 'race'; it binds the longing, the acknowledged need, for contact and community with the antithetical drive to dominate and control colonial others. As McClintock emphasizes, the fetish can be deployed 'for a variety of political ends – some progressive, some subversive, some deeply reactionary' (202). Unquestionably,

Kipling recruits Stalky, and the later, more intensely invested Kim, in the service of an enduringly racialist and authoritarian imperial politics. Yet his production of such hybridized fetish-images calls into question the insularity of British imperial authority and must perturb 'the official metropolitan culture' Parry invokes. The fetish enables one to sustain contradictions rather than to resolve them; it is the object of compromised passion, a site where the unresolved contradictions of power and desire are written, and where they can be read.

4
Kim: Disciplinary Power and Cultural Hybridity

In this first of two chapters on *Kim*, I consider hybrid Kim's participation in the Great Game of post-Mutiny British imperial
management. Questions of racial and cultural identity and difference are raised in the novel's opening passages, even as the hybrid
boy is proffered as a mediator, a 'go-between', for British power. The
hybrid adolescent lives and moves within Wurgaft's 'gap' – the gap
that, after the Mutiny, is presumed to divide and separate British
and Indian cultures – functioning as the enabling, indeed indispensable, intermediary for the post-Mutiny project of detached
domination. Kipling's imagining of power–knowledge applications
in India entirely depends on the hybrid Kim, who negotiates and
sustains the relationship, at one remove, between imperial power –
most notably embodied in the abstracted, Olympian Creighton
(military officer, administrator, and ethnologist) – and the bustling
multiplicity of Indian colonial subjects Kim encounters in the cities,
in the countryside, on the trains, on the Grand Trunk Road.
Although the imperial Great Game evidently exists before Kim's
recruitment, Kipling's specific representation of its workings clearly
requires the culturally liminal adolescent, whose ability to 'blend
in' signals his special capacity for the bearing of confidential information, for surreptitious surveillance, for cross-cultural
information-gathering. As in the previous chapter, however, my
analysis will consider the hybrid boy as both a productive and also
a potentially disruptive figure within Kipling's representation of the
British imperial project in India.

My study has led me to consider Kipling's novel as a consolidating document of British imperial culture but also as a potential source of decolonizing initiatives. My analysis strives therefore to show how Kipling's representation of Kim registers the potentially disruptive, problematizing effects that may be occasioned by the introduction of a hybridized subject to modern imperialism's culturally divided world. I begin by outlining the issues that arise around Foucault's work on the modern 'disciplines'. I subsequently consider Kim's unstable identity, his undecided relation with paternity, and therefore, the uncertainty of understanding him in relation to socially empowered systems of meaning and interpretation. Returning again to questions of disciplinary power and its practices, I show how the attempt to contain the marvelous boy within the regime of imperial discipline succeeds, and also how it falls short. Having noted the perturbatory effects of multiple and hybrid ethnicities upon the disciplinary economy of Kipling's fictional, post-Mutiny Indian Empire, I will proceed, in Chapter 5, to consider the ethnographic aspects of *Kim* more closely.

The disciplines and the law

In 'Can the Subaltern Speak?' Spivak argues that to accept 'a self-contained version of the West is to ignore its production by the imperialist project' (291). The work of Michel Foucault, she finds, is curiously symptomatic of the tendency to envision a self-contained West' insulated from its global, imperial investments. She observes that Foucault's multi-volume analysis of the history of Western modernity can be read as a peculiarly allegorical 'miniature version' of the history of modern imperialist projects: Foucault focuses upon the 'management of space – but by doctors'; upon the 'development of administrations – but in asylums'; upon 'considerations of the periphery – but in terms of the insane, prisoners, and children'. Spivak concludes that the various topics of Foucault's scholarship – the clinic, the asylum, the prison, the university' – all seem to function as 'screen-allegories that foreclose a reading of the broader narratives of imperialism' (291).

It is most specifically Foucault's investigation of the constitution and development of the disciplinary society that Spivak targets for critique. Disciplinary power, 'the new mechanism of power [emerging] in the seventeenth and eighteenth centuries ... is secured', in

Spivak's view, '*by means of* territorial imperialism ... "elsewhere"' (290). Spivak, unfortunately, does not pause to detail and document the connection she notes here. Yet, given that the 'new mechanism of power', what she aptly characterizes as 'power-in-spacing' (290ff.), functions most characteristically by distributing and hierarchizing a multiplicity of subjects within mapped and managed space, it seems likely that the spaces of empire would provide key sites – perhaps, indeed, inaugural sites – for the experimentation and elaboration of disciplinary techniques. That is to say, it seems entirely probable that the acquisition of far-flung, culturally diverse colonies posed new problems of governance and social control – new problems that spurred the development of what Foucault has called 'the disciplines'.

Her critical caveats notwithstanding, Spivak concedes that Foucault's analysis of the mechanics of the disciplines can still provide a useful critical pathway for postcolonial scholarship, a pathway I intend to pursue in this chapter. As Spivak's intervention clearly reveals, however, Foucauldian theory needs to be revaluated in the light of the modern European imperial project. To manifest its pertinence for the elaboration of a decolonizing cultural criticism, this theory needs to be used to critique articulations of power whose focal points are not 'metropolitan centers' but rather 'colonial margins'. Kipling's *Kim* provides an excellent opportunity for just such a critical maneuver, offering the postcolonial critic a literary work that uncannily foreshadows Foucault's sociopolitical analyses, a colonial text that registers the insinuation of the Foucauldian 'disciplines' between the two terms of imperialism's much-invoked dyad, law and order. In Kipling's representation of British India, discipline, not law, is the predominant force that makes and maintains imperial order.

As Spivak duly notes, 'the law' constitutes a key discursive system in and by which 'the history of Europe as Subject is narrativized' (271). Crucial to the alibi of the 'civilizing mission' is the notion of the rule of law, the notion that the colonizer initiates and sustains law and order in otherwise lawless lands. The colonizer's claim to moral authority is seated upon his paradoxical promise of 'freedom under the law'; in the words of imperial poet Alfred Noyes, one must 'Reign by that law which sets all nations free' (qtd. in Morris *Pax* 176). However, the text of *Kim*, as I will show, implicitly sets itself at odds with this fundamental legitimizing myth of the British imperialist project.

As a necessary first step to specifying the India Kipling imagines for *Kim*, one must consider the role of the Utilitarian legacy in the shaping of British India. The Utilitarian thinkers' powerful influence runs through the nineteenth century to the time of Curzon's vice-royalty and Kipling's confirmation in the role of bard of the Indian Empire. As Eric Stokes makes clear in *The English Utilitarians and India*, to consider the question of the 'rule of law' in British India is perforce to confront the decisive contribution of the Utilitarian thinkers. Jeremy Bentham's contribution to the elaboration of colonial rule in India ordered itself around his foundational conviction that 'government cannot operate but at the expense of liberty' (123). As Stokes puts the case, Bentham represented an authoritarian and paternalistic political philosophy, a conviction that 'Sovereignty was single and indivisible; its instrument was law speaking the language of command'. Government, in his view, should function as a rational political machine embodying the Enlightened virtues of 'speed, efficiency, economy, regularity, and uniformity' (Stokes 72). Closely aligned with Bentham, James Mill approached the reconstruction of British Indian government as a problem of law; his resolution of the 'destructive anarchy' he perceived in early nineteenth-century British colonial administration resided in 'an accurate code, an adequate judicial establishment, and a rational code of procedure' (521). James Fitzjames Stephen, the main political thinker of the post-Mutiny Indian Civil Service and the most prominent and influential inheritor of the Utilitarian legacy, advocated the rule of law as the governmental articulation of imperial conquest. He was supported in this by his friend and ally John Strachey, who exerted considerable influence on viceroys Mayo and Lytton in the 1870s. The two together shaped the Utilitarian tradition for the post-Mutiny Raj: for Stephen, as for Strachey, an aloof pragmatism was the basis for an enduring foundation of law and order. As Strachey concludes in his influential *India* of 1888, the duty of British government in India is 'to use the power which we possess for no other purpose than to govern India on the principles which our superior knowledge tells us are right, although they may often be unpopular, and may offend the prejudices and superstitions of the people' (367). 'The English in India', states Stephen, more tersely, 'are the representatives of peace compelled by force' (qtd. in Strachey 367).

The influence of Utilitarian political thought upon Kipling's work is unmistakable. In *Kim*, however, I would affirm that Kipling distances himself somewhat from the Utilitarians' fundamental commitment to law, bringing to the forefront other less obvious aspects of their governmental legacy. *Kim* certainly evidences the Utilitarian faith in dispassionate, rational, efficient administrative practice. Also inscribed here is the Benthamite notion of individual administrative actors carefully controlled by accountability and 'inspectability'. At the same time, Kipling manifests in *Kim* a Benthamite belief in 'the need for the intervention of the protecting arm of the State in native society' (Stokes 157). The Kipling who envisions the Great Game of *Kim* also evidently shares with the Utilitarians a dream of a colonial administration founded upon a military analogy. As Stokes puts the case, 'The cohesion, discipline, and perfect subordination of a military body, which worked almost in silence with the minimum of discussion and a few crisp commands, appeared to such minds a thing of intellectual beauty' (309). Kipling, moreover, applies to the India of *Kim* a political machinery remarkably similar to that of the Panopticon – an application its inventor, Jeremy Bentham, never proposed.[1] Just as pertinently, Kipling presents his version of Lord Macaulay's Utilitarian faith in the governmental utility of colonial mediators; his commitment to a bicultural, in-between group, shaped by contact with the West, which, in Macaulay's words, 'may be interpreters between us and the millions whom we govern' (*Selected Writings* 249).

I must certainly acknowledge, however, that a case can be made for Kipling as an advocate of the authoritative yet ultimately beneficent force of law. Indeed, Shamsul Islam has made such a case. In *Kipling's 'Law'*, Islam finds in Law 'the unitive principle around which the complex web of Kipling's thought is woven' (11). 'The Law', Islam states in his conclusion, 'can ... be understood as a principle of order that is essential for the growth of both society and the individual', and he adds: 'The nature and function of this master idea of Law is most fully expounded in the fables of *The Jungle Books*' (146).

It is understandable, given the substance of his argument, that Islam should emphasize *The Jungle Books*. Jungle Law does indeed provide the governing principle of jungle society: it is a world-making law, an empowered code that constitutes and informs its subjects, that acts upon subjects who, in response to its demands, enact it in turn. As Mowgli learns from Baloo, this Law, whose injunctions are 'many and mighty', is 'like the Giant Creeper, because it drop[s] across every one's back and no one [can] escape' (*Jungle Books* 149). Yet this Law, as John Murray astutely remarks, has no ethical dimension. It is a pragmatic, expedient code of imperatives and constraints, propounded by sovereign authority and sustained by 'threat of sanction' (Murray 5ff.); it clearly reveals its affiliation with the 'analytical positivism' informing much English jurisprudence and, more particularly, the legal theory of the Indian Civil Service, during Kipling's time of writing (Murray 2–4). In Kipling's Jungle Law, as in positivist legal theory, the crucial opposition is not between 'right' and 'wrong', but rather, as Murray emphasizes, between 'discipline' and 'lawlessness' (7), and 'the ultimate sanction', ensuring obedience and order, 'is the deliberate, premeditated, disciplined use of force' (10).

Although in Murray's discussion 'discipline' has no specialist, Foucauldian inflection, it is nonetheless likely that the Jungle Law Murray discovers – a pragmatic, non-ethical code aimed at assuring a given social order – would be susceptible to infiltration by the mechanisms and techniques of the Foucauldian 'disciplines'. And indeed, when the adolescent Mowgli ascends to the status of Master of the Jungle, it becomes clear that, in Bagheera's words, 'There is more in the Jungle now than Jungle Law' (187). The black panther's somewhat cryptic comment is elicited by a renewed demonstration of Mowgli's capacity to 'stare down' even the most powerful of his jungle companions. Mowgli's special power, the more than lawful power, takes shape as a gaze that commands the submission of those upon whom it falls. Mowgli, in childhood a subject under the law, manifests in youth a new kind of power, previously unknown in the Jungle and unmistakably disciplinary. Nor is Mowgli's gaze-of-power the only manifestation of the jungle's disciplinarization. As I observed in my earlier discussion of Kipling's jungle tales, Mowgli's triumph over Shere Khan and his destruction of the Indian village both involve disciplined practices – systematic surveillance, multiple-source information gathering, the carefully orchestrated management of space and spatial relations.

Already in *The Jungle Books* the 'disciplines' are present as the unsettling supplements of lawful social order. As I noted in the preceding chapter, disciplined imperial practices inform the action of *Stalky & Co.*, a text in which the place and purpose of law or code is never clearly established. In *Kim* the law is a decidedly discreet, oddly abstracted presence, a noteworthy element in the transcendental philosophy of the Tibetan lama, but one that does not assert itself in relation to the worldly practicalities of the novel's narrative developments. In this novel, which is among other things a spy novel, disciplinary techniques definitively take precedence over legal principles and practices, as its adolescent hero becomes a secret agent, an initiate and practitioner of the Great Game of imperial espionage. Kipling represents a British India administered by means of surreptitious surveillance, by the gathering and circulation of politically charged information. Social order under Kipling's fictive Raj is maintained not by the public and explicit operation of law but by the secret, 'unofficial' workings of discipline.

Even a cursory examination of *Kim* reveals that the authority of law, so insistently (if at times somewhat equivocally) asserted in the earlier *Jungle Books*, is now very much open to question. The first tale of *The Jungle Books* opens with a poetic invocation, at once benediction and appeal, culminating with 'Oh hear the call! – Good hunting all/ That keep the Jungle Law!' *Kim*, by contrast, addresses its verse opening, rather disparagingly, to 'ye who tread the Narrow Way'. And, as one quickly learns, the central character and eponymous hero of this novel is not to be numbered among these 'treaders'. This text's prose opening implicitly challenges the authority of law by situating Kim in delinquent relation to legal codes, by seating the boy, 'in defiance of municipal orders' (1), atop the Zam-Zammah gun. Kim is introduced, very literally, *en flagrant délit*: he enjoys the forbidden pleasure of Zam-Zammah, not surreptitiously, but jubilantly, triumphantly, obstreperously.

Identity and the law

Evidently, Kim enjoys a special dispensation in his relations with the law. The peculiar character of this relationship is most tellingly marked in terms of another relationship, Kim's relationship with paternity. In an amulet-case, the orphan Kim carries, along with his birth certificate, a Masonic document bearing his father's name and the cautionary subscript '*ne varietur*'. The amulet-case, fashioned by Kim's 'half-caste' foster-mother, serves to contain a mysterious and fearful magic power. She knows, as Kim does, that the identification papers, if presented at the 'Jadoo-Gher' ('Magic House'/Masonic Temple), would land the boy in an orphanage (2). Kim's experience of his social world has taught him, as a general rule, to steer clear of that grave, respectable sort of European who tends to ask inconvenient questions. The continuance of Kim's free and easy way of life evidently depends not simply upon his being an orphan but, more crucially, upon the undisclosed nature of his familial legacy.

Placing his own work in relation with the findings of structuralist anthropology (most notably that of Lévi-Strauss), Jacques Lacan emphasizes the crucial symbolic importance of the marriage tie in social organizations, asserting: 'The primordial Law is ... that which in regulating marriage ties superimposes the kingdom of culture upon that of nature.' This same primordial Law he posits as 'identical with an order of language' (what Lacan will elaborate as 'the Symbolic'). 'For without kinship nominations', he reasons, 'no power is capable of instituting the order of preferences and taboos which bind and weave the yarn of lineage down through succeeding generations' (66). Marriage ties and kinship structures thus situate themselves at the core of a sociogenetic *lex*icon, a social order at once lawful and verbal, which discovers its organizing, sustaining symbol in the *name of the father*: 'It is in the *name of the father* that we must recognize the support of the Symbolic function which, from the dawn of history, has identified his person with the figure of the law' (67). The patronym assures the father's child's claim to a legitimate place in social networks, but also marks that child as subject to the law of the father, to the socializing system of constraints and interdicts – all the various Thou-shalt-nots – pronounced in the father's name. In *Kim*, however, the boy's relationship with the patronym is deferred, suspended – indeed, literally suspended in the amulet-case that hangs around Kim's neck. The initial delineation of Kim thus suggests a boy who is not yet marked by the *name of the father* nor entirely subjected to paternal law.

Not surprisingly, therefore, Kim is a shape-shifter, a boy who has as yet no fixed, assigned place within the social order (as the child of the father whose name he bears), and who therefore enjoys an exceptional degree of freedom in the negotiation of his social status and identity. Kipling's evocation of the boy's life experience, moreover, does not evidence the regulated desire paternal law demands. On the contrary, Kim lives a life of 'Arabian Nights' extravagance (3), immersing himself in libidinal delights, giving himself to the unbridled and polymorphous pursuit of his pleasure. The boy is a fabulous interloper, a teaser of social boundaries, a tester of taboos.[2] Unlike Mowgli, whose place in the Seeonee wolf-pack is determined at the Council Rock by due process of Jungle Law, Kim cannot be adequately understood as a subject under the law. Freely and pleasurably transfiguring his person, identity, and social station from moment to moment, from situation to situation, Kipling's street-bred orphan eludes legal definition: he has no fixed identity, no dependable place of residence, no established social position; he keeps questionable company and is no stranger to shady deals. The boy, certainly, is not presented as an 'evil' lad, though it is affirmed that he knows 'evil' intimately (3). Opportunistic and disabused, he nonetheless evidences a sense of 'fair play', particularly in relation to the lama-newcomer, to whose naivity he responds not exploitatively but indulgently and protectively, to whose high quest he quite sincerely, if a little ironically, pledges himself. Yet this penchant for fairness (which, certainly, is not uncompromised) does not change the fact that Kim, from a legal perspective, represents nothing more or less than an exotic, attractive version of the juvenile delinquent. His lack of parental authority and guidance, his indeterminate social status, his vagrancy, his preferred company and milieus – all these aspects of his characterization attest to such a designation.[3]

The disciplines at work

As I mentioned earlier, Foucault's scholarly project is, in large part the study of new practices of power, which he calls 'the disciplines' and the consequent transition, in modern Western societies, from the lawful order of sovereignty to the disciplinary order of administration and surveillance. In *The History of Sexuality*, Foucault concedes that 'in Western societies since the Middle Ages, the exercise of power has always been formulated in terms of law' (87), but he posits a difference between the conventional representation of social power and the realities of its workings. He argues that 'the juridical system', sustained by sovereign authority, 'is utterly incongruous with new methods of power whose operation is not ensured by right but by technique, not by law but by normalization, not by punishment but by control, methods that are employed on all levels and in forms that go beyond the state and its apparatus' (89). The disciplines operate, as it were, on the underside of the law, infiltrating and transforming pre-existing social institutions. As Foucault emphasizes in *Discipline and Punish*, the disciplines 'effect a suspension of the law. ... Regular and institutional as it may be, the discipline, in its mechanism, is a "counter-law"' (223). Discipline is concerned not with justice and the common weal but with the efficient practice of power; it addresses not the what and why but rather the how of social order.

Kim's delinquency, as I have noted, is first indicated by his claiming of the Zam-Zammah perch, which he does as part of an illicit game of king of the castle he plays with two other boys. This game establishes Kim in playful, insouciant relation with a massive phallic emblem of paternal law. (Indeed, employing imagery that combines alluring wish-fulfilment with the grotesque, Kipling allows Kim to take possession of the forbidden phallus, to seat himself astride the great bronze gun, which protrudes, almost absurdly, from between his boyish thighs.) It would be worthwhile to consider the politics of this game, given that it constitutes the novel's first staging of social relations, given, moreover, that this little game orients the opening passages of a novel whose overall plot structure will be dominated by the Great Game of imperial intelligence. Although its actions and its object are at odds with the law, the game is nonetheless explicitly concerned with power and social order, reproducing in little a real sociopolitical struggle. The Zam-Zammah cannon, as one learns, is popularly acknowledged as the symbol of social and political authority in the Punjab: 'Who hold Zam-Zammah ... hold the Punjab.' Kim's success thus figures an English success, by which it is authorized; real British power is the boy's 'justification' (1). Although Gail Ching-Liang Low rightly observes that the Zam-Zammah game is marked by 'the narrator's joking reference to the historical realities of Empire' (212), she also acknowledges that the 'joke' initiates a racialized political allegory, which needs, in the last analysis, to be considered seriously.

Evidently, Kim need not display any of the usual markers of British colonial authority – white skin, English language, social standing, wealth. The issue of 'race' is authoritatively, yet rather paradoxically, segregated from uncomfortable questions of ethnicity and acculturation: Kim *is* 'white', although poor, bazaar-fostered, and 'burned black as any native'; he *is* 'English', even though his spoken English is a 'clipped uncertain sing-song' (1). Kim's 'racial identity' is guaranteed by the *name of the father*, a kind of trump card secreted in the amulet-case, which Kim can play if and when he chooses. The importance of Kim's 'racial identity' manifests itself in the way it affects the social situation: its invocation, by Kipling's narrator and subsequently by Kim, clearly upsets the fraternalistic 'perfect equality' supposedly characterizing Kim's dealings with Lahore's bazaar-boys (1). Kim's claim to 'whiteness' and 'Englishness' unbalances power relations and enables a hierarchical classification of individuals. Abdullah, although the son of a bazaar sweetmeat-seller, is Muslim and takes precedence over Chota Lal, who, although of extremely wealthy parentage, is Hindu. King of the castle Kim places both, in relation to himself and to each other: he jubilantly reminds his playmates that the Muslims 'fell off Zam-Zammah long ago!'; that the Hindus also fell, 'pushed' aside by Muslims (4). 'White', 'English' Kim thus situates his achievement within a historical narrative of subcontinental political transformations: the English unseat and replace their Muslim predecessors who had previously overcome Hindu dynasties. What is more interesting, however, is that the playmates tacitly acknowledge Kim as a representative of English authority: the Indian boys do not contest their own contingent designation as representatives of specific subaltern groups; the Hindu and Muslim contestants both give over their bid for possession of Zam-Zammah.[4]

In its development and still more clearly in its resolution, the king of the castle game enacts a social order that is sustained not by the authoritative force of law but by insidious workings of the disciplines. Defining the game in relation to a tacitly understood tacitly accepted imperial proverb – 'Who hold Zam-Zammah .. hold the Punjab' – Kim makes his own success a 'rule' of the game

He recreates the 'hierarchizing pyramid' of disciplined social structure. As Foucault points out, disciplinary power functions to assure 'the ordering of human multiplicities' (*Discipline* 218): 'the disciplines characterize, classify, specialize; they distribute along a scale, around a norm, hierarchize individuals in relation to one another and, if necessary, disqualify and invalidate' (223). Just so, Kim's disciplinary maneuver allows him to situate all players of the game in relation to an empowered 'norm' ('whiteness' or 'Englishness'), to actualize a 'non-reversible subordination' of Indian by European and, simultaneously, to maintain a secondary hierarchy of Muslim former conqueror and doubly vanquished Hindu.

Disciplined identity through education

Kipling's novel thus thematizes the disciplinarization of Indian society even before Kim is initiated to the practice of imperial espionage. Already evident, as well, is the dubious, paralegal dimension of this disciplinarization. One should not be surprised, therefore, to find that Kim takes to the disciplinary practices of the Great Game like a fish to water, nor that he takes in stride a fellow operative's later announcement that players of the Game stand 'beyond protection' (200). The Great Game has no official, legal status, nor do its agents. But then, Kim is accustomed to living without the provisions and circumscriptions of the law.

Of course, the early movements of Kipling's plot are energized by a quest for the father, or rather, for the solution to the cryptic message contained in the *name of the father*, which is imaged in suitably awe-inspiring and heraldic terms: Kim's papers assure him of an 'exalted' destiny to be discovered between splendid 'pillars' and in the company of numerous 'first-class devils' and their red-bull god (2). Quite promptly, Kim fulfills his quest and discovers his relation with the father's name and law, returning to the father's regiment and, rather less fortunately, to the father's regimen. Indeed, the destiny proclaimed in the name of the father falls well short of its glorious promise. When Kim's paternity is revealed, his identity fixed, he briefly glimpses the decidedly less than exalted life of the 'regimented' orphan. He must endure the deadening, Dickensian oppression of the Military Orphanage and its third-rate schooling, the 'closely watched' days of confinement passed among narrow-minded, bullying boys and unsympathetic masters (106) – the whole dreadful panoply of underprivileged life-under-the-law, the very life the earlier Kim had so scrupulously avoided.

Yet Kim's confinement under the law proves to be only a prelude to his release. His lawful destiny is ultimately nothing more than a harrowing sojourn: following three miserable days, Kim is rescued, temporarily by the dashing heroics of Mahbub Ali, and more permanently by the sager efforts of Creighton and the lama, who contrive (with different ends in mind) to send the boy to St Xavier's at Lucknow, the top-notch school for India's sons of empire. Here, Kim learns to be a 'Sahib', receiving an empowering education in imperial disciplines, which prepares him (officially) for a career as a surveyor and (unofficially) for a career as an operative of the Great Game.

Certainly, one can assume that life at St Xavier's is not carefree and free-wheeling. The school is a place of bounds and rules. Kim nonetheless finds the means to pursue his pleasures, as the record of his indictments reveals; he is chastised for out-of-bounds excursions, smoking, and also for using that 'full-flavoured' verbal abuse that is a key aspect of the boy's street-savvy sociability (123). Kipling, however, significantly chooses not to detail Kim's St Xavier's life in any thoroughgoing way. Twice, the narrator blandly affirms its lack of real interest and pertinence (123, 164). The Lucknow school is not prominently placed among the pleasure zones of the boy's narrative landscape, although clearly, as Robert Moss affirms, it contributes significantly to the transformation of 'an ill-bred, illiterate bazaar boy into a full-fledged sahib' (135). Kim's story does include, on the other hand, an abundance of information about the boy's exotic, alternative education under Lurgan Sahib. St Xavier's represents only one half, and not the better half of the boy's educational prospects; his real 'finishing-school' is elsewhere.

In Lurgan's house, which the proprietor characterizes as a different sort of *madrissah* (school), Kim perfects disciplines of mind and body by applying himself once again, but more exactly this time, to the games of his childhood at Lahore: the ever-watchful boy plays jewel-oriented games that teach him to see and remember more precisely; he rediscovers the pleasures of shape-shifting, reproducing a wide variety of cultural 'identities' with ever greater exactitude. Lurgan's shop, with its extravagant array of exotic objects, reminds Kim of the Lahore Museum, one of the favorite haunts of his earlier boyhood, and this new *madrissah* is indeed the Museum's 'entertaining and eroticized counterpart' (Low 209). Lurgan himself calls to Kim's mind a Lahore fakir with whom the younger boy had been familiar. Once again, as in childhood's lawless days, pleasure, power, and intrigue come together enticingly: Kim is initiated to the tantalizing secrets of the new Wonder House and engages mind against mind with the wily and more than slightly sinister Lurgan (a Fagan-fakir in the service of the Empire). If, at St Xavier's, the boy learns to apprehend himself in terms of the privileged yet constrained subject position of the 'Sahib', under Lurgan's tutelage he is taught to make disciplined use of his libidinally charged liminality. Lurgan's instruction puts finishing touches on the St Xavier's education, but more importantly, it teaches the boy to make disciplined use of his earlier self; it serves to revive, reshape, and redirect the subjectivity that existed before the advent of lawful constraints.

Lurgan's ultimate test, his ultimate lesson, concerns the establishment of a disciplined relationship between the two poles of Kim's subjectivity, his ultimately dominant 'Englishness' and his ultimately subordinated 'Indianness', a relation that is revealed in the ordeal of the broken jar. Focusing his pupil's attention upon a jar shattered a moment before, Lurgan attempts, by hypnotic suggestion, to make the boy see the jar whole again – 'Look! It shall come to life again, piece by piece' (153). In the invitation to an envisioning of renewed coherence and wholeness, there is pleasure, even a subtle eroticism. Lurgan's hand settles caressingly on the back of Kim's neck. Feeling this touch, hearing the words whispered in familiar Hindi, Kim's 'blood tingle[s] pleasantly' (153). Lurgan's mesmeric appeal clearly addresses itself to the 'Indian' portion of Kim's personality; as the jar reassembles, Kim is 'thinking in Hindi'. Despite the pleasure he experiences, his mind – another portion of his mind – recoils from an enveloping 'darkness' (154).[5] Kim takes refuge in English language and, more particularly, in a Lucknow-learned rote rehearsal of multiplication: 'The jar had been smashed – yess, smashed – not the native word, he would not think of that – but smashed – into fifty pieces, and twice three was six, and thrice three was nine ...' (154). Only after he has successfully dispelled the

illusion does Kim allow himself to return to Indian words, eve
then announcing his triumph – 'Look! *Dekho!*' (154) – first i
English, only subsequently in Hindi.

In the episode of the jar, Kim, to maintain his self-sovereignt
must choose 'English' analytic thought and vision over an 'India
synthesizing orientation, must choose 'English' Symbolic logic ov
the 'Indian' Imaginary disposition. In the fate of the jar is image
the predicament of its perceiver's self and, at the same time, th
self's relationship with its world: either one synthesizes or or
analyzes; either one experiences oneself as whole and coherent,
one with a world reflecting back that coherence, or one acknow
edges the fragmentation of self and world, the multifacetedness
both. Both orientations are available to Kim, but his usefulness as
player in the Great Game depends on his retaining a capacity fo
analytic distance with respect to himself and his world. He mu
never be entirely swallowed up by any otherness in which he parti
ipates, by any Indian identity he assumes, or by any sociocultur
situation in which he involves himself. The Game requires one t
experience culture not as a sublime and seamless whole but rathe
as a matter of discrete parts; it requires one to see differences, t
make distinctions, to order and distribute the piecemeal of the rea
Kim's aptitude for secret service, most notably manifested in h
marvelous talent for role-playing (which, like his success in the ja
trial, distinguishes him from his otherwise exceedingly gifte
Hindu fellow-pupil), is thus not so much a matter of Imaginar
involvement and becoming as of Symbolic detachment and discerr
ment, not a matter of being 'Indian' but of reading and representir
'Indianness'. The boy must perform, ongoingly, a decoding an
recoding of self in contingent relation with the complex deman
of a multicultural, power-fragmented world.[6]

Powers and pleasures

Despite the self-disciplining rigours involved in his initiation to th
intelligence Game, Kim is not required to forsake his pleasures. H
is, of course, made to pursue them more self-consciously and mo
purposefully, to recognize and exploit their instrumentality. He
not called upon to choose power over pleasure, but rather to choos
the pleasures of power (pleasures which, as my preceding analysis

the Zam-Zammah game reveals, have never been entirely unknown to him). After a year at St Xavier's (and following an adventurous time of 'going native' in the service of Mahbub Ali), Kim goes to Lurgan at Simla with a fairly clear awareness of the gratifications that 'Sahib' status can procure. What he discovers much more thoroughly with Lurgan are the specific pleasures and powers of the *India-bred* 'Sahib'; he is initiated to the complex play of sociocultural participation tempered by an ever-alert detachment. Kim's several years of schooling and training are, of course, regularly punctuated by noteworthy episodes of zestful self-indulgence and adventure. Even as a graduate of St Xavier's and a fully-fledged player of the Great Game, Kim manifests unimpaired appetite and energy in his pursuit of 'the pleasures of imperialism' (Said, *Culture* 132ff.). The much-matured Kim who undertakes to disguise the fugitive E.23 approaches the maneuver as a game and experiences 'a boy's pure delight' (205), the same delight that had characterized the child of the novel's earliest passages. Upon the successful completion of the maneuver, he enjoys a 'thrice-heaped contentment' (210). Kim's hedonistic propensities, which have been cultivated rather than curbed, will save him, one feels certain, from the world-weary alienation so frequently represented by the imperial functionaries who people several of Kipling's earlier 'Indian' tales.[7] For all that he will know trial and perplexity, which spur the repeated question 'Who is Kim?', this boy can always return, as he does in the novel's final passages, to the revitalizing embrace of Mother India.

By envisioning the imperial enterprise in disciplinary rather than lawful terms, Kipling is able to present a pleasure-productive imperialism, an Indian Empire in which domination and administration take shape as a Great Game. The pleasures of Kim's career signal the primary and perhaps the most significant advantage recommending imperial disciplinarization over the rule of law: unlike the fundamentally repressive and prohibitive apparatus of law, disciplinary modes of power manifest, typically if not invariably, a *productive* relationship with pleasures, as Foucault first makes clear in the inaugural volume of his *History of Sexuality*. In the *History*, Foucault argues that disciplinary power accesses 'the most tenuous and individual modes of behavior, ... penetrates and controls everyday pleasure – all this entailing effects that may be those of refusal, blockage, and invalidation, but also incitement and intensification' (11). He contrasts sovereign authority, encoded as law and sustained by 'the right to *take* life or *let* live' (136), with the more modern methods of power that undertake 'the calculated management of life' (140). Elaborating upon this distinction, Foucault writes: 'The law always refers to the sword. But a power whose task is to take charge of life needs continuous regulatory and corrective mechanisms. It is no longer a matter of bringing death into play in the field of sovereignty, but of distributing the living in the domain of value and utility' (144). The life drives and the pleasures these entail are no longer submitted to the Procrustean schema of the licit and illicit so much as they are scrutinized, catalogued, administered, and productively deployed. Individual pleasures are not so much prohibited or restricted or 'permissively' ignored as organized and put to use. Kim's pleasures, which are recruited to the service of empire, clearly provide a case in point. In the figure of Kim, Kipling embodies the possibility of an imperialism that knows power, order, and enjoyment, in more or less equal portions and at the same time. Kipling's narrative of the liminal boy at play in the Indian Empire, having once discovered the potentialities of disciplinary regulation, can offer the imperial satisfactions of spectacle, adventure, and intrigue in full measure without ever turning its attention from the crucial concerns of imperial power.

Efficient delinquency in historical context

The particular character of Kim's career recommends itself not only by its marvels and pleasures, but also by its efficiency as imperial power practice. If one considers the question of imperial efficiency in historical terms, the choice of Kim as the focal subject in a disciplinary order of empire appears remarkably apt. As S. P. Mohanty points out in 'Kipling's Children and the Color Line', the Indian uprisings of 1857–58 'made the issue of Empire an urgent racial one' (27–8). During subsequent decades, therefore, '"poor whites" who lived close to the "natives"' posed, more than ever, 'a threat to the racial image that colonial whites wished to present to the India they ruled'. Members of this 'awkwardly intermediate class' were generally 'confined to workhouses and made "invisible" and "useful" at the same time' (30). (Kim's early years, I should recall, are marked by the fear of being sent to an orphanage – a fate that very nearly overtakes the boy.) Kipling, however, offers a daring and ingenious alternative to the historical Raj's more or less arbitrary and inefficient exercise of legal prerogatives: Kim, a poor white orphan, is initiated to the disciplines of imperial espionage. This street urchin's intimate involvement in the Indian scene is re-envisioned as a source of potentially valuable 'know-how'. Equipped with his knowledge of Indian languages and customs, his seemingly innate instinct for observation and his talent for disguise, Kim can make British power effective in sites where domination by military force or by legal sanction is least practical – notably in the dispersed, multicultural spaces of rural India.

City-bred Kim, once in the service of the Raj, makes the best use of his talents in rural India. Upon being engaged in the Great Game by Mahbub Ali, a Pathan operative, Kim immediately sets off on a trek across the Indian countryside, which remains the preferred sphere of secret-agent activity throughout the novel. Kim, in his ongoing initiation to the Great Game, repeatedly travels out and away from the novel's urban centers (most notably Lahore and Lucknow). This foregrounding of rural settings is by no means incidental, but rather is informed by the real historical development of the Raj and directly related to Kipling's envisioning of effective imperial power politics. As Mohanty points out in 'Drawing the Color Line', the late nineteenth-century Raj is characterized by strategies of 'invisibility and spectacularization', which are selectively deployed: 'Spectacles – exhibitions, *durbars*, the ritualization of the monarchy and its public activities – seem to be confined to the cities, both in England and in colonial India, while the concern with invisibility reveals itself in the contact with the colonial countryside' (340). Kim may be a city boy, but his capacity to 'blend in', socially and culturally, recommends him for service in the countryside, which poses a particularly nettled problem for British colonial government.

As Mohanty stresses, although the later nineteenth-century history of the Raj is largely one of successful consolidation, British authority met with 'perennial resistance' in rural India: 'the radical forms of political-economic change – forced patterns of migration and settlement, dispossession and relocation – led to both explicit and mediated kinds of anticolonial rebellion' (323). The potential threat to British rule, here suggested, is enormous. At the end of the nineteenth century, the population of British India approaches two hundred million. The British presence in India, both military and civil, does not exceed 150,000. Moreover, only about one-tenth of the Indian population is urban; whereas British numbers are concentrated in the cities. By mobilizing poor white Kim as an imperial agent, Kipling not only places a problematic subject within the Empire's containing grasp, but also enables British power to infiltrate, more thoroughly, more effectively, the relatively unknown and unpredictable spaces of rural India.

Kim's delinquency is as useful to the Empire as his pleasures (which, of course, are frequently represented in relation to delinquency). And if one considers the other principal operatives of the Great Game, it becomes evident that Kim's delinquency does not represent an isolated case. Kim's fellow-agents are also questionable characters, are also members of refractory, or potentially refractory, social groups. E.23, although a minor character, provides an intriguing case in point. Lurgan, one learns, takes a particular pride in having transformed E.23 from 'a bewildered, impertinent, lying, little North-West Province man' into an effective agent of the Raj (176). It is noteworthy that when this creature of the Empire's unstable frontier zones makes his first appearance in the novel, he is desperate, marked by violence, and disguised as a Mahratha. As Percival Spear records, the Mahratha confederacy presented, from the time of Hastings into the twentieth century, one of the most enduring and intransigent sites of resistance British power confronted: 'Mahratha revivalism', spearheaded by the actions of Nana Sahib (a Mahratha chieftain), played a powerful role in the developments of the 1857 rebellion (143); the Mahrathas' 'regionalist' struggle for independence 'set an example and was an important influence on ... [India's] modern national movement (159). It is therefore singularly significant that Kim, in his effort to save his hunted fellow-agent, decides to refigure – that is, disguise – a politically charged Mahratha as a politically disengaged Saddhu mystic. Kipling's narrative thus figures forth, in a single scene, his general strategy for representing the confrontation between power and resistance in British India.

Moving on to Kim's more significant cohorts, one may consider Mahbub Ali. Edward Said remarks, 'Mahbub Ali, Creighton's faith ful adjutant, belongs to the Pathan people, historically in a state of unpacified insurrection against the British throughout the nineteenth century, yet here [in *Kim*] represented as happy with British rule, even a collaborator with it' (*Culture* 148). As for Hurree Chunder Mookerjee, another imperial agent, he is a Babu, a Western-educated Bengali. The very type of the much-despised 'mimic-man', Hurree is cowardly yet wily, a matchless dissembler. The colonized subject most able to turn the weapons of the master against the master, he is a figure strongly marked by subversive potential. As Gauri Viswanathan points out in her *Masks of Conquest*, the Babu represents the failed promise of the British attempt, in the latter half of the nineteenth century, to follow the proposal of Macaulay's 1835 'Minute' and create a Western-educated class of colonial mediators. The Babus were very rarely admitted to higher positions within the British imperial administration, the very positions for which their education seemed to prepare them. By the late nineteenth century, Western-educated Bengalis were voicing their discontent, emerging as a significant subversive force in the Indian press.[8]

Kipling's Babu, neither administrator nor journalist, finds his niche as a gifted spy. As he proves, when confronted with non-British Europeans (the French and Russian enemy-agents), Hurree can play the discontented Babu, can stage in person what the Russian describes as 'the monstrous hybridism of East and West' (239). Making brilliant tactical use of the colonial stereotype of the Babu, Hurree feigns drunkenness in the company of the enemies: 'He became thickly treasonous, and spoke in terms of sweeping indecency of a Government which had forced upon him a white man's education and neglected to supply him with a white man's salary.' Hurree's lamentations upon 'oppression and wrong' promptly become tearful, before drifting finally into befuddled versions of Bengali 'love-songs'. The narrator caps the scene with an ironic reflection: 'Never was so unfortunate a product of English rule in India more unhappily thrust upon aliens' (237). Of course, Hurree is in fact a disciplined collaborator, who never turns his shifty talents squarely against the Raj. His representation of the Babu malcontent reproduces historical actualities, but from the British imperial perspective (as the scene's parodic aspects demonstrate) and in the service of British interests.

The mobilization in imperialism's Great Game of such potentially refractory elements as Kim, E.23, Mahbub, and Hurree manifests a signal characteristic of disciplinary society, what Foucault calls 'the differential supervision of illegalities'. As Foucault points out, 'although the juridical opposition is between legality and illegal practice, the strategic opposition is between illegalities and delinquency' (*Discipline* 277). In a disciplinary society, the force of law does not exert itself most vigorously to eliminate delinquency but rather to administer it. What occurs is the emergence of 'enclosed illegality', a dispersed, heterogeneous class of known delinquents, a class which, once isolated and infiltrated, can be used to detect and circumvent the more dangerous illegalities – those that present a real threat to the established social order. Even as the 'ex-con', the prostitute, the pimp, the vagrant are employed, in modern Western societies, as informants, as agents that extend the scope of generalized social surveillance, so the poor white boy, the Mahratha, the Pathan, the Babu come to serve, in Kipling's fictive India, as instruments of imperial domination. And it is precisely their location upon the potentially disruptive margins of the imperial social order that constitutes their utility. As Foucault states the case, delinquency, once duly administered, 'functions as a political observatory' (*Discipline* 281).

To speak of 'a political observatory' is, of course, to evoke the idea of the Panopticon, Jeremy Bentham's intricately designed supervisory apparatus, in which Foucault finds 'the architectural figure' of social control in disciplinary societies (*Discipline* 200–9). And indeed, once Kim and his fellow agents are disseminated throughout the core regions of British India – in the cities, in the countryside, on the roads, and in the trains – they articulate what is effectively an Indian Panopticon. Kipling thus offers, in the virtual absence of legal apparatus, a post-Mutiny fictional actualization of the orienting ideals of the Utilitarian project in India, staging the efficient, rational, impersonal application of governmental power. In keeping with the post-Mutiny mentality, he imagines a disciplinary apparatus that produces a detailed abundance of demographic and ethnological knowledge, but minimizes at the same time direct confrontational contact between the Raj's empowered officials and its subject peoples. In Kipling's India, imperial power is not simply represented but also enacted by intermediaries. British power-knowledge is gathered and applied not by cross-cultural encounter and exchange but by mediated observation. Kipling fulfills Macaulay's dream of efficiently mediated colonial government, though his vision focuses more on political technique than on education.

Envisioning a pacified India

As Foucault stresses, disciplinary power's most notable, most efficient instrument is 'permanent, exhaustive, omnipresent surveillance, capable of making all visible' (*Discipline* 214). Collectively, Kim and his cohorts, the surreptitious 'overseers' of imperial order, transform the novel's social world into a perceptual field held together by alert, mobile, networked gazes. Not surprisingly, therefore, Kim most typically witnesses a bustling India whose happenings are manifestations of nothing more than 'happy Asiatic disorder' (64); India under Kim's eyes is 'happy' under the Raj. Offering a more disturbingly suggestive statement of the case, Kinkead-Weekes writes, 'the world is strangely disinfected as it passes through Kim's eyes' (217). Speaking in Foucauldian terms, the gaze-of-power is a pacifying gaze: it produces the docility of the dominated, the docility of all those who know their actions may be observed, their words overheard, by some unseen representative of power. One cannot adequately account for Kim's India, as Edward Said wishes to do, by suggesting that Kipling did not, indeed could not, imagine an India 'unhappily subservient to imperialism' (*Culture* 145). In *Kim*, Kipling does not wishfully imagine an India 'at peace' with the Raj, but rather stages a sophisticated system of sociopolitical domination to produce and maintain the desired 'peace'. In Kipling's fictive India, precise, detailed information gathered from dispersed sources moves rapidly from the peripheries to the centers of power. The Raj sees and knows promptly, concentrates and applies the required force without delay. Understandably rare as these may be, insurgent initiatives (such as the hostile princely alliance of the novel's early chapters) are nipped in the bud, put down by means of a pre-emptive military maneuver.

   The India of *Kim* is not, of course, historically referential in any rigorous sense. The Raj was never so efficient, the peoples of India never so docile. However, as Wegner puts the case, 'while *Kim* represents neither India nor empire in its "real truth", the narrative does illuminate important aspects of the specific historical terrain on which it unfolds' (132). Its imperialist utopianism notwithstanding, Kipling's text represents the real, if less colorful attempt to discipline an India that, during the mid-century rebellion notably and in subsequent decades, demonstrated its intractability to British rule. The novel envisions a post-Mutiny Raj disengaged from its own power-practice, a strangely abstracted Raj exercising power at a distance, elaborating a structural, administrative system of domination that locates in the subject peoples (beginning, of course, with the intermediaries themselves) 'the principle of [their] own subjection' (Foucault, *Discipline* 203). Kipling recognizes that modern imperialist expansion and consolidation raise issues of social control with new and unprecedented intensity; that, at least in the area of governmental administration, the possibility of any stubbornly enduring 'colonial belatedness' must be ruled out. For Kipling, the most modern, most sophisticated administrative techniques are required 'out there' in the colonies – and most particularly in populous and culturally diverse India, where the colonizing few are called upon to supervise and control the multicultural many.

In *Kim*, power discovers itself in practical, situational, opportunistic ways. Kipling's novel, when examined in the light of Foucauldian theory, offers a staging of systems of social control produced by and within a process of colonial domination. It does not enact a law brought from afar so much as it elaborates itself 'on site' in response to the *specific* demands of the post-Mutiny imperial project in India. Kipling stages an efficient political machinery *for British India*. Therefore, this novel does not sustain an envisioning of a sovereign, self-contained 'West' exerting itself, unaffected, upon its colonies. Notwithstanding its representation of a disengaged Raj whose practice of power is thoroughly mediated, *Kim* presents a vision of a 'West' that shapes itself in its effort to reshape and dominate other cultures, other worlds. Moreover, the imperial culture's involvement with the colonized culture is manifested most clearly by the same elements that enable its putative detachment, that is, by the mediating subjects – the indigenized white boy, the co-opted Pathan, the Western-educated Bengali – all of whom are marked by effects of cultural hybridization.

My argument thus returns to questions I touched on earlier, questions concerning the colonizing subject's involvement with the societies and cultures of the colonized, concerning also the pertinence of that involvement to imperial authority and agency. Citing John McClure, Wegner asserts that, 'despite his expressed desire to reform the practice of imperial rule, Kipling in no way questions the deeper ontology of empire – an "authoritarian view of the world as a place structured in dyads of dominance and submission, obedience and isolation, power and pain"' (132). I find, however, that the case of *Kim* (the text to which Wegner refers) is perhaps not so clear-cut. Kim does stage multicultural India in relation to a more than tacit power divide, which is promptly drawn by the 'racialized' assertion of Kim's 'white', 'English' identity and by the power-play of that identity in the Zam-Zammah game. Yet as the narrative progresses it becomes increasingly clear that cultural and ethnic identities are not always susceptible to such sharp delineation, such unimpeachable hierarchization. Kim, although he provides the most spectacular instance, is not the only example of a character who straddles, crosses, and recrosses imperialism's power divide. Mahbub aligns himself unfalteringly with British power, yet is unapologetically a Pathan and, despite moments of jovial self-ironizing, outspokenly adheres to the religion and culture of his people. One may also speak of Hurree Chunder, the Western-educated Bengali who combines Royal Society ambitions with atavistic superstitions, or of Lurgan, whose ethnicity remains as mysterious as his status in the hierarchy of the Great Game.[9] Whereas Colonel Creighton's sociocultural and political location is represented unambiguously – Hurree's peremptory affirmation that Creighton is European requires no qualification – other prominent, more active if less powerful Great Gamesters are difficult to classify, difficult to situate within the normalizing, hierarchizing systems of disciplinary order.

Disciplinary power and ethnic indeterminacy

As my preceding discussion has made clear, disciplinary power functions by situating subjects within a social field, by classifying, distributing, hierarchizing. The mechanism of the Panopticon, as Foucault stresses, aims to maximize the efficiency of *any* project of subject formation and social control – to facilitate supervision in the prison or the asylum, education in the school, productivity in the factory: 'The Panopticon is a marvelous machine which, whatever use one may wish to put it to, produces homogeneous effects of power' (*Discipline* 202). The enabling key, however, is sure knowledge of the subject's assigned position within the supervisory architecture, a position that need not be continuously verified if it is at all times verifiable. A multicultural, ethnically diverse, and increasingly hybridized social context might therefore pose problems with respect to an imperial application of disciplinary systems. The emplacement of the disciplines may not be impeded, but the end they serve may become, at least to some degree, multiple and divided. Disciplinary power does not flow vectorally from the upper to the lower echelons of the social body. It is relayed through a multiplicity of subjects; it circulates through all social levels. In a social context such as one finds in *Kim*, the disciplines may serve, therefore, to enable transgressions of the power divide inscribed by imperialist intervention, may serve to unbalance the dyad of dominance and submission.

A close consideration of the following scene from *Kim* should serve to clarify these last points and render my suggestions more concrete. Having carried Mahbub Ali's secret message to Creighton, Kim professes news of war to a group of Indian listeners. To prove his story, he performs a mimicking description of his source, the Commander-in-Chief of the Indian Armed Forces, looking to a retired Indian officer for confirmation of the truth of his performance. The ragged *chela* walks like the 'great man', talks like him, and mimes his characteristic gestures, setting the crowd a-shiver and leaving the old soldier 'inarticulate with amazement'. As a final proof that his knowledge is not built up from hearsay, Kim is called upon to reproduce the Commander's manner of giving an order:

'He rubs the skin at the back of his neck – thus. Then falls one finger on the table and he makes a small sniffing noise through his nose. Then He speaks saying: "Loose such and such a regiment. Call out such guns."'
The old man rose stiffly and saluted. (48)

Making a shrewd rhetorical move, the boy translates 'the clinching sentences' for his listeners, ending with a Hindi version of the Chief

Officer's 'It is not war – it is a chastisement. Snff!' Overcome by the performance, the retired soldier exclaims at last, 'It is He!' (48)

On first examination, this little scene seems clearly to confirm, in an unproblematic way, the disciplinary force of imperial power. Functioning as a proxy, Kim makes the Commander-in-Chief, and the authority he embodies, compelling and effective even in absence: the crowd of Indian listeners remains 'breathless-still' throughout Kim's performance and draws one 'long, quavering breath' at its conclusion (47, 48); the retired soldier goes so far as to salute, then stands for some time 'at attention' (48). Closer and more extensive consideration reveals, however, that the scene cannot be read so simply and unequivocally. To begin with, Kim's performance is duplicitous, literally doubled: Kim represents a low-caste Hindu boy representing the British Commander-in-Chief. In so doing he undertakes what is, in the context of the novel as a whole, a singular, implicitly forbidden action – the representation of a white man (and a highly placed, powerful white man at that) by an Indian. The representation, moreover, is enabled by a preceding act of surreptitious, exacting surveillance, detailed right down to the idiosyncratic and tell-tale 'Snff!' The 'great man' is thus captured within the narrative's generalized disciplinary schema, seen rather than seeing, represented rather than self-representing. His person, his decisions and actions, and his secret information (the receipt and distribution of which should be his more or less exclusive prerogative) are offered to an Indian collectivity for discussion and evaluation. The boy's actions submit crucial military intelligence to the economy of rumor, whose unpredictable, potentially subversive effects played an important role in the early development of the great revolt of 1857.[10]

The scene of Kim's performance, despite its optimistic affirmation of just and uncontested British authority, is in fact haunted by the specter of the Mutiny. Kim brings news of anti-colonial initiatives of sufficient moment to necessitate the fairly massive military response represented by 'eight thousand redcoats' with artillery support (47). As Kim begins his performance, the narrator briefly recalls the Mutiny; shortly after the performance, the old soldier recites 'tales of the Mutiny' (50), preparing for the extensive discussion of the Mutiny story that soon follows. No anti-imperial enunciations find their way into the immediate dramatic situation, but discourse of insurrection provides a context. Indian colonial subjects, moreover, are offered politically charged information that should not be theirs and are thus enabled to evaluate and judge the workings of the governing power. Unquestionably, Kim's undecided ethnicity is the key factor in the creation of this situation. His European heritage, together with the supplement of Indian acculturation, recommends him for secret service, but also allows him surreptitiously to acquire privileged information. His easy familiarity with the codes and customs of Indian sociability and his tacit validation of Indian society (as evidenced by his drive to be a success, to distinguish himself within that social context) motivate and facilitate his disclosure. These same factors also augment the social effects of his performance.

Multivalent, hybrid ethnicity thus associates itself with a disorderly proliferation of disciplinary power. Kipling's text registers the destabilizing potential of such proliferation, yet affords it a place in the cultural framework of the Raj. Ethnicity such as Kim's, although undecidable and at times unpredictable in its expression, is not unknown and unknowable; it is, like other aspects of the Indian cultural scene, susceptible to documentation. 'In Kipling's novel', writes Deirdre David, 'imperialism is a notably efficient operation, appropriating, for instance, the newly established scientific discipline of ethnography' (134). To supplement and, as it were, guarantee the *imperial* effectiveness of the political practice of 'the disciplines' his novel stages, Kipling employs a modern scholarly 'discipline'. The ethnographic rendering of colonial India works to produce a controlled distribution of multiple, shifting ethnicities, to contain the potentially disruptive energies of hybridization and unbridled intersubjective, cross-cultural exchange – what Pratt describes as transculturation in the contact zone. Ethnography represents the crucial and decisive gambit in Kipling's 'Great Game' of imperial domination. In the chapter that follows, I will examine the ethnographic aspects of *Kim*, seeking to document, describe, and evaluate the overall ethnographic project of the text; and focusing my attention upon the figure of the liminal boy, whose centrality within the textual economy will be once again and still more clearly confirmed.

5
Kim: Ethnography and the Hybrid Boy

The suggestion that *Kim* can be approached as an ethnography immediately raises a question about Kipling's status as an ethnographer. As James Clifford observes in his introduction to *Writing Culture*, ethnographic writing is normally governed by generic determinations and 'is usually distinguishable from a novel or a travel account' (6). Clifford nonetheless acknowledges that ethnography 'is an emergent interdisciplinary phenomenon' that 'blur[s] the boundary separating art from science' (3). The ethnographer, for Clifford, is a text-maker whose work ineluctably requires 'expressive tropes, figures, and allegories that select and impose meaning as they translate it' (7). The textual practices of ethnography and literary art are thus potentially compatible. Although *Kim* is not an ethnography in the purest sense, it includes ethnography; it evidences an ethnographic project. The India of *Kim* is clearly not exotic backdrop or *trompe l'œil* conforming more to the urges of imagination than to the exigencies of cultural documentation and representation. This text provides ample evidence of what one might call the ethnographic impulse, the writerly drive to grasp and document cultural realities. If, as Arnold Krupat suggests, ethnographers are most fundamentally, most crucially, the 'providers of data for the understanding of other worlds' (80), then Kipling must be granted a certain status as an ethnographer.

More specifically, one can consider Kipling an *imperial* ethnographer. Invariably, as George Marcus avers, 'closely observed cultural worlds are imbedded in larger, more impersonal systems' and must be studied in integral relation to a determining 'context of historical political economy' (166, 167). Ethnographies, writes Clifford, 'are systems, or economies, of truth. Power and history work through them, in ways their authors cannot fully control' ('Introduction' 7). One should read Kipling's representation of India, therefore, in relation to the implicit and explicit relations it establishes with British imperialism in India. In this chapter I will show, first, how Kipling's ethnographic practices enact and confirm imperial power-knowledge and, subsequently, how the organizing figure of the hybrid boy both enables and problematizes the project of imperial ethnography.

Ethnography, orientalism, power–knowledge

The ethnographic impulse manifests itself in *Kim* a variety of ways. The novel's opening scenes, which serve admirably to orient the action and to introduce the principal themes, occur in and around the museum of ethnology in Lahore. Kim's subsequent relationship with a Tibetan lama has significant ethnological implications, as do his relationships with Mahbub Ali and Hurree Chunder Mookerjee. Both Hurree Babu and Colonel Creighton, the 'unofficial' head of the novel's imperial spy network, are ambitious ethnographers. And this connection between spying and scholarship is not, of course, coincidental; ethnology and ethnography are crucial aspects British intelligence. As Kim learns from Lurgan Sahib, careful attention to ethnological data – right down to its most minute details – is the key to success as an imperial agent: it enables Kim to become a master of cross-cultural disguise – enables him, that is, to stage an ethnology 'in person', to embody and enact an ethnography.

Implicit and explicit linkages of knowledge and power, of ethnology and imperial practice, occur throughout Kipling's novel. In the initial encounter between the Red Lama and the curator of the Lahore Museum, Indian culture is presented as a British possession. Although Kipling pictures eager Indian peasants flocking to Lahore's Wonder House to see Indian handicrafts, the Museum, as Kim duly informs the inquisitive holy man, is 'the Government's house' (6). All those seeking knowledge of India – including, of course, those who are natives of India and, as such, producers of its culture – must consult British holdings and solicit the explanations of the wise, white-bearded curator-Sahib.

Encouraged by Kim, the lama enters the Museum and immediately confronts imagery attesting to the precedence and enduring pre-eminence of Western cultural achievements in relation to those of the East; in conformity with the principles enunciated by Said in *Orientalism*, this ethnological museum presents the visitor with 'derivative' Eastern masterpieces, which strive to recapture an earlier, more masterful Western artistry. As soon as he is through the turnstiles the scholarly holy man stands before 'Greco-Buddhist sculptures', which are admirable insofar as they manifest a 'mysteriously transmitted Grecian touch' (6). European superiority, however, is most tellingly a matter of knowledge. Western 'savants', Kipling's text assures us, know virtually everything there is to know of the 'mysterious' East. The curator (clearly to be numbered amongst these 'savants') produces an enormous book containing photographic images of the lama's own lamasery. He knows the details of the Buddha's life, which is represented by the museum's carvings and also in abundant books – learned works in French or German by reputed Europeans. To questions concerning 'Oriental' cultures, the curator can answer with authoritative simplicity, 'It is written. I have read' (9). Although his expertise finds its limit with respect to the lama's mystic river, whose waters promise release from the Wheel of worldly attachments, the curator's knowledge of the Wheel itself, that is, of the sociocultural life of the subcontinental world, seems to comprehend both generalities and minutiae. Aptly, his parting gift to the lama, a pair of spectacles of European manufacture, bears the promise of a clearly detailed, far-reaching 'envisioning' of the material, phenomenal world. Thus, in his novel's opening movements, Kipling represents an amply documented 'Orient' whose sociocultural realities are securely encompassed by a European knowledge *imperium*. The Museum passages posit an 'Orient' that is not 'mysterious' but objectively known, an accountable 'Orient' whose concrete elements can be located and delineated, authoritatively organized and represented.[1]

Temporality, oriental and occidental

The Orientalist and orientalizing propensity, which situates 'the East' in meaningfully subordinate relation to 'the West' (see Said, *Orientalism* 49–73), persists throughout the text of *Kim*. Kipling's narrator repeatedly makes generalizing, authoritative statements upon Oriental character and custom. Orientals, for example, possess a penchant and a talent for fabrication and duplicity: Kim, for instance, can 'lie like an Oriental' (23) – that is, spontaneously, unscrupulously, elaborately, and well. Most typically and most significantly, however, such Orientalist statements address issues of temporality. As Mahbub Ali comes to clear awareness of the pressing nature of an intelligence mission, one learns that he has, characteristically, 'an Oriental's views of the value of time' (22), but can bestir himself to act promptly when occasion demands. Similarly, as Kim and the lama enter a benighted yet crowded train station, the narrator affirms that 'All hours of the twenty-four are alike to Orientals' (26). Particular, Oriental relationships with time are also made evident when the narrator observes that one anna per rupee is 'the immemorial commission of Asia' (27), or when he details the movements of Mahbub's caravan, which breaks camp '[s]wiftly – as Orientals understand speed' (142), which is to say, in an ambling, ill-directed way – not swiftly at all.[2]

Mahbub's Oriental-style breaking of camp merits attention insofar as it contrasts sharply with an earlier description that calls attention to the wondrous speed and efficiency with which the Maverick regiment sets up camp: 'The plain dotted itself with tents that seemed to rise, all spread, from the carts. Another rush of men invaded the grove, pitched a huge tent in silence, ran up eight or nine more by the side of it, unearthed cooking-pots, pans, and bundles … and behold the mango-tope turned into an orderly town' (81). In this passage, Kipling represents the efficient use of time – the everyday practice of the time-mastering European, 'the routine of a seasoned regiment pitching camp in thirty minutes' (82). Oriental time thus discovers its relation to an alternative model; ambling, undifferentiated Oriental time contrasts with European time, which is apportioned, regimented – quite literally, pressed into service. Just as clearly, European time is the time of imperial enterprise, the time that enables the Mavericks, together with their duly marshaled 'crowd of native servants' (81), to 'invade' the virgin mango grove and to make of it, in 30 precisely measured minutes, 'an orderly town'. Considered in relation with the narrator's statements upon Eastern temporality, the Mavericks' pitching of camp offers itself as a representative staging of a grander spectacle – the productive mastering of a timeless 'East' by a time-binding 'West'.

To specify and characterize Oriental temporality from a Western perspective is, of course, to make an ethnographic distinction, one that clearly is not lacking in significant sociopolitical implications. In Kipling's text, the 'allochronism' of ethnographic discourse (Fabian 32ff.), which constitutes a strategic difference between the time of the observed, cultural other and that of the Western observer, does not serve merely to affirm, once again, the superiority of European cultural paradigms. It also reveals something of the method and the means by which that illusion of superiority is secured and maintained. As Clifford notes, the power to represent cultural realities typically rests on the Western writer-observer's claim to a special capacity to apprehend time 'objectively'. The traditional discourse of anthropology 'speaks with automatic authority for others defined as unable to speak for themselves ("primitive," "pre-literate," "without history")' (Clifford, 'Introduction' 10). Kipling's India is represented as being 'without history' in the sense that it is submitted to what Clifford calls 'synchronic suspension' ('Ethnographic Allegory' 111). As Ronald Inden observes in *Imagining India*, the 'India' represented by Western Indologists is a place of long-standing cultural stasis – a stasis Kipling renders in predominantly temporal terms. In Kipling's Wonder House, India's different times are presented in spatial contiguity, compartmentalized in such a way that a time or period constitutes not a distant and distinct past but rather another supplementary, adjacent, equally 'present') manifestation of an eternal, essentially unchanging 'India'. The Greco-Buddhist sculptures, fashioned by 'forgotten workmen' (6), are important in that they manifest an aspect of 'India' – as do the contemporary regional handicrafts of an adjoining hall. These and other holdings contribute to a broadly inclusive, largely transhistorical reading of 'India'.

India as text

As Talal Asad ascertains, deeply embedded in the traditions of Western anthropology is the tendency to transform the 'notion of culture ... into the notion of a *text* – that is, into something resembling an inscribed discourse' (141). *Kim*, in this respect, presents an interesting case. The ethnologically, historically informed gaze, which is exercised most saliently by Kipling's narrator, does not restore history to the Indian scene, but rather employs the 'historical sense' to perceive and confirm the effective absence of a *dynamic* history. The timelessness of Kipling's 'India' allows for its treatment as a text, as an assembly of signifying elements whose order is necessary, invariable – fixed, as it were, for all time. To deprive India of a dynamic historical temporality is to exclude the very possibility of innovation and change. It is to create an India whose cultural manifestations are *pre-scribed*, written in advance, an India that ceaselessly recites itself. Thus, when the Kipling narrator affirms that India is a land of 'dreamers, babblers, and visionaries', he adds, 'as it has been from the beginning and will continue to the end' (32). Ostensibly, Kipling's novel does not remake India as a text so much as present a reading of the text India always-already is. For all that it is multifaceted, the cultural object of study is perceived as something stable, as a kind of museum-text to which one can return, again and again; as it was, so it shall be. The elements of the cultural text can be located, specified, classified, with the assurance that locations, specifications, and classifications are not susceptible to historical contingencies. Such 'synchronic suspension', Clifford argues, 'effectively textualizes the other, and gives the sense of a reality not in temporal flux, not in the same ambiguous, moving historical present that includes and situates the other, the ethnographer, and the reader' ('Ethnographic Allegory' 111). Under the eye of the alert and informed reader-observer, the bustle and flux of India – its 'happy Asiatic disorder' (64) – becomes its pageantry, its spectacular, strangely ceremonious reproduction of itself.

The narrative process of *Kim* inscribes in its own way the kinds of methods and procedures that characterize the Great Game and affirms, as does the Great Game, that India in all its diversity can be known and controlled. Like the Great Game, Kipling's ethnologically informed narrative organizes and reproduces a vast assembly of information. In Kipling's India, as is confirmed by the exhausted Kim's reviviscence in the final pages, the ordering consciousness of the trained observer can always 'lock up anew on the world without', with a 'click' as sure as that of the museum's visitor-counting turnstiles. Things will find their 'proper proportion'; meaning and purposes will be revealed. One will walk the roads, inhabit the houses, till the fields, and talk to the women and men who are there, of course, 'to be talked to'. Everything, in short, will reveal itself in the end as 'real', 'true', and 'perfectly comprehensible' (282).

The hybrid boy as ethnographic instrument

Although Kim's consciousness ultimately is presented as a site of perfect knowledge, as a fluid, self-adjusting ethnological archive, one must nonetheless recognize that the boy typically appears as something of a rogue element within the controlled and controlling knowledges deployed by Kipling's novel. Amidst the timeless, changeless pageantry of India, Kim consistently discovers and enacts the new and unprecedented. He drums his heels upon the austerely symbolic Zam-Zammah, keeps company with fakirs, catches forbidden glimpses into the feminine world behind the *purdah*, roams the bazaar and kicks a holy cow in the nose (while dressed as a low-caste Hindu boy). A friend to all castes and creeds, Kim freely traverses discrete social spaces, exchanges castes and creeds, scrambles categories, obscures distinctions. His antic life seems, on first consideration, to challenge the adequacy of the ethnological science which the Lahore Museum displays and the Great Game puts into practice.

One should not conclude, however, that the boy has no productive role in Kipling's imperial ethnographic project. As Inden argues, the image of India as meticulously distributed cultural stasis does not reflect inherent social structures, but is rather a sense-making imposition of the categories and concepts of Western Indology, which produce a deeply determined, essentialized India informed by 'the mind of Hinduism' (85ff.) and ordered upon archaic, supposedly fixed and unchanging stratifications of 'caste society' (49ff.). Kim's gay liberty is constituted as exceptional, and thus contrasts with and sets in relief an Indological 'India' of self-imposed social stricture and constraint. India is imaged in *Kim* as doubly controlled – by imperial authority and its sustaining power-knowledge, certainly, but also by codes and taboos of 'Indian culture'. In the figure of Kim, Kipling discovers the means of representing a freewheeling 'experience' of Indian culture, one that is characterized by unrestricted access and mobility yet does not significantly unsettle the representation of India as a discretely ordered multiplicity, as a static society of fixed (and therefore fully knowable) social forms. The boy's irreverent transgressions remind us of the boundaries that inscribe Indological India. Kim provides, moreover, a subjective and fully participatory perspective that does not perturb so much as it supplements the objective knowledge contained in archives, artifacts, documents, and maps. He creates the possibility of maintaining the 'delicate balance of subjectivity and objectivity' that a thoroughgoing ethnography is expected to produce (Clifford, 'Introduction' 13).

Evidently, then, the election of Kim as the central, organizing character of an ethnographic fiction is by no means arbitrary. Indeed, the marvelous boy recommends himself in a variety of ways as an enabling figure for an imperial ethnography of British India. As I have shown, Kipling's narrative discourse articulates an Orientalist representation of India as part of a timeless, eternal East, as a place that is somehow outside history. It is the business of the Great Game, moreover, to secure India from the perturbations of history: illegitimate princely alliances must be nipped in the bud; Russian incursions must be stopped at the frontier. Not so surprisingly, a boy plays an important role in this Great Game. Spaces like the India of *Kim*, spaces outside history, seem to solicit the figure of the boy, even as this figure solicits such spaces. One may recall, in this regard, the 'Neverland' of J. M. Barrie's *Peter Pan* (1904, 1911) or the island of the Crusoe myth, which is appropriated for boys in R. M. Ballantyne's *The Coral Island* (1857). In the popular imagination of Victorian Britain, it would seem that the boy is situated outside history, at least in the sense that he is not in it *yet*. As Jacqueline Rose has observed, the child of later Victorian and Edwardian imaginings is insistently envisioned as 'a pure point of origin' in relation to language and the social (8). The child – or, as in the present case, the boy of imperial fictions – is therefore presumed to have an intuitive, unmediated, 'natural' relation with his world. The boyish presence thus dehistoricizes, depoliticizes. The boy provides an alibi of disinterestedness, operating as an embodiment of what Krupat calls 'the putatively innocent eye of the observer' – an eye that was presumed to function without the aid of 'aprioristic theory' (Krupat 89–90), an eye whose innocence was a crucial article of faith for early ethnographers such as the highly influential Franz Boas (a contemporary of Kipling).

The value of the hybrid boy as an instrument for imperial ethnography is also very much in evidence in the intersubjective realm, where he serves to mediate cross-cultural colonial relations. Occupying a middle ground between the (adult, male, European) colonizer and the (adult, male, non-European) colonized, a boy like Kim has no stable identity; his subject position – always in flux – can never be reliably assigned. Alternatively, Kim identifies, and is identified, both with the colonizer and the colonized. European by birth, he is called upon to represent imperial authority. Yet he is also a subject under that authority – as is his counterpart, the colonial 'native', whom the discourse of colonialism insistently represents as a child.[3] The figure of the boy has a function akin to that of the 'median category' described by Said in *Orientalism*. The 'median category', Said suggests, 'allows one to see new things ... as versions of a previously known thing'. And yet 'such a category is not so much a way of receiving new information as it is a method of controlling what seems to be a threat to some established view of things' (58–9). As a site of knowledge that is somewhat charted and familiar, the 'median category' allows the Orientalist or the anthropologist or the ethnographer to apprehend and negotiate radical difference. It effects a familiarizing displacement: the relatively familiar 'Near East' mediates the confrontation with the 'Far East'; similarly, the familiar figure of the boy mediates the confrontation of the European imperial subject with the potentially uncanny colonial other. One establishes a putative control over this other by envisioning him as a kind of child. This supposed affinity, between the child and the colonial subject, begins to account for the atmosphere of mutually acknowledged peerage characterizing Kim's relations with subcontinental adults – with fellow Great Gamesters, Mahbub and Hurree, and with the lama, who is, paradoxically, Kim's master and his dependant.

Of relatively unfixed, indeterminate identity, the boy is highly susceptible to 'indigenization'. Mowgli with his wolves and Tarzan with his apes represent variations on this theme. The boy, however, suffers little from the stigma generally associated with 'going native'. The adult colonizer who 'goes native' is beyond recuperation – ruined, lost. One may consider Conrad's Kurtz or, for that matter, Kim's father, who is represented as a renegade soldier, a bazaar loafer, an opium addict. The indigenized boy, on the other hand, is simply taken in hand, recruited, disciplined, and schooled. Unlike the man, the boy does not betray and abandon a European selfhood; he has yet to acquire one. Just as the wolfish Mowgli is not yet human, so Kim, the boy of the bazaar, is not yet European. The boy's true nature and identity are secured, however, by the invocation of an essentially racialist notion of the relationship of nature to nurture, a notion Jean-François Gournay names as 'l'intangibilité de l'inné' (389), the intangibility of the innate. As Kipling's text insists at the outset, Kim is 'English' and 'white' despite appearances; 'the color "white" functions', Gail Low observes, 'as a residual "truth" which cannot be erased' (213). The boy of imperial myth thus lives and moves within a circular teleology, progressing toward a 'true character' already inscribed in his origin.[4] More importantly, however, once he has been reclaimed, once he has been adequately, if not entirely, disciplined and subjected, the indigenized boy is an invaluable tool: Kim's continuing access to subcontinental culture and society enables him to provide imperial power with a view from the inside. Access to the insider perspective, observes Clifford, can provide an ethnographic project with 'new angles of vision and depths of understanding' ('Introduction' 9).

The boy as potential site of resistance

Upon cursory consideration, Kipling's articulation of his ethnographic project in close relation to a hybrid boy seems to resolve the kinds of questions raised in James Clifford's *The Predicament of Culture*, a deconstructive analysis of the history of Western ethnographic practices. How can the supposedly objective outsider effectively and accurately observe a culture? But then, if ethnographic practice is oriented in terms of involvement or even immersion, how can the ethnographer reliably represent an otherness in which she or he is deeply implicated? Is one a participant or an observer? Does not involvement seriously compromise ethnographic authority? Kipling's proposed answer to all these troubling queries is Kim, the indigenized white boy who is able to mediate the ethnographer's relationship with the otherness of India.

In relation to India, the cultural object of study, Kim stands as an insider/outsider, as the principal *agent* but also as the spectacular, highly engaging, preferred *object* of the cross-cultural gaze. Speaking in ethnographic terms, Kim has a function akin to that of the 'participant observer' and also to that of 'native informant'. By recognizing the dualities that inform his role, one can begin to appreciate how the hybrid boy may complicate as well as enable an imperialist ethnographic representation of cultural alterity. As the fieldworker who participates and observes, Kim clearly aligns himself with British imperial authority, that is, with the power that represents. As the native informant, however, Kim is tacitly or implicitly aligned with the objects of power, with those who are represented. Situated on both sides of imperialism's power divide, he is an ambivalent figure, a site for the deployment of imperial power, but also, at least potentially, a site of resistance.

Certainly, the process of Kim's initiation to imperialism's Great Game reveals the boy's capacity to resist, at least partially, the power that plays upon him. During his inaugural mission, Kim dutifully delivers Mahbub Ali's message to Colonel Creighton, then proceeds to spy upon the Colonel and to eavesdrop upon his highly confidential conversation with the Commander-in-Chief of the Indian Armed Forces. As I observed in the preceding chapter, the impetuous boy subsequently relates what he has seen and heard to a crowd of eager Indian listeners. As a schoolboy, Kim periodically slips out of the confines of St Xavier's, to visit his lama or simply to indulge in the pleasures of the town. Disregarding the plans Creighton has made for him, the fledgling agent disappears without a trace during his first three-month school holiday. An esoteric and unauthorized Indian rite of passage marks Kim's accession to the status of fully-fledged agent: the boy becomes a Son of the Charm, a member of a secret organization within the secret organization of the Great Game. This exclusively Indian clan, invented by Hurree Babu, is 'strictly unoffeecial' and, if one can trust Hurree's word, entirely unknown to Creighton (182). Kim's insider status, his intimate knowledge of the Indian scene, makes him both a valuable and an uncertain imperial agent. His insider knowledge provides him, moreover, with the means to ensure that his terms are respected. The boy claims he can disappear, if he chooses, into the life of India – 'Once gone, who shall find me?'(146) – a claim even the canny Mahbub Ali seems to take seriously.

One must acknowledge nonetheless that neither Mahbub nor the Colonel is greatly worried by Kim's errant escapades (in so far as they are aware of them). The Pathan horse-dealer concludes that the colt has spirit; the colonial administrator that the insolent boy has 'resource and nerve' (142). In the end, as both these senior players correctly surmise, Kim will play the Great Imperial Game and play it well – even if it means endangering Teshoo-lama and compromising the holy man's quest for salvation and enlightenment. Similarly, Kim proves, as I have suggested already, a very serviceable ethnographic agent, processing ethnological data ever more thoroughly and efficiently, staging 'in person' various Indian cultural 'identities', generally enabling imperial power to maneuver within and manipulate the cultural contingencies of British–Indian colonial encounter.

Narrative enunciation: distinctions and identifications

The ethnographic project of *Kim*, however, is not ordered by the hybrid boy alone, but by the relationship between the boy and the narrator. It is the narrator's indispensable function to detail the boy's thoughts, feelings, and actions, to gaze upon the boy in the imperial contact zone, then to document both the boy and the India he experiences. The narrator of *Kim* is not disengaged from the actions he records. Although something less than an obstreperous presence, Kipling's narrator nonetheless manifests himself as a personality, as one who guides affective and imaginative responses and actively assists the sense-making process of his reader.

The enunciation of *Kim* evidences both authoritative detachment and sympathetic engagement; it is marked, as Moore-Gilbert observes, by 'fluctuations in the narrative perspective' ('Bhabhal 130). In the novel's first sentence, the narrator refers to the 'Ajaib-Gher – the Wonder House, as the natives call the Lahore Museum' Here, the narrator speaks knowingly, yet maintains his authoritative distance, offering first the vernacular name, then immediately translating it and marking it as 'native'. What 'the natives' call the 'Ajaib-Gher', the narrator calls the Lahore Museum, and he, quite clearly, knows more and better than they do. In this enunciative moment, the narrator presents something that comfortably approximates 'the viewpoint of a metropolitan British audience

('Bhabhal' 130); he assumes with respect to India a certain mastery but also maintains distance. When one turns the page, however, the narrator introduces the 'Jadoo-Gher – the Magic House, as we name the Masonic Lodge'. As before, the vernacular name, then the translation – but to whom does this 'we' refer? Certainly, 'we' know the Masonic Lodge is the Masonic Lodge, so one can assume that 'we' are not 'natives'. The group with which the narrator identifies would seem to be the acclimatized 'Anglo-Indian' community. Noteworthy, here, is the suggestion that this ostensibly European group prefers to use the vernacular names for things, even for such 'un-Indian' things as the Masonic temple. The narrator who represents the hybrid boy now identifies himself not with the home-bred English but with a partially hybridized group whose characteristic habits and attitudes have been inflected by experience of India.

Kim's opening passages raise the question of cultural difference or, more precisely, of cultural differentiation, not only in relation to Kim but also in relation to a 'we' proposed as the site of narrative enunciation. Although different from 'the natives', this 'we' shares a language with them. Yet, as one soon learns, the accessing and ordering of cultural difference in the world of *Kim* cannot be achieved by means of a singular idiom shared by 'natives' and partially assimilated colonizers. The opening proposition – that 'the natives' call the Museum the 'Ajaib-Gher' – is a misleadingly simple statement, which presents an ultimately untenable envisioning of 'native' homogeneity. The Indian populous, which may concur in designating the Museum as a 'Wonder House', would nonetheless use a plurality of terms to name it as such. Kipling's text, as it develops, registers a multiplicity of competing codes – English, Urdu, Hindi, Punjabi, Pushtu – none of which is clearly constituted as definitive and authoritative. English, of course, predominates, but it is not so much a language of preference as one of necessary, if often partial and imperfect, translation. Kipling's narrator not only acknowledges but employs a multiplicity of linguistic codes. His narration stages in a variety of ways the heteroglossia of British India, a heteroglossia that must undermine the early, too easy rendering of the readily negotiable binary of 'we' and 'they', of Anglo-Indians and colonized, subordinate 'natives'.

The language of *Kim* is necessarily hybrid, yet – this must be stressed – more hybrid than it need be. The narrator chooses to use a variety of 'alien' terms, not all of which are marked as such by italics, many of which have no accompanying English translation. Certainly, the narrator's easy familiarity with subcontinental languages may be seen to augment his claim to ethnographic authority. However, as Robert Young observes, the hybridizing of a code must ultimately undermine rather than sustain authoritative discourse. Working within the frame of Bakhtinian theory, Young argues, 'Authoritative discourse ... must be singular'; it cannot speak through the fundamentally dialogistic, 'double-voiced' effects of 'linguistic hybridization' (20–2). Authority, moreover, is not the only issue. The narrator betrays a taste for subcontinental vocabulary and inflection, using many foreign terms not once (to show he knows them) but repeatedly. He offers up essentially untranslatable puns, such as the word-play that links '*yagi* (bad-tempered)' with '*yogi* (a holy man)' (13). He retains curious instances of hybridized English such as '*tikkut*' and '*te-rain*'. The dialogue the narrator-ethnographer records is generally rendered in a formal, highly figurative, archaic English, a stylistic decision that tends to situate speech and action in the timeless realm of fable, certainly, but also one that foregrounds the act of translation. By mimicking the forms and figures of subcontinental languages, the dialogue recalls that English is very rarely the spoken language of *Kim*.

The narrator does not, moreover, sharply and consistently distinguish his own voice from that of his characters. The lama's first appearance, for example, is rendered in this manner: 'for there shuffled round the corner, from the roaring Motee Bazar, such a man as Kim, who thought he knew all castes, had never seen' (4). The phrase 'for there shuffled' does not ring as early twentieth-century English usage, nor does the eccentric syntax of 'such a man as Kim'. A reader will also note, perhaps with relish, that the bazaar roars. Similarly curious stylistic touches mark the brief passage that ushers in the novel's final movement: 'Towards evening, when the dust of returning kine made all the horizons smoke, came the lama and Mahbub Ali ...' (283). Here, archaic 'kine' are framed by a horizon that smokes. These picturesque kine combine with an unusual inversion of plural subject and main verb to evoke something very like the fictive world of the fabulist. The narrator's discourse, as evidenced in this passage and the preceding one, is often like the novel's dialogue – richly figured, faintly archaic, syntactically idio-syncratic.[5]

The language of *Kim* fails to create for the narrator a singular and separate position of synoptic transcendence. Unquestionably, the totalizing voice of ethnographic (and imperial) authority asserts itself when the narrator offers peremptory statements upon the Orient. And yet, this same narrator, on occasion, records outlandish manifestations of the Indian folkloric imagination with dispassion-ate equanimity, as if rendering yet another cultural fact: a *churel*, as it happens, is a particularly dangerous female ghost; 'her feet are turned backwards on the ankles, and she leads men to torment' (138). When Kim and the lama take to the Grand Trunk Road, the narrator notes that they encounter 'strong-scented Sansis with baskets of lizards and other unclean food on their backs' (71). Thus briefly but tellingly, the narrator acknowledges and employs a notably non-visual mode of cultural recognition, manifesting a capacity to distinguish and interpret scents. One may also observe that, in relation to British food standards, lizard would be straight-forwardly disgusting rather than 'unclean' – a term that would sound quite Pentateuchal and archaic to the modern, metropolitan, English ear. A change of identification, positionality, and perspec-tive is evident here, a change that takes a more extreme form when the narrator disparages 'careless, open-spoken English folk' (148), as if referring to an alien group, or when he alludes, with casual distaste, to Europeans' 'dull fat eyes' (118). Evidently, 'the English', as much if not more than 'the natives', find their position in the 'they' of narrative enunciation.

It is most notably in delineating the relationship between the narrator and the hybrid boy that Kipling negotiates what Zohreh Sullivan describes as his 'fantasy of integration between the opposi-tional roles of colonizer and colonized and of the master who rules and the child who desires' (148). The narrator, as one would expect, keeps very close to the boy. Kim's alluring presence provokes and, in a sense, justifies the shifting of the narrator's position, away from authoritative, informed detachment and toward sympathetic involvement. The narrator is quick to suggest that he, like Kim, is one of those who prefer to speak in the vernacular. Like Kim, he confronts subcontinental folklore with the casual imperturbability of an insider. For the narrator, as for Kim, the Sansis are specifically, meaningfully 'strong-scented'. For both of them, a cultural hygier that pronounces lizards 'unclean' is familiar, commonplace. Fc both, 'the English' constitute a more or less antipathetic, alie group. Clearly, the narrator identifies with Kim and strives t demonstrate that he has access to Kim's experience, that he can se the world through the boy's eyes.

Adult, child, cultural other: the undoing of ethnographic authority

Ethnographically speaking, once again, the narrator and Kim seen at least upon cursory examination, to enjoy a fairly workabl complementary relationship. The two together reproduce the tw faces of the ethnographer as participant observer. The first face, a outlined by Clifford, is that of the child in the process of discove ing and learning; the second is that of the knowing adult-initiat who later writes the experience (*Predicament* 40). Clifford, howeve characterizes this dyadic paradigm as a 'fable of rapport', observin that the crucial transition, the progress from the child's ofte intense experience to the adult's 'confident, disabused knowledge is generally an achievement of style, a ruse of the finished te» (40–1). The question to be asked of Kipling's narrator, then, is th same as that which Clifford poses for the ethnographer wh involves himself in the culture he studies: 'If ethnography produce cultural experiences through intense research experiences, how unruly experience transformed into an authoritative writte account?' (25) Clifford finds that intensive involvement with th culture of study invariably undermines the ethnographer's capacit to maintain stable, coherent positionality as a subject of discours the ethnography of involvement tends to be composed, as *Kim* i from 'a series of discontinuous discursive positions' (33).

Kipling reproduces the paradigmatic adult–child dyad of cros cultural knowledge-gathering and writing; in so doing, he inscribe a certain instability in his novel's enunciative process. The knowin adult, rather than establishing his authoritative distance and diffe ence, alters his subject position in response to the charming boy The fully hybridized Kim enjoys powers of access and pleasures c involvement that the Kipling narrator can only experience, as were, vicariously. For this narrator, Kim, evidently, is both an objec of imaginary identification and a site of desire. Kim provides an appealing image of freedom, of plenitude, of 'being' not yet fully regimented in and by the Symbolic; as Abdul JanMohamed observes, Kim inhabits 'a world of pure becoming. . . . Endowed by the narrator with special talents, he can do anything and become anybody' (97). Yet, at the same time, Kim embodies the narrator's lack-of-being; the boy ostensibly experiences, lives, what the narrator merely observes and documents. Anthropologist Stephen Tyler notes that 'ethnography can perform a therapeutic purpose in evoking a participatory reality', but emphasizes that 'non-participatory textualization is alienation – "not us" – and there is no therapy in alienation' (128). If it is true that the narrator's representational mastery presupposes a certain degree of detachment or objectivity, it is also true that the figure of Kim tends to situate the experience of India *elsewhere*, outside and beyond the narrator's ken. Yet by aligning himself with Kim, by sporadically identifying with him, the narrator-ethnographer therapeutically restores himself, at least momentarily, to a subject position where knowledge and rich, enlivening experience come together. The narrator therefore vacillates back and forth between seeing and being, between the site of authoritative, 'objective' (but ultimately alienated) representation and the site of the restorative but unruly experience of involvement and cross-cultural identification.[6] By examining closely the relationship between narrator and hybrid boy, one confirms the validity of Lane's assertion that, in Kipling's rendering of empire, 'colonial and psychic mastery fundamentally are untenable' (26); one discovers, too, at least the suggestion that 'external colonization is part congruent with internal crisis' (30). In the last analysis, the Kipling narrator clearly manifests desire for Kim's desire, for his identification with and urge to become the cultural other. The text thus precariously ventures beyond 'the *erotics* of the same' (Lane 25), beyond the carefully managed economy of desire and pleasure between male colonizers, which mobilizes the hybrid adolescent as a mediating figure for the exploration of cross-cultural fantasies and fascinations.

Quite apart from ethnographic considerations, however, the relationship between the adult who represents and the child who is represented is curiously fraught. In *The Case of Peter Pan or The Impossibility of Children's Literature*, Jacqueline Rose argues that

Freudian psychoanalysis, with its discovery of the unconscious, radically problematizes the traditional envisioning of the chronology of a human life. The unconscious undermines the claim to a stable, coherent identity, to a unified self emerging out of a history it somehow transcends. After Freud, therefore, it becomes impossible to envision childhood merely as a temporary stage of the passage from infancy to adulthood. On the contrary, asserts Rose, 'childhood is something in which we continue to be implicated and which is never simply left behind. Childhood persists. ... It persists as something which we endlessly rework in our attempt to build an image of our own history' (12). This quest for coherent personal history and identity necessarily entraps us in a mirror-maze of self-representations – of the stable, adult self one (supposedly) is, and of the child one was. The adult cannot therefore speak of or for the child from a position of representational mastery, because the boundary that separates the child from the adult is not clear-cut. Re-examined in the light of Freud's discovery of the unconscious, this boundary is no longer obvious. Still less secure, I should add, is the distinction that separates adulthood from the adolescent in-between.

The question of representation in *Kim*, however, is complicated further by the fact that the figure of the boy is intimately linked with representations of the colonial subject – ethnography's other. Two figures are caught up in a complex metonymy: to invoke the boy is to invoke the colonial subject and vice versa. And it is important to recognize that the two terms are not exactly equivalent, that their relation tends to be metonymic rather than metaphorical. The play of similarity and difference characterizing their relation is precisely what allows the two terms to function within a discourse of domination: each term can be used to mediate and manage, to render meaningful and comprehensible, the ethnographic speaking subject's relation with the other. The speaking subject, however, can also be drawn into the play of similarity and difference. To attempt, from the point of view of the adult, to represent the liminal boy and to attempt, as an involved ethnographer, to represent imperialism's cultural other, this is the doubly complex – Rose might say, doubly impossible – ambition enacted by Kipling's text. In his relation both with the hybrid adolescent and with the cultural other, the Kipling narrator's claim to representational mastery is deeply compromised. In both cases, the boundary between the representing subject and the represented other reveals itself as tenuous, uncertain. And, of course, the metonymic linkage between the two objects of representation redoubles the complexity of the undertaking, making it all the more difficult to manage.

Liminality in/as textual process; enigma, crisis, collapse

Elucidation of my last points requires a return to the text of *Kim* for a closer consideration of Kipling's project in process. Following an extensive, confidential discussion on the topic of the Great Game, Kim and Hurree Chunder Mookerjee take leave of each other: 'Hurree Babu stepped back a pace or two into the crowd at the entrance of Lucknow station – and was gone. Kim drew a deep breath and hugged himself all over' (184). What, one must ask, is the affective content of Kim's gesture? Adequate evaluation of that content demands, in my view, an appreciation of its ambivalence: joy *and* anxiety inform the gesture. Both of these affects are regis- tered by Kipling's text, which evokes first, Kim's 'glad rapture' (184), then shortly after, his 'sudden natural reaction' (185), his self-questioning and sense of self-alienation.

Certainly, Hurree is a potentially unsettling character, as his sudden uncanny disappearance testifies. He is enormously fat and yet his excess of flesh is like so much clay that he can mould to his will. He is a master of disguise, able to hoodwink even fellow-spies (as he has earlier proved to Kim) – a very slippery character, or rather 'oily', to use Kipling's own oft-repeated adjective. The surface, the boundary, of his person is slick, elusive, ungraspable. Here Hurree melts into a crowd; elsewhere he stows about his body the various elements of a large intelligence trove, then transforms his entire aspect and demeanor, all the touchstones of his identity, while passing through a doorway. The Hurree Kipling has imagined possesses a liminal body, a liminal selfhood. And although there is evidently a certain joyful freedom in the experience and experi- mentation of this liminality, one must recall that it is 'glad *rapture*', the sudden seizure of the self by that which is Other. It may be apt to speak, therefore, of ecstasy, of joyful self-alienation and self-loss, or of *jouissance*, the extreme, excessive pleasure that radically chal- lenges the claim to coherent self-sameness. Hurree is produced as an uncanny other and, as such, he is a potential site of anxiety. Manifestations of his liminal selfhood challenge any secure division between self and other, any secure sense of an insular, individualized identity. Even Kim, who also knows the ecstatic pleasures of shape-shifting, becomes anxious. Kim, after all, is at this point a graduate of St Xavier's. He has been schooled to a bounded British sense of self. He has become, rather like his creator, an Anglo-Indian, a divided subject whose identity vacillates between contradictory assertions: 'I am a sahib'; 'I am not a sahib.' As Hurree duly informs the boy, he will need an ample, unsupervised 'leave' to become 'de-Englishised' (184).

In the act of hugging himself, Kim discovers keys to his identity which serve, at least momentarily, to reassure him. He feels for his new revolver and old dependable amulet, assuring himself also that 'begging gourd, rosary, and ghost-dagger ... [are] all to hand, with medicine, paint-box, and compass' and the exquisite purse that holds his 'month's pay' (184). Kim's process of self-seeking immediately returns him to his 'props'; he can recover himself only by taking stock of his personal possessions – his weapons, cultural curios, scientific tools, money – the little bits of identity that others have given him. Kim is the product of an eclectic *bricolage*; his identity, it seems, can never be more than contingent. Self-hugging, then, performs a 'suturing' of self, a joyful self-possession – 'Yes! it's all mine, and I *can* hold it all together!' – and, at the same time, an anxious self-seeking, a questioning of self – 'Am I really here? Am I the sum of these various parts?'

As he has done before, but more insistently this time, Kim poses the identity question: 'Who is Kim – Kim – Kim?' The narrator chooses, once again, to implicate himself in Kim's subjective process:

> A very few white people, but many Asiatics, can throw themselves into a mazement as it were by repeating their own name over and over again to themselves, letting the mind go free upon speculation as to what is called personal identity. When one grows older, the power, usually, departs. ... (185)

The liminal identities of the adolescent and the colonial subject are thus brought into close association: the 'power' of profound self-questioning pertains to 'many Asiatics'; it usually diminishes or disappears 'when one grows older'. The narrator nonetheless implicates himself in Kim's bewilderment: maintaining a contemplative, almost confessional tone, he pushes to the limit his tacit claim to knowledge of Kim's interiority, implicitly affirming a personal, experiential understanding of the boy's crisis of identity. More than this, his reflections serve to generalize the import of Kim's question, casting doubt upon the concept of stable, definable selfhood – '*what is called* personal identity'. Thus, in relation to the hybrid boy, Kipling poses the question of personal and cultural identity within a multicultural, imperial context and then leaves the question unresolved. The recurring question 'Who is Kim?' is, must be, the crucial question of *Kim*, which employs the boy, in a variety of ways, to mark cultural distinctions and to posit identities in relation to those distinctions. To ask 'Who is Kim?' or, as the question is finally posed, 'What is Kim?' (282), is to recall the radical and multiple indeterminacies that attend cultural hybridization in the contact zones of the empire. An enigma resides at the core of Kipling's ethnographic project; but it is this enigma, the hybrid boy, that provides the project with its energizing, enabling figure.[7]

As Sara Suleri astutely remarks, Kim's marvelous boyhood is unsurpassable. In a moment of muted tragedy buried in the very core of his text, 'Kipling supplies a casual but crucial anticipation of the collapsibility of Kim' (127), fatefully linking the richness of Kim's gifts with the brevity of their duration; even as the text celebrates India-bred Kim's 'quickness' and seemingly unquenchable vitality, it anticipates 'the half-collapse that sets in at twenty-two or twenty-three' (*Kim* 124; qtd. in Suleri 127). Robert Moss, to a degree, anticipates Suleri's argument, focusing attention on the collapse, in more than a 'half' measure, that overtakes an exhausted Kim who is not yet 18. Working from this collapse, Moss ascribes to Kim an unresolved adolescence, with loyalties undecided and 'conflicts unreconciled' (141). Suleri, however, states the case more strongly: the figure of Kim 'become[s] the image of the colonizer, but one that is elegiacally mourned in the passing of its prematurity' (129); the text of *Kim* becomes an imperial allegory of education troubled by the discovery 'that in its adolescence is its end' (131). Kim's unimaginable 'maturity', like that of the empire he is called upon to represent, must therefore be interminably deferred. Kipling's novel ultimately reinscribes rather than resolves the tensions that inform its progress, concluding, as it must, with the enunciation of two incommensurate promises: Kim is pledged to enlightenment and to an ongoing imperial career, to service upon the Wheel and yet, at the same time, to freedom from it. As Mahbub rather facilely states the case, 'now I understand that the boy, sure of paradise, can yet enter Government service' (285). Disciplined imperial endeavor and the quest for spiritual fulfillment and autonomy must continue their uneasy coexistence. The boy, still in the care of two partial and incompatible fathers, Mahbub and Teshoo Lama, is left suspended upon the brink of an impossible manhood. The predicament implied by Kim's truncated *Bildung*, his insuperable adolescence, mirrors the problem of imperial consolidation, the problem of an empire that has not discovered – that may never discover – its appropriate coming of age.

Ethnography as salvage; the passing of empire

Kipling's *Kim* mutedly but unmistakably gives voice to what Clifford has called the ethnographic 'allegory of salvage'. Such allegory, Clifford argues, is 'implied by the very practice of [ethnographic] textualization'. Ethnography 'translates experience into text', capturing and recording the furtive moments of cultural 'life'; it is written against (and yet in tacit or explicit acknowledgment of) the ineluctable transience of 'words and deeds' (115). Typically, therefore, the ethnographer laments 'the vanishing primitive' his text records, announces 'the end of traditional society' and the disappearance of his object – 'the other [who] is lost, in disintegrating time and space, but saved by the text' (112). Typically, too, ethnography is informed by the assumption that 'the other society is weak and "needs" to be represented by an outsider (and that what matters in its life is its past, not present or future)' (113). The pertinence of the allegory of salvage for the reading of *Kim*, which close analysis of its adolescent protagonist most tellingly confirms, is also suggested by the novel's frequently fond and nostalgic tone and by its detailed evocation of a remembered world – the India of the 1880s, the India that, at the time of *Kim*'s appearance in 1901, its author has not witnessed for ten changeful years. Moreover, the text presents occasional, explicit inscriptions acknowledging India's historical transformation: the narrator remarks upon 'the mixture of old-world piety and modern progress that is the note of India to-day' (11), records various manifestations of 'India in transition' (239). And indeed, as I noted earlier, the Great Game presumes to preserve a timeless, changeless India; its relation with India is energized by an allegory of salvage.

Yet the India of *Kim*, as the salient presence of the Great Game confirms, is not so much archaic India as it is India under the Raj. It is the Raj during a period Percival Spear has characterized as 'The Imperial Heyday' (145ff.) that Kipling seeks to capture, to preserve against the inevitable violence of time. *Kim*, despite the considerable sustenance it offers to the imperial 'illusion of permanence' (Hutchins), announces in its ethnography the passing of the Raj. Its assiduous efforts in the realm of cultural description assert a knowledge *imperium*, yet at the same time evidence an anxious desire to grasp and retain fugitive cultural realities; its narrative implies an eventual dispossession and loss of power. *Kim* is an ethnographic text that implicates its readers in complex, hybrid forms of subjectivity and cultural participation; it also involves British imperial identity and authority in compromising maneuvers of cross-cultural confrontation and negotiation. The text ultimately confirms what Tyler calls the 'first law of culture': 'the more man controls anything, the more uncontrollable both become' (123).[8] Kipling's Indian Empire and his wondrous hybrid boy elude the controlling, containing grasp of imperial and ethnographic authority; both escape toward what is, from Kipling's historical perspective, an unforeseeable, unrecognizable future. *Kim*, once considered and evaluated as ethnography, reads as the Raj's celebratory swan-song.

Conclusion

In Kipling's time, the reality of a global British Empire inscribe itself fully and confidently in the realm of cultural production; th imperial boy thus takes shape in relation to Euro-imperialism 'consolidated vision' (Said, *Culture*). Kipling's boy represents a energizing yet carefully circumscribed process of transculturatior Called upon to negotiate the contact zones of empire, this limina boy asserts the imperial project's capacity to manage colonial alter ity, to respond creatively and productively to the challenges pose by multifarious cultural contexts, by 'heterogeneous cultures . yoked by violence' (Suleri 5). The figure, at once extraordinary an familiar, provides a pleasing, reassuring site of identification for th imperial imagination. As Mohanty affirms, Kipling's tales c boyhood 'tell a distinct and specifiable political story in whic adventure is indistinguishable from surveillance, pleasure is inte twined with power ...' ('Drawing the Color Line' 326). Kipling boy, far from being merely a figure of fantasy and facile wish-fulfil ment, engages ever more intimately and intensely with the affai: of empire. To follow, moreover, the trajectory of the Kipling bo from the Mowgli saga through *Stalky & Co.* to *Kim* is to witness th figure's arrival upon the center-stage of the Eastern Empire.

Yet the British Empire's time of confidence is also its time c anxiety, of doubt and self-questioning, and this paradoxical dispc sition manifests itself in Kipling's treatment of the imperial boy Posing the figure of the boy as a site of critical inquiry for both colc nial and postcolonial cultural studies, my writing situates Kipling i a period marked by the consolidation *and* destabilization of th modern empires. Kipling's rendering of the boy manifests an confirms an imperial world-view, yet raises at the same time som of the key questions orienting initiatives of contemporary pos colonial criticism and theory. Sustained analysis reveals the figure overdetermination and, ultimately, a susceptibility to the breal down and collapse that is literally inscribed in the text of *Kin* Envisioned complexly and intensively as a hybrid subject, Kipling boy takes shape as an ambivalent figure that serves yet disrupt:

asserts yet subverts, imperial authority and ideology. The figure thus provides a significant literary manifestation of the hybridity of the colonial signifier and the inescapable ambivalence of the discourse of empire. In various ways, Kipling's treatment of the boy opens up new possibilities for a deconstructive, decolonizing critique of British imperialism's cultural legacy.

As my introduction announced, one of my orienting critical concerns is European imperialism's production of a strategically divided world, in which postcolonial societies are discursively distributed in subordinate relation to 'Europe' or 'the West'. Against this mapping of the modern globe as an assembly of distinct, differently empowered cultural zones, I put forward a critique guided by a notion of transculturation – the reciprocal transformation of the cultures imperial expansion brought into protracted confrontation. Following Spivak's example, I posit a 'Subject of Europe' that constitutes itself through a generalized othering of colonized cultures. The study of Kipling, whom I consider as a representative voice of late nineteenth-century British imperial culture, enables specific, detailed examination of this self-constituting representation of cultural alterity. As I observe, moreover, Kipling's work registers a singularly important cultural confrontation, that which opposes yet binds together Britain and India. Exemplifying a post-Mutiny consciousness, an imperial consciousness in crisis, Kipling functions as a reassuring myth-maker for a British Empire that must consolidate itself in the face of contestation and resistance.

Accompanying, however, the enunciation of enduring confidence in the British imperial mission is the more muted acknowledgement of anxiety and uncertainty. Kipling's work offers support to notions of cultural superiority and difference, which set British and Indian cultures apart and at odds, and which justify and sustain the British imperial intervention. However, this work also acknowledges an irresistible, reciprocal process of transculturation or hybridization – a process of which Kipling and his fictions are noteworthy products. Kipling envisions youthful, enterprising, imperial protagonists who, as sites of circumscribed transculturation, represent 'a borderline position that incorporates, polarizes, dialogizes, and bridges the worlds of colonizer and colonized, ... [of] England and India' (Sullivan 126). This 'borderline position' is also a mediating position, which bears the promise of symbolic resolution of the ambivalencies and contradictions that inhere in the world-view of a writer whose cultural sympathies and identifi cations are radically divided. Kipling's staging of imperial enterpris by the mediation of the boy is a consolidating cultural interventior one that draws upon and rearticulates a quite varied array c cultural precedents, one that enunciates an imperial envisioning c the nature and meaning of boyhood. The adolescent protagonis reconfigures the terms and meanings of cross-cultural encounter thus confirming a Eurocentric imaginative domination of th spaces and subjectivities of colonized cultural others.

From his first emergence as a distinct, recognizable figure withi: the social text of early modern Europe, the boy is enmeshed i issues of social differentiation and hierarchization. Both as 'specia ized child' and as the focal, representative subject-in-process of civilizing process, the figure of the boy participates intimately i the rearticulation of modern European societies. Furthermore, h early evidences his sense-making function in relation to th encounter of expanding European 'civilization' with 'uncivilizec others. Kipling makes full use of his cultural patrimony in his val dation and consolidation of the key values, themes, and concept informing an imperial vision of boyhood. His writings represent ' cultural self constructed during decades that saw radical revisions i European understanding of the identity of the subject, of gende: the psyche, the child, and the "native"' (Sullivan 127). His repeate inscription of the boy at the center of narratives of empire reir forces the envisioning of European imperialism as masculin endeavor and arranges structuring, sense-making categories – th subject, the child, the 'native' – according to a masculinist perspec tive.

However, Kipling's portrayal of the boy conforms to, and draw sustenance from, a masculinist bias within childhood's Europea: history, one that is instituted in childhood's specialization and **i** confirmed, notably, in Rousseau's highly influential pedagogica philosophy. Kipling's boy, a liminal subject-in-process, is deployec like Ariès's specialized child, in contingent relation with variou others whose subject positions are thereby established. Around th liminal boy, both imperial and colonial subjects are distinguishec distributed, and hierarchized. The subjectivities and spaces c cultural alterity are thus mapped as the territory of a consolidate *imperium*. Kipling locates in the figure of the boy, as did Rousseau, a special capacity to organize the representation of the relationship between imperial Europe and its subject peoples. In his deployments of the figure, Kipling adheres to the notion of a 'time of the other' distinct from that of modern Europe, placing his boy in relations of peerage with much more mature and experienced 'native' characters. Sustained in his initiative by a prodigiously productive half-century of empire-affirming school and adventure narratives of the boy, Kipling refashions the figure Edmund Burke had construed as British imperialism's inept intruder as an efficient imperial agent, one who mediates cultural difference and renders it malleable to imperial purposes.

Kipling's boy represents the possibility of staging imperial subjectivity coherently, in relation to both Imaginary and Symbolic orders of experience. Kipling's fictions of imperial adolescence provide abundantly the Imaginary gratifications of adventurous self-discovery, self-testing, and self-assertion among admiring cohorts and engaging, but never indomitable adversaries. The worlds of Kipling's boy, however, also manifest a complex Symbolic dimension – the Jungle Law, the 'official' and the delinquent codes of the 'Coll.', the Great Game – in relation to which the young protagonist must define and situate himself. By the adept manipulation of modes of Imaginary and Symbolic identification, Kipling strives to strike a balance between the typically contrary demands of the two orders of subjective experience. Notwithstanding this drive to coordinate the Imaginary and the Symbolic, Kipling's imperial fictions entail divided identifications and a certain fragmentation of meanings. In the fictions of adolescence, the imperial boy provides a site for identification, for self-affirming fantasies and for broadly shared meanings and values. Yet, paradoxically, the political, representational content of the figure is compromised and perturbed by the cultural liminality that lends it its imaginative allure.

Lupine Mowgli is a hybrid whose allegorical *Bildung* refashions imperial story and history – most notably, the story and history of the Indian insurrection of 1857. Kipling's allegorical restagings of Mutiny scenes are sense-making maneuvers, attempts to symbolically manage troubling, refractory aspects of Mutiny history. The hybrid adolescent of *The Jungle Books* overcomes the antipathy and resistance his difference inspires both in the jungle and the village, progressing through partial and selective assimilation to the domination and mastery that allow for the mapping of both his alternative worlds as spaces of imperial action and endeavor. The Mowgli saga, however, allegorically recapitulates more than it transforms the Mutiny story upon which it is posited: despite the capacity to negotiate differences that Mowgli's liminality implies, the boy resolves antagonistic encounters by acts of violence, which signal the Mutiny's status as the limit-text of pro-imperial myth-making. If Mowgli does not display, to the same degree as Stalky or, better still, Kim, a talent for the negotiation and manipulation of cultural difference, it is due in large part to his status as a displaced site of hybridization.

Although my study considers that Kipling's boy, in every case, configures and renegotiates issues of British–Indian encounter, it is important to recognize that both the wolf-boy and his divided world offer no explicit address to questions of colonial cross-cultural confrontation and hybridization: Mowgli's two antithetical worlds are not 'Britain' and 'India', but India as 'jungle' and 'village'; the liminal place of Mowgli's subjectivity is not articulated between British and Indian cultures, nor even between the jungle society and the *Indian* society of the village, but between the feral and the human. Although Mowgli facilitates the mapping of the imperial project onto an allegorized India, he does not represent a meeting place or point of contact for British and Indian cultures. Kipling's jungle saga never directly acknowledges the process of transculturation – the very process that makes a figure like hybrid Mowgli imaginable – as an aspect of British–Indian cross-cultural engagement. This series of allegorical tales is so deeply informed by the Mutiny trauma that it can only represent a displaced hybridity, one that has no immediately recognizable reference to shared cultural history and actuality, one that evokes but never directly refers to the intensely troubling issue of post-Mutiny British–Indian encounter.

Kipling's rendering of Mowgli does, however, signal the general allegorical significance of the imperial boy, the boy who stages the formation of an imperial subject for a global, multicultural Empire. Similarly, the case of Mowgli saliently reveals that the hybrid boy needs to be understood as a site of displacement for imperial subjectivity. While the degrees of displacement may vary, the boy is in all cases a contained, controlled site where the hybridization of imperial subjectivity can be acknowledged and enablingly deployed: feral Mowgli commands the jungle to the service of the Empire; in the guise of a Sikh, Stalky stages an affirmative resolution of British imperial ventures; Kim, as a 'white' Indian boy, serves within, and ultimately must justify, the complex system of post-Mutiny British imperial order in India. Mowgli, like Stalky and Kim, discovers in hybridization the path to power. At the same time, however, Mowgli's experience of the splitting of his group identifications registers, in a few noteworthy moments, the 'identity crisis' that is a salient element in Kipling's overall characterization of Kim.

In *Stalky & Co.*, Stalky's cultural hybridization coincides with and in large part accounts for his accession to a position of power and privilege in the contact zone of the Indian Empire. The effects of this hybridization are curtailed by an essentialized, racialized conception of cultural difference. Yet Kipling is clearly aiming toward a new, more integrated envisioning of British imperial actuality, an envisioning of an Empire composed of various analogous spaces of struggle and endeavor, inhabited by various analogous subjectivities. And certainly, the text of *Stalky* represents an imperial world in which autonomous cultural unities, such as 'the British school' or, more broadly, 'the British nation', no longer exist; these seem to have given way to a world of hybridized cultures and subjects. The final rendering of the boyish British officer as Sikh, moreover, raises the question of the imperial hybrid and thus of British–Indian transculturation. *Stalky* introduces but does not yet explore the key topic of *Kim*; the hybridity of Stalky's imperial subjectivity is traced, sketched out, rather than extensively examined.

Although a color line is drawn in the first few paragraphs of *Kim*, its delineation, as I have remarked, is both peremptory and strangely fraught with qualifications. As this peculiar enunciative maneuvering suggests, the color line is drawn, here, not to elude the troubling complexities of cultural and subjective hybridization, but to initiate a controlled, circumscribed meditation upon them. Within an encompassing framework informed by panoptical, administrative disciplines and ethnological documentation, *Kim* stages – as *Stalky* does not – the multidimensional, often ambivalent agency of the radically hybridized imperial subject. I have undertaken therefore a reading of *Kim* that focuses upon the role of the hybrid boy, who maneuvers within the 'gap' post-Mutiny ideology opens between British and Indian cultures; who, as the crucial, mediating link, enables yet also potentially disrupts the functioning of two distinctly modern, ostensibly objective and disengaged power-systems – administrative panopticism and ethnological science. The hybrid boy is situated within British imperial order not as a subject under the law but as one acted upon by disciplinary systems in relation to which he must discover both his subjection and his agency. Kim first takes shape as a potent, productive instrument for imperial power. By learning to pursue his pleasures in the service of the imperial cause, the boy is able to fulfil the destiny foreshadowed by his early role, as the startlingly unlikely representative of British power and authority, in the allegorical Zam-Zammah game. Kim's career asserts British imperialism's capacity to discipline, subordinate, and mobilize effectively the uncertain elements of the colonial social body. Kim's India becomes an administered space inhabited by a catalogued multiplicity.

However, the mobilization of hybrid Kim within imperial disciplinary systems entails certain liabilities. Cultural hybridization, which Kipling's novel registers in its representation of Kim and his Great Game cohorts, complicates disciplinarization by creating mobile subjects whose cultural identification is unstable and whose agency is therefore politically uncertain. Kim, especially, tends to obscure imperialism's power divide by deploying the disciplinary power of the Raj in ways that submit it to disorderly proliferation Ethnography is the supplementary 'discipline' Kipling employs in his attempt to contain the disruptive energies of transculturation and the hybrid subject it produces. Like the knowledge production of the Great Game, the ethnographic treatment of India renders i as fully knowable and controllable.

Notwithstanding the hybrid boy's various recommendations a an instrument of imperial ethnography, I characterize Kim as a problematic figure for imperial representation. An object and an instrument of representation, the boy reveals himself as a site o identification for the narrator, for the authoritative speaking subject. Writing the other and, by extension, writing India as th cultural Other are revealed as highly contingent negotiations c imperial representation, as compromised writings of the subjectivity of the speaker and, by extension, of the much more broadly based Subject-status of 'Europe', of 'the West'. The question 'Who is Kim?' must, I therefore affirm, be read as a radical interrogation of formations of the subject constituted by the modern imperial project. Finding that the text poses but cannot resolve Kim's question, I locate in it the enunciative instance that enables a deconstruction of Kipling's dream-vision of an ideal Indian Empire. The hybrid boy (who cannot identify himself, who cannot be securely identified) confounds the ideology of cultural difference upon which the post-Mutiny Raj is founded; the figure collapses the binary, oppositional formulation of the British imperial subject and the Indian colonial, of sovereign 'West' and subordinate 'East'. In the figure of Kim, British imperial culture acknowledges the unsettling productivity of its encounter with India.

I have tried in my preceding analyses to discover in the figure of the imperial boy a means of questioning the 'authoritative subjectivity produced in the colonizing process', a way of revaluating 'the process of identification in the negotiations of cultural politics' (Bhabha 233). Imperial subjectivity – the subjectivity constituted for the British imperial project, in and by the cross-cultural confrontations that project necessarily entails – does not, in Kipling's fictions of the boy, manifest its deep and dependable 'embeddedness' in the culture of the British 'homeland'. Imperial subjectivity manifests instead its contingent formation upon the *limen* that emerges between the cultures of imperial 'home' and the colonial 'outland'. Indeed, as the fictions I have considered make abundantly clear, the formation of subjects in an imperial world is not to be understood, simply and unambiguously, in terms of discrete sociocultural spaces and identities. Kipling's boy situates himself between cultures in confrontation. Produced to negotiate and sustain the sharply drawn post-Mutiny distinction that opposes British colonizer to Indian colonized, Kipling's boy nonetheless calls this same clear-cut binary formulation into question. The imperial figure of the boy must be read as a hybrid figure, in this case, as the figure for an imperial subject marked by the trace of the colonial other. As such, the figure occupies 'a space of cultural and interpretive undecidability' (Bhabha 206) – an undecidability Kipling represents, very tellingly, as 'adolescence'.

Kipling consistently represents adolescent liminality in intimate, seemingly interdependent relation with cultural hybridization: the tales of wolf-boy Mowgli displace this relation and render it allegorically; the treatment of the schoolboy, at once little savage and little imperialist, enunciates the imaginative association of adolescence and hybridity even before the presentation of Stalky as boyish British officer and Sikh; in the figure of Kim, the experiences of adolescence and of cultural hybridity are intertwined to such a degree that both find their summary enunciation in the inevitable question, 'Who is Kim?' Kipling figures the transculturation of the imperial subjectivity as an adolescence, and in so doing articulates the subjective register of the post-Mutiny, imperial 'crisis of consolidation' (Stokes). Here resides the special importance of Kipling's contribution to cultural productions of the imperial boy. The boy who mediates an envisioning of imperial subjectivity also, by that very mediation, dislocates and displaces this subjectivity, opening a bounded, authoritative 'self' to 'adolescent' doubt and self-questioning.

Although Kipling's boy-protagonists invariably serve energetically and productively within the fictive Empire, they also introduce 'adolescent problems' to the imagining of the imperial enterprise. The adolescent (especially the hybrid adolescent) is uncertain as to his sociocultural identifications. Rather than embodying constituted authority, he is more typically at odds with it. If he shapes his world, he is also shaped by it; if he defines his others, they also define him. The election of the hybrid adolescent as a representative subject of the British imperial project signals a destabilization, by the force of crisis, of that project's foundational assumptions and premises. It attests to doubt about self-sovereignty and authority at the individual and the cultural level; it reveals uncertainty about the place, power, and meaning of the Other (which serves to constitute and define the cultural Subject of the imperial enterprise). It articulates an 'identity crisis' of British imperial culture.

Kipling's representations of the imperial boy intervene in perturbatory ways in the imaging of an empowered, self-sovereign and authoritative imperial subject, thus disarticulating, to a certain degree, the ideology that sustains both that subject and the Empire of which he is a representative. The cultural production of the bo as a principal representative of the British imperial enterprise enacts a figurative displacement in the self-representation of the imperial subject. Imperial fictions of the boy effectively remake an authoritative, self- and other-determining, masculine subject as a liminal, contingent 'adolescent'. Although Kipling is by no means alone in narrating boyhood and its empire, his fictions deserve special attention because they manifest clearly yet complexly the tensions informing imperial ideology and subjectivity. Unlike a Ballantyne or a Henty, Kipling not only registers but represents the forces of disruption that initiate and impel the production of the boy as the British Empire's representative protagonist.

Kipling's narratives of imperial adolescence thus intervene in and transform the signifying practices of post-Mutiny British imperial discourse and ideology. To consider the decades following the 1857 Mutiny as a period of cultural, ideological crisis is to appreciate the full force of contradiction informing the confrontation of post-Mutiny isolationist and separatist ideology with the unignorable fact of cultural hybridization, which two centuries of cross-cultural encounter must necessarily entail. Registering this crisis and responding creatively to it, Kipling produces an imperial boy who is not simply a hybrid figure forged in the press of cultures in confrontation, but indeed the very sign of cultural hybridization, the figure allowing British imperial representation to register transculturation in the contact zones of the Indian Empire. However, Kipling's deployments of the boy do not negotiate the post-Mutiny crisis of consolidation with unqualified success. As a hybrid figure whose cultural identifications are split, Kipling's boy offers ambivalent service to the discourse of late nineteenth-century British imperialism in India. If Kipling's representations of boyhood confirm and consolidate the boy as an imperial figure for an 'Age of Empire' (Hobsbawm), they also signal the fissuring impact of colonial, cross-cultural confrontation upon British imperial subjectivity and upon the imaging of the imperial enterprise.

Notes

Introduction

1 Amongst available scholarly works, one should note particularly Christopher Lane's *The Ruling Passion*, which scrutinizes the racial and erotic aspects of Kipling's fictive fraternities.

2 Spivak's use of the category of the subject and, more particularly of the Subject (with an upper-case 'S') reveals an indebtedness to Althusserian theory of ideology as it is elaborated in 'Ideology and Ideological State Apparatuses'. Having first established the subject as the *sine qua non* of all ideological functioning, Althusser goes on to argue that ideology posits 'a Unique, Absolute ... *Subject*', by which it is centred and stabilized (166). The individual subject is only '*a subject through the Subject and subjected to the Subject*' (167). The Subject is thus the condition of individual subjectivities. Spivak's coding of this Subject as 'Western' or 'European' suggests that, within the contemporary structuring of global relations, all subjects are predicated in relation to a Eurocentric paradigm.

3 Anne McClintock has more recently examined the production of 'métissage' in imperial discourse, arguing that the demand for the racial and cultural purity of children is a way of controlling women's sexuality both in the imperial homeland and abroad (47–8).

4 In *Girls Growing Up in Late Victorian and Edwardian England*, Carol Dyhouse stresses, as Phillips does, the middle-class origins of modern adolescence. Although her study focuses on adolescent girls, she acknowledges that the new time of life is mainly ascribed to males and reflects socially sanctioned masculine privilege.

5 In *Kipling's Indian Fiction*, Marc Paffard adopts a similar line of argument, suggesting that, in large part through Kipling's mediation, India became for the 1890s British public 'a subject inevitably bound up with national identity and self-esteem' (30). In *Culture and Imperialism*, Edward Said makes a strong case for the mutual transformation of colonized and colonizing cultures, suggesting that India makes modern England as much as England makes modern India. He argues, as I do, for the decisive importance of Kipling's work 'in the definition, the imagination, the formulation of what India was to the British empire in its mature phase' (133).

6 Given that the Kipling fictions I consider stand at a distance of four decades from the events of 1857–58, my stressing of the determining significance of the uprisings may seem somewhat strange. As my chapters on Kipling demonstrate, however, the Mutiny has a prominent place in Kipling's imaginative rendering of India and of British–Indian relations. His emphasis on its importance moreover, reflects, contem

porary British attitudes. Eric Stokes argues that the Mutiny initiates and sets its mark upon a 'decisive historic phase' that endures until the advent of Gandhi (*Peasant* 1–2). Karl de Schweinitz, like Wurgaft, fore-grounds the change in British attitudes and the inception of 'more efficient, if more impersonal rule' (175). Taking a different view, Francis Hutchins argues that the rebellion 'crystallized' incipient British percep-tions of India, setting the tone and establishing the core notions of British thinking about India throughout 'the latter half of the nine-teenth century' (x). However, despite their differences of project and perspective, Stokes, Schweinitz, and Hutchins concur in considering the Mutiny as an organizing referent for thinking about British India both before and during Kipling's time of writing.

7 The 'gap', for example, that is presumed to stand between British 'civil-ity' and Indian 'barbarity' is most emphasized during a historical moment when the two terms are enacted as resemblance. As Sharpe notes in *Allegories of Empire*, the Mutiny drama is played out amidst the 'retributions' of an outraged 'civility', which mirror, and even surpass, the 'savage excesses' they are intended to punish and correct.

8 I invoke, here, the core notion informing and organizing theories of the subject regardless of the particularities of their orientation – psychoan-alytic, ideological, or poststructuralist. To speak of a 'subject' rather than a 'self' is always to acknowledge that this 'subject' is not autonomous, not self-sovereign, but rather deeply determined by exter-nal structures and forces – by that which is other than itself. The dynamic tension sustaining the subject is to be located in the subject's drive to assert its autonomy in the face of this determination, this inscription, by the other. What I characterize here as the core notion of theories of the subject is, of course, clearly evident in Spivak's descrip-tion of a 'Subject of Europe' that constitutes itself as self-sovereign by disavowing its formation in relation to its Other. In my writing, I refer to the 'other' or to 'others' to designate individuals or groups represent-ing cultural difference for a certain community of subjects – that is, difference of disposition, belief, social practice. When my concern is more particularly with otherness as a self-structuring, self-constituting category, shaped by and for a subject or community of subjects, I will use an upper-case 'O' as Spivak does.

9 Of these three designations, 'Anglo-Indian' (the acclimatized English colonial) is the most apt, if one takes seriously the cultural liminality it would seem to name. Yet Kipling, even during his early career in India, cannot be easily, seamlessly, identified with the views and attitudes of the late nineteenth-century 'Anglo-Indian' community – given that the foibles, prejudices, ethnocentric alienation and eccentricity of Anglo-Indian society are often ridiculed in the early poems and stories that appear in *Departmental Ditties* (1886) and *Plain Tales from the Hills* (1888). A thorough consideration of Kipling's cultural affiliations can be found in Bart Moore-Gilbert's *Kipling and 'Orientalism'*, which argues a distinction between metropolitan and Anglo-Indian perspectives with

respect to India. Although Moore-Gilbert more commonly links Kipling with Anglo-Indian thought and writing, he is alert to the author's tendency to swing back and forth between the metropolitan and Anglo-Indian perspectives.

10 My discussion of liminality draws upon the anthropology of Victor Turner, as developed in his *Dramas, Fields, Metaphors*. Turner finds the social function of liminal figures in their testing and transgressing of social boundaries, which serve ultimately to knit social structures together, to give to the totality of these structures a more organic coherence. Expanding upon this function, I want also to consider liminal figures as imperial agents who facilitate, and also at times disrupt, the ideological mapping of colonial societies.

11 I understand 'growing up' to entail, necessarily, a stabilizing and fixing of identity. Thus Mowgli, the young man who enters into imperial service under Gisborne, is not entirely 'grown up', in so far as he is still very much a liminal being, enduringly enjoying uncanny powers of woodcraft. Stalky the young officer in India is virtually indistinguishable (in his tactical 'stalkiness' and in his perturbed relation with 'higher authorities') from Stalky the shifty schoolboy.

1. The Genealogy of the Imperial Boy

1 Certainly, Ariès's account of childhood's history has not gone entirely unchallenged. In 'The Evolution of Childhood', Lloyd DeMause, an early and still notable anti-Ariès scholar of childhood, questions the thesis of childhood's 'invention'. According to DeMause, the assertion, grounded in the study of medieval art, that 'a separate concept of childhood was unknown' in the society of the early Middle Ages, 'leave[s] the art of antiquity in limbo' and, moreover, 'ignores voluminous evidence that medieval artists could, indeed, paint realistic children'. The idea of an early modern 'invention' of childhood, DeMause concludes, 'is so fuzzy that it is surprising that so many historians have recently picked it up' (5). DeMause does not, however, offer any challenge to Ariès's fundamental, and for me, most compelling thesis: childhood, beginning in the later fifteenth and early sixteenth centuries, was subjected to profound transformations, what Ariès calls its 'specialization'. In my view, this specialization of childhood constitutes, if not its 'discovery' or 'invention', at least its culturally significant reconstruction in new terms and along new lines.

2 The influence of Montaigne's essays, especially the essays on educational topics ('Of Pedantry' and 'Of the Education of Children'), is noteworthy. R. H. Quick, in his introduction to *Some Thoughts Concerning Education*, notes numerous 'parallel passages' linking Locke's treatise to the texts of the *Essays* (Locke lix). Quick goes so far as to suggest that 'the chief importance of the Thoughts is due to the prominence given by Locke to truths which had already been set forth by Montaigne' (li).

3   I should mention here the enormous success of Locke's little book both in Britain and on the Continent. Sommerville notes that it rapidly 'became the most popular book on child rearing in its day, with at least 26 editions before 1800. It had a European reputation, enjoying 16 French editions in that same period, as well as 6 Italian editions and translations into Dutch, German, Swedish, and Spanish.' Sommerville adds, pertinently, 'Locke did not have to wait to be discovered; the public was ready for his views' (121).

4   In tracing the genealogy of the savagery/civilization opposition, José Luis Abellán draws attention not only to Montaigne, but to the work of other writers of the early sixteenth century: Bartolomé de Las Casas, Pedro Mártir de Anglería, Luis Vives and, most notably, Antonio de Guevara, whom Abellán considers 'the true author of the barbary-civilization opposition that gives positive meaning to the first term and pejorative meaning to the second' (410, my translation).

5   This is not to say that the Christian view of history ceases to be culturally pertinent. Indeed, it would be difficult, in the absence of such a view, to fully account for Victorian belief in progress and in the civilizing, Christianizing mission of colonialism. Fabian's point is that the secular time of 'natural history' becomes the principal time in relation to which knowledge is gathered, organized, understood.

6   Both Locke and Rousseau conclude their works on education by considering the role and value of travel. Both, moreover, are re-evaluating a widespread, established practice of persons of means. Émile's education culminates with travel to foreign lands, which takes him away from the already beloved Sophy, who must, of course, remain behind. Unlike Locke, who treats the question of educative travel with considerable circumspection (184–7), Rousseau, despite a few reservations of his own, sees it as indispensable. Émile, however, will travel not for pleasure but for knowledge; he must learn 'to travel as a philosopher'. In Rousseau's view, 'The child observes things till he is old enough to study men. Man should begin by studying his fellows' (418). And 'any one who has only seen one nation', he states categorically, 'does not know men' (415). Although Émile does not pass beyond the bounds of Europe, his journeys initiate him to a knowledge-gathering practice that will, ultimately, embrace the world as the field of its endeavours.

7   I must stress this theme of interlinkage. I do not intend to present either 'child' or 'primitive' as the origin or first cause in terms of which the other is to be understood. My point is that modern notions of 'child' and 'primitive' emerge, each in conjunction with the other, during the same historical period and within the shared context of specific socio-cultural developments.

8   Adventure writers of the last decades of the nineteenth century become increasingly self-aware with respect to the imperial implications of their work and increasingly sensitive to the topical enthusiasms bred by the imperial venture. Henty's career is in this respect illustrative: abandoning the 'classical' adventures set in ancient Greece or Rome, which had

dominated his unsuccessful early career, Henty, to great acclaim, 'modernizes' his contents and goes on to become the most popular fictional chronicler of modern imperial exploits (see Bristow 146–7).

9   The discourse of adolescence, as Sommerville points out, is (like the discourse of childhood) focused upon boys. Girls are considered less likely to 'exhibit the stress that was now [in the later nineteenth and early twentieth century] associated with adolescence' (204). Adolescence comes to be construed as a 'disease' that plagues masculine development most particularly. The corresponding conclusion is, 'Girls were not so commonly afflicted as boys and had milder attacks' (205).

2. *The Jungle Books*: Post-Mutiny Allegories of Empire

1   'Victorian accounts of the Mutiny', Brantlinger observes, 'display extreme forms of extropunitive projection, … an absolute polarization of good and evil, innocence and guilt, justice and injustice, moral restraint and sexual depravity, civilization and barbarism' (200). In the immediate aftermath of the event and throughout the remaining decades of the century, British Mutiny writing is typically marked by sensationalism and 'a general racist and political hysteria' (202).

2   As Brantlinger briefly acknowledges, Kipling's *Kim*, although it is not a Mutiny novel, does address the Mutiny topic (294n.).

3   Lane, who shares my concern with the allegorical dimension of imperial representation, provides a good definition of 'allegory' as I intend it: 'a rhetorical structure that substitutes partial and fragmentary emblems for subjective entities, thus organizing otherwise disparate groups and individuals into effective political units' (2).

4   The urge to remember the Mutiny vividly and concretely, and at the same time to maintain the pre-established, sociogenetic 'lines' of its interpretation, is clearly manifested in the post-Mutiny production of monuments and memorials. As Stokes observes, 'The shell-pocked Kashmiri Gate at Delhi … was left to point its moral. At Kanpur (Cawnpore) a weeping angel carved in marble by Marochetti was placed as a shrine …. At Lucknow the shattered remains of the Residency were left unrepaired, and from the tower the Union Jack continued to be flown day and night, as through most of the siege. … So long as the Raj endured, the living force of these symbols remained' (2).

5   As Brantlinger observes, the Mutiny story is so deeply resonant that the Victorian imagination can submit it, on occasion, to various forms of fictive displacement. First finding in Dickens's 'The Perils of Certain English Prisoners' a restaging of the East Indian crisis in a West Indian setting (207–8), Brantlinger subsequently draws attention to noteworthy inscriptions of the Mutiny in *The Tale of Two Cities* and in Wilkie Collins's *The Moonstone* (208, 295n.). Young, more recently, has noted journalistic remapping of Mutiny discourse onto the slave society of the American South in relation to Lincoln's Emancipation Act and its anxiously forecast sociopolitical consequences (138).

6 John McBratney, in his recent examination of Kipling's jungle saga, offers a similar argument, affirming 'the decisive importance of the British Raj' in the resolution of Mowgli's 'rival allegiances to bestial and human cultures' (287). He also notes that the jungle-man finds (in addition to a wife) 'a new father-figure' in Gisborne, a European, imperial 'father' to replace his 'bestial fathers ... Kaa, Baloo, and Bagheera' (288).

7 Homi Bhabha affirms in a different way the importance of Lacan's conception of the Imaginary for colonial discourse theory: a process of Imaginary identification, which enables the subject 'to postulate a series of equivalences, samenesses, identities, between the objects of the surrounding world', establishes and assures the colonial subject's relationship with the colonial 'stereotype', which is, for Bhabha, a fundamental figure within imperialism's discourse of domination (76–7).

8 Given Kipling's characterization of Gisborne, Inden's use of the figure of the 'jungle officer' is quite startling. As one might expect, Inden is borrowing the figure from the Indological discourses he criticizes. I am certainly tempted to surmise that Gisborne is drawn, at least in part, from the same sources.

9 To place this affirmation of the tiger's outsider status in relation with Inden's scholarship, I should emphasize that Shere Khan's symbolic affiliation is not with 'Hindu' India but, as I have begun to reveal, with Moguls and 'Indo-Aryan' conquerors.

10 Kipling's imaginative participation in an imperial thematics of the tiger-hunt is most clearly revealed in 'The Tomb of His Ancestors' (*The Day's Work*), in which young John Chinn, a newcomer to colonial service, successfully undertakes an initiatory tiger hunt and thus confirms himself as the rightful successor – indeed, the reincarnation – of his grandfather, John Chinn, a revered district administrator.

11 This idea that anarchy precedes British rule and would follow upon British withdrawal can be found in much British writing on India – by Macaulay, Strachey, and others. In *Pax Britannica*, James Morris sums up the British attitude quite nicely: 'By the end of the [nineteenth] century most people assumed, not least the public and the policy-makers at home, that an India without the British would fall apart in communal violence, and relapse into the chaos from which the Empire was supposed to have rescued it' (125).

12 The Cawnpore 'Judith' is famously imaged in an illustration from Charles Ball's 1858 history of the Mutiny (see Brantlinger 198). Here, the porcelain-pale 'Judith' (ostensibly the youngest daughter of General Wheeler of Cawnpore) is shown with blazing pistol in hand, stalwartly defending herself against notably 'black-faced', attacking Mutineers. According to Mutiny lore, the indomitable 'Judith'-Miss Wheeler was taken captive by a rebel, but later 'killed her captor and his family' (Brantlinger 295n.).

13 Although I do not offer any analysis of 'Red Dog' and 'Rikki-Tikki-Tavi', I think both these tales could be brought into a more extensive

discussion of the Mutiny's inscription in *The Jungle Books*. In the former tale a vicious dog pack, marked significantly by the color of blood, pursues a career of terror and destruction, which puts Mowgli's 'Free People' in fear of annihilation. In the latter, as Paffard remarks, one can find a 'more benign parable' to pair with 'The Undertakers', one that presents the mongoose as the 'loyal native' who protects the endangered English family (91).

3. *Stalky & Co.*: Resituating the Empire

1   Argumentative lines similar to that which I propose here have been developed by noteworthy critics whose contributions, although different from mine, deserve mention. Martin Green characterizes the Kipling of the later Victorian and Edwardian periods 'as celebrant of overt imperialism and subverter of literature-as-a-system' (264). Kipling, for Green, subverts the norms of British literary 'high culture', by inscribing propaganda within its putatively disinterested esthetic, by forcing the repatriation of the 'exiled' topics of empire and adventure. More recently, Stephen Arata has undertaken an extended revaluation of Kipling's cultural placement and impact: 'The familiar image of Kipling as popular apologist for the dominant ideology has obscured our view of the turbulence which his initial appearance on the literary scene provoked' (8). Arata proceeds by linking Kipling of the 1890s with 'the transgressive quality of *fin-de-siècle* writing, its calculated and often spectacular deviances' (7).
2   I borrow the phrase 'combat zone' from Carole Scott, who, in 'Kipling's Combat Zones', considers *Stalky & Co.* as an 'otherworld' permeated by violence, a world 'where the expected structural order is consistently sabotaged, and various codes of behavior vie with each other for supremacy' (63). Scott also pertinently notes 'the absence of a clear dividing line between the "Coll." and the "real world"' (65).
3   'Stalky', the first story of *The Complete Stalky & Co.* of 1929, also situates the bulk of its action out of bounds. The reader of the 1929 *Stalky*, having perused the volume's first two stories, 'Stalky' and 'In Ambush', has spent a great deal of time following out-of-bounds shenanigans and very little time within the bounds of the school space.
4   Although he does not squarely confront the issues I raise here, Green remarks upon the repeated inscription of '"savage" and "primitivist" perspectives' in Kipling's school tales and supports the observation with an extensive catalogue of textual citations (273–4).
5   The characterization of the Sergeant represents a key site of the Mutiny's inscription in *Stalky*. Foxy, the Mutiny veteran who will later fulfill the role of drill-master of the cadet corps, codes school struggles not simply as imperial contests but, much more specifically, as displaced re-enactments of the insurgency and counter-insurgency of 1857–58. The presentation of the boys as Orientalized insurgents in 'Slaves of the Lamp, Part I' similarly recalls the Mutiny even as it foretells future careers in the Indian Empire.

6 It is important to note that Buchanan's article inscribes itself within an intensely contested ideological arena. Buchanan's dissenting voice, which flies in the face of Kipling's contemporary lionization in both the political and cultural spheres, provokes various responses, most notably from Walter Besant and Clive Holland. Besant's 'Is It the Voice of the Hooligan?' (also appearing in the *Contemporary Review*) calls Buchanan's ethics and motives into question and approvingly evaluates Kipling's artistry, morality, and politics. Holland, publishing in *Literature*, tends to steer a middle course between Buchanan and Besant, but finds in Kipling's work, and especially in *Stalky & Co.*, a grievous lack of accuracy and verisimilitude. The Kipling debate apparently commanded considerable public attention, as is evidenced by the publication, in 1900, of *The Voice of 'The Hooligan': A Discussion of Kiplingism*, which brings together in book form the disparate views of co-authors Buchanan and Besant.

7 Clearly, the overall movement of my 'hooligan' argument posits a special resonance for 'Ireland' and 'the Irish' within British imperial discourse: both are taken to evoke at once the imperial centre and its peripheries. Such a stance is not, however, without precedent. Wegner notes Kim's double position as a subject to be located both in 'the colonial periphery and the centre'. Citing Fredric Jameson, Wegner goes on to observe that occupied Ireland represents 'the unique national analogue of this double position' (154). Considering then the question of Kim's Irish identity, Wegner suggests that *Kim* may be 'about' Ireland as much as it is 'about' India: the text would thus perform 'a utopian reconstruction of increasingly restive Irish populace; a neutralization of the Sinn Fein movement that had been founded only two years before the publication of *Kim*' (155).

8 Stalky's special prestige in the Sikh community is tellingly confirmed by the fact that his name can be deployed in lieu of the more conventional signs that order and facilitate intersubjective exchange. Affiliation with Stalky, the right to use his name, is as good as money: concluding his anecdotal narrative, M'Turk relates, ''Told me ... that if I wanted any supplies I'd better say I was Koran Sahib's *bhai* [brother]; and I did, and the Sikhs wouldn't take my money' (296).

9 This 'color line' is derived from W. E. B. Du Bois, who coined the phrase, in 1903, to name the 'problem of the Twentieth Century' (qtd. in Mohanty, 'Drawing' 314). Mohanty elaborates upon his source in his account of the post-Mutiny 'racialization' of British imperial ideology, arguing that the category of race became, after 1857, fundamental to the coding and hierarchizing of the various subject communities of British India.

10 Cultural hybridization briefly becomes an issue in Hobson's chapter 'Imperialism in Asia', where he laments that 'the conditions of free, close, personal contact between British and Indians are virtually non-existent', adding that 'inter-marriage, the only effective mode of amalgamating two civilizations', is even less in evidence. Yet the histo-

rian goes on to observe that, from the European perspective, the Indian mind presents 'a series of baffling psychological puzzles', and to assert, regretfully, 'the impossibility of ... close, persistent, interactive contact of mind with mind' (301).

4. *Kim*: Disciplinary Power and Cultural Hybridity

1 Stokes notes an unmistakable influence of Panopticon in the construction of the nineteenth-century prisons at Poona and Ratnagiri, and remarks that Viceroy Elphinstone favoured a project for a panoptical penitentiary on Bombay Island. James Mill also was among Panopticon's admirers, and one who favoured Indian applications (see *English* 149–50, 325n.).

2 Kim's mobile, socially unbounded selfhood, his capacity to cross and recross cultural boundaries, receives extensive consideration in Judith Plotz's 'The Empire of Youth'. Aptly characterizing Kim as 'an adolescent inhabitant of the border territory between childhood and manhood' (112), Plotz observes: 'All India, especially that which is out of bounds, is Kim's province' (115).

3 Foucault, in *Discipline and Punish*, documents a nineteenth-century French juvenile delinquent whose case provides a fairly precise analogue to that of Kim. Béasse is brought before the law in 1840. Foucault pieces the interrogation together from contemporary journalistic accounts: 'The Judge: One must sleep at home. – Béasse: Have I got a home? – ... What is your station in life? – My station: ... I don't work for anybody. I've worked for myself for a long time now.... I turn cartwheels on the avenue de Neuilly; at night there are the shows; I open coach doors, I sell pass-out tickets; I've plenty to do.... – Does not your father wish to reclaim you? – Haven't got no father. ... No mother neither ... free and independent' (290–1). Béasse is able to offer an ironic challenge to legal process because, jovial and *sans regrets*, he refuses to provide any of the 'handles' (residence, occupation, familial affiliation) by which the law may apprehend and locate him as a legal subject. In the figure of Béasse, as the leftist press is prompt to affirm, 'crime manifests "a fortunate irrepressibility of human nature"' (289). Foucault observes, 'All the illegalities that the court defined as offenses the accused reformulated as the affirmation of living force: the lack of a home as vagabondage, the lack of a master as independence, the lack of work as freedom, the lack of a time-table as a fullness of days and nights' (290).

4 The deployments of race and ethnicity I describe here clearly reflect what S. P. Mohanty characterizes as the post-Mutiny 'racialization' of intercultural relations under the Raj. This racialization entails the production of an essentializing, hierarchizing discourse of race that 'narrates conditions of political and ethical possibility, defining and reshaping ideas, ideologies, and interests' ('Drawing' 314). Clearly, it is only in the context of such racialization of the colonial Indian cultural scene that Kim's 'Englishness' and 'whiteness' can be asserted in the face

of the concurrently acknowledged peculiarities of his acculturation. Racialization must therefore be understood as an important aspect of the disciplinarization of the Indian Empire, which I will shortly be delineating.

5 As Inden observes, the Indological imaging of Indian culture as a 'sponge' is almost as commonplace as the 'jungle' metaphor (85ff.). The 'sponge' is clearly implicit in the evocation of a 'darkness' that engulfs or swallows.

6 Mohanty remarks that India unfolds under Kim's eye in ways that 'mark *potential* distinctions and discriminations in ways of seeing and knowing' ('Drawing' 318) – hence the importance of seeing as reading. Kim is called upon to develop a 'specific faculty of perceiving unities and differences as *interpretable* social facts', to become 'a competent and reliable reader of texts, ultimately, in fact, of society as text' ('Drawing' 317–18). In Chapter 5, also on *Kim*, I discuss Kipling's remaking of Indian culture as text.

7 Particularly striking evocations of imperial alienation occur in 'Thrown Away' (*Plain Tales from the Hills*), 'At the End of the Passage' and 'The City of Dreadful Night' (*Life's Handicap*).

8 For a fuller account of the problems besetting the Anglicizing initiative of the Raj, see Viswanathan's sixth chapter, 'The Failure of English'. Concluding this chapter, she focuses upon 'the tension between the upward mobility promised by modern studies and the limited opportunities open to the colonized for advancement. ... At one level, education as part of the state is complicit with the reproduction of an economic and social order. But because education is also expected to provide opportunities for advancement, it becomes an arena of social conflict' (164). Moreover, 'The colonial subject's resistance to British rule occurs in the ideological space created by this contradiction, transforming education in its dual aspects of social control and social advancement into the supreme paradox of British power' (165).

9 The black-bearded, fakir-aspected Lurgan is perhaps to be understood as Eurasian, a possibility suggested in Kim's ambivalent appraisal of him: 'He was a Sahib in that he wore a Sahib's clothes; the accent of his Urdu, the intonation of his English, showed that he was anything but a Sahib' (151).

10 In the chapter 'By Bread Alone' of *The Location of Culture*, Homi Bhabha presents an extensive discussion of the relationship between rumor and insurgency, emphasizing rumor's 'indeterminacy', its 'performative power of circulation' and, most crucially, its close, energizing link with 'panic' (200).

5. *Kim*: Ethnography and the Hybrid Boy

1 In accord with Saidian scholarship, the quotation marks enclosing 'Orient' are intended to mark it as a concept and to question it as a

designation of a cultural actuality or locale. Having thus noted the dubi-
ousness of 'Orient' and 'Oriental' as terms of cultural description, I will
henceforth omit the quotation marks.

2 In '*Kim* and Orientalism', Patrick Williams isolates Orientalist 'knowledge' as an 'adjunct of colonial control', which, in Kipling's novel, most
often takes 'the form of bold syntheses, universal norms, invariant
truths about Orientals' (41). For Williams, '[f]oremost among such
truths is that of the duplicitous, perpetually untruthful Oriental' (42); I
stress, however, Kipling's production of 'truths' about Oriental time.

3 The treatment of Teshoo-lama provides an instructive case in point.
From his first appearance a thematics of childhood attaches to the character. He is pictured as 'helpless'(5), unable to make his own way in the
world – in need of direction, incapable of effectively providing for his
fundamental need for food. He promptly manifests guilelessness (a
childish trait with which the precocious Kim is not burdened) and a
capacity for wonderment. Explicit inscriptions of the child-figure soon
follow: the lama presents the curator with a note of introduction bearing
'clumsy, childish print' (7); touring the museum, the holy man is
'delighted as a child at each new trove' (8); 'Simply as a child' (13), the
old man delivers his begging-bowl to Kim; he discusses future projects
with his new-found disciple, speaking as 'hopefully as a child' (34).

4 Juniper Ellis has recently analyzed Kim's role in the cultural production
of 'whiteness'. She also acknowledges, however, that characters like Kim
and Hurree Babu register 'the formation of a new subjectivity ... as a
result of colonial contact' (318).

5 Judith Plotz notes the foregrounding of 'linguistic "code switching"' in
Kim, affirming that 'The India of *Kim* is not a babel but a harmony of
many voices' (115) and that 'Kipling's single *Kim* idiom contains all the
differing codes' (116). While I would not contradict either statement, I
would observe that neither acknowledges the narrator as a character
who speaks various voices and participates in various codes.
Considering the narrator as an authoritative yet involved speaker
complicates considerably the issue of 'code switching'.

6 My focus is upon the narrator's relationship with Kim. I do not posit
Kim as a pure site of being and belonging – an untenable position
insofar as Kim's engagement in the Great Game seriously compromises
his insider status with respect to Indian culture and involves him in the
same subjective dilemmas I have ascribed to the narrator.

7 As Plotz points out, 'By a genial touch "Kim" means *who* in Turkish, so
that "who" is "Kim" and "Kim" is "who".' However, the unfortunate
boy, 'necessarily self-unknowing, "knows no Turki"' (114). This canny
reader's translation of 'Kim' (a translation that neither the boy nor any
other character within the text seems capable of performing) only
serves, however, to further encrypt the mystery of identity: the question
becomes who is who and what is who.

8 Colonel Creighton, to and through whom a vast amount of ethnological and political information flows, comes very close to an imperial

restatement of Tyler's 'first law': 'The more one knows about natives the less one can say what they will or won't do' (111). For Bart Moore-Gilbert, Creighton's startling admission of the limits of his ethnological expertise manifests 'Kipling's deep scepticism about ... the extent of colonial knowledge and power' ('Bhabhal' 121) and stands as a decidedly perturbing challenge to the view of Kipling as an unwavering upholder of 'imperial certainties' (121, 119).

Works Cited

Abellán, José Luis. *Historia Crítica del Pensamiento Español*. Vol. 2. Madrid: Espasa-Calpe, 1979.

Althusser, Louis. 'Ideology and Ideological State Apparatuses'. *Lenin and Philosophy and Other Essays*. Trans. Ben Brewster. New York: Monthly Review Press, 1971. 121–73.

Arata, Stephen D. 'A Universal Foreignness: Kipling in the Fin-de-Siècle'. *English Literature in Transition (1880–1920)*, 36.1 (1993): 7–38.

Ariès, Philippe. *Centuries of Childhood: A Social History of Family Life*. New York: Knopf, 1962.

Asad, Talal. 'The Concept of Cultural Translation in British Social Anthropology'. Clifford and Marcus 141–64.

Baden-Powell, R. S. S. *Scouting For Boys: A Handbook for Instruction in Good Citizenship*. London: n.p., 1908.

Ballantyne, R. M. *The Coral Island*. London: Puffin, 1982.

Barrie, J. M. *Peter Pan*. London: Puffin, 1982.

Bentham, Jeremy. *The Works of Jeremy Bentham*. Ed. John Bowring. Vol. 9. Edinburgh: William Tait, 1843.

Besant, Walter. 'Is It the Voice of the Hooligan?'. *Contemporary Review* 77 (Jan. 1900): 27–39.

Bhabha, Homi K. *The Location of Culture*. London: Routledge, 1994.

Blake, William. *Selected Poems*. Ed. P. H. Butter. London: Dent, 1982.

Boas, George. *The Cult of Childhood*. London: Warburg Institute, 1966.

Brantlinger, Patrick. *Rule of Darkness: British Literature and Imperialism, 1830–1914*. Ithaca: Cornell UP, 1988.

Bristow, Joseph. *Empire Boys: Adventures in a Man's World*. London: HarperCollins, 1991.

Buchanan, Robert. 'The Voice of "the Hooligan"'. *Contemporary Review* 76 (Dec. 1899): 774–89.

Buchanan, Robert Williams and Sir Walter Besant. *The Voice of 'the Hooligan': A Discussion of Kiplingism*. New York: Tucker, 1900.

Burke, Edmund. *The Writings and Speeches of Edmund Burke*. Vol. 5: *India: Madras and Bengal, 1774–1785*. Ed. P. J. Marshall. Oxford: Clarendon Press, 1981.

Burroughs, Edgar Rice. *Tarzan of the Apes*. New York: Ballantine, 1983.

Chaudhuri, Napur and Margaret Strobel. Introduction. *Western Women and Imperialism: Complicity and Resistance*. Ed. Chaudhuri and Strobel. Bloomington: Indiana UP, 1992.

Chaudhuri, S. B. *Theories of the Indian Mutiny (1857–59)*. Calcutta: World Press, 1965.

Clifford, James. 'Introduction: Partial Truths'. Clifford and Marcus 1–26.

—— 'On Ethnographic Allegory'. Clifford and Marcus 98–121.

—— *The Predicament of Culture: Twentieth Century Ethnography, Literature, and Art*. Cambridge Mass.: Harvard UP, 1988.

Clifford, James, and George E. Marcus, eds. *Writing Culture: The Poetics and Politics of Ethnography*. Berkeley: U of California P, 1986.

Conrad, Joseph. *Heart of Darkness*. London: Penguin, 1973.

David, Deirdre. 'Children of Empire: Victorian Imperialism and Sexual Politics in Dickens and Kipling'. *Gender and Discourse in Victorian Literature and Art*. Ed Anthony Harrison and Beverly Taylor. DeKalb: Northern Illinois UP, 1992. 124–42.

Defoe, Daniel. *Robinson Crusoe*. London and New York: Oxford UP, 1972.

DeMause, Lloyd. 'The Evolution of Childhood'. *The History of Childhood*. New York: Psychohistory Press, 1974. 1–73.

Demos, John, and Virginia Demos. 'Adolescence in Historical Perspective'. *Journal of Marriage and the Family* 31.4 (Nov. 1969): 632–8.

Dickens, Charles. *Oliver Twist*. Oxford: Oxford UP, 1982.

Dingley, Robert. 'Shades of the Prison House: Discipline and Surveillance in *Tom Brown's Schooldays*'. *Victorian Review* 22.1 (Summer 1996): 1–12.

Dunae, Patrick. 'New Grub Street for Boys'. *Imperialism and Juvenile Literature*. Ed. Jeffrey Richards. Manchester: Manchester UP, 1989. 12–33.

—— 'Penny Dreadfuls: Late Nineteenth-Century Boys' Literature and Crime'. *Victorian Studies* 22.2 (Winter 1979): 133–50.

Dyhouse, Carol. *Girls Growing Up in Late Victorian and Edwardian England*. London: Routledge & Kegan Paul, 1981.

Elias, Norbert. *The Civilizing Process: The History of Manners*. Vol. 1 of 2. Trans. Edmund Jephcott. New York: Urizen, 1978.

—— *The Civilizing Process: State Formation and Civilization*. Vol. 2 of 2. Trans. Edmund Jephcott. Oxford: Basil Blackwell, 1982.

Ellis, Juniper. 'Writing Race: Education and Ethnography in Kipling's *Kim*'. *Centennial Review* 39.2 (Spring 1995): 315–29.

Fabian, Johannes. *Time and the Other: How Anthropology Makes Its Object*. New York: Columbia UP, 1983.

Farrar, F. W. *Eric: Or, Little by Little*. New York, Garland, 1977.

Foucault, Michel. *Discipline and Punish: The Birth of the Prison*. Trans. Alan Sheridan. New York: Vintage, 1979.

—— *The History of Sexuality. Volume 1: An Introduction*. Trans. Robert Hurley. New York: Vintage, 1990.

Freud, Sigmund. 'The Uncanny'. *New Literary History* 7 (Spring 1976): 619–45.

Gillis, John R. *Youth and History: Tradition and Change in European Age Relations, 1770–Present*. New York and London: Academic Press, 1974.

Gournay, Jean-François. 'Ésquisse d'une lecture anthropologique de *Kim*'. *Études Anglaises: Grande Bretagne, États Unis* 35.4 (1982): 385–95.

Green, Martin. *Dreams of Adventure, Deeds of Empire*. New York: Basic Books, 1979.

Guha, Ranajit. 'The Prose of Counter-Insurgency'. *Selected Subaltern Studies*. Ed. Ranajit Guha and Gayatri Chakravorty Spivak. New York: Oxford UP, 1988. 45–86.

Hall, G. Stanley. *Adolescence*. 2 vols. New York: Arno and New York Times, 1969.

Henty, G. A. *The Young Colonists: A Story of the Zulu and Boer Wars*. Glasgow: Blackie, 1898.

Hobsbawm, E. J. *The Age of Empire, 1875–1914*. London: Weidenfeld & Nicolson, 1987.

Hobson, J. A. *Imperialism: A Study*. London: Allen & Unwin, 1954.

Holland, Clive (Charles James Hankinson). 'Rudyard Kipling and His Critics'. *Literature* (London) 6 (Feb. 1900): 153–4.

Hughes, Thomas. *Tom Brown's Schooldays*. Oxford: Oxford UP, 1989.

Hutchins, Francis. *The Illusion of Permanence: British Imperialism in India*. Princeton: Princeton UP, 1967.

Inden, Ronald. *Imagining India*. Oxford: Blackwell, 1990.

Islam, Shamsul. *Kipling's 'Law': A Study of His Philosophy of Life*. London: Macmillan, 1975.

JanMohamed, Abdul R. 'The Economy of Manichean Allegory: The Function of Racial Difference in Colonialist Literature'. *'Race', Writing, and Difference*. Ed. Henry Louis Gates, Jr. Chicago: U of Chicago P, 1986. 78–106.

Kinkead-Weekes, Mark. 'Vision in Kipling's Novels'. *Kipling's Mind and Art*. Ed. Andrew Rutherford. Edinburgh: Oliver & Boyd, 1964. 197–234.

Kipling, Rudyard. *The Complete Verse*. London: Kyle Cathie, 1990.

—— *The Day's Work*. Ed. Thomas Pinney. Oxford: Oxford UP, 1987.

—— *Departmental Ditties. Barrack-Room Ballads, and Other Verses. The Five Nations. The Seven Seas*. Garden City, NY: Doubleday, Page, 1927.

—— *The Jungle Books*. Ed. W. W. Robson. Oxford: Oxford UP, 1992.

—— *Kim*. Ed. Alan Sandison. Oxford: Oxford UP, 1987.

—— *Life's Handicap*. Ed. A. O. J. Cockshut. Oxford: Oxford UP, 1987.

—— *Plain Tales from the Hills*. Ed. Andrew Rutherford. Oxford: Oxford UP, 1987.

—— *Soldiers Three. The Story of the Gadsbys. In Black and White*. London: Macmillan, 1960.

—— *Something of Myself and Other Autobiographical Writings*. Ed. Thomas Pinney. Cambridge: Cambridge UP, 1990.

—— *Stalky & Co*. Ed. Isabel Quigly. Oxford: Oxford UP, 1987.

Krupat, Arnold. *Ethnocriticism: Ethnography, History, Literature*. Berkeley: U of California P, 1992.

Lacan, Jacques. *Écrits: A Selection*. Trans. Alan Sheridan. New York: W. W. Norton, 1977.

Lane, Christopher. *The Ruling Passion: British Colonial Allegory and the Paradox of Homosexual Desire*. Durham, NC, and London: Duke UP, 1995.

Locke, John. *Some Thoughts Concerning Education*. London: Cambridge UP, 1934.

Low, Gail Ching-Liang. *White Skins/Black Masks: Representation, Colonialism and Cultural Cross-Dressing*. New York: Routledge, 1996.

Macaulay, Thomas Babington. *Critical and Historical Essays*. Vol. 2. London: Dent, 1907.

—— *Selected Writings*. Ed. John Clive and Thomas Pinney. Chicago and London: U of Chicago P, 1972.

McBratney, John. 'Imperial Subjects, Imperial Space in Kipling's *Jungle Book*'. *Victorian Studies* 35.3 (Spring 1992): 277–93.

McClintock, Anne. *Imperial Leather: Race, Gender and Sexuality in the Colonial Contest*. New York: Routledge, 1995.

McClure, John A. *Kipling and Conrad: The Colonial Fiction*. Cambridge, Mass.: Harvard UP, 1981.

Macdonald, Robert H. *Sons of the Empire: The Frontier and the Boy Scout Movement, 1890–1918*. Toronto: U of Toronto P, 1993.

Macherey, Pierre. *The Theory of Literary Production*. Trans. Geoffrey Wall. London: Routledge & Kegan Paul, 1978.

Marcus, George E. 'Contemporary Problems of Ethnography in the Modern World System'. Clifford and Marcus 165–93.

Marryat, Captain. *Masterman Ready*. New York: Garland, 1976.

Mill, James. *The History of British India*. 2nd edn. 6 vols. London: Baldwin, Cradock, & Joy, 1820.

Mohanty, Satya P. 'Drawing the Color Line: Kipling and the Culture of Colonial Rule'. *The Bounds of Race: Perspectives on Hegemony and Resistance*. Ed. Dominick LaCapra. Ithaca: Cornell UP, 1991. 311–43.

—— 'Kipling's Children and the Colour Line'. *Race & Class* 31.1 (1989): 21–39.

Montaigne, Michel de. *Essays and Selected Writings*. Bilingual Edition. Trans. Donald M. Frame. New York: St. Martin's Press, 1963.

Moore-Gilbert, Bart. '"The Bhabhal of Tongues": Reading Kipling, Reading Bhabha'. *Writing India, 1757–1990: The Literature of British India*. Ed. Bart Moore-Gilbert. Manchester and New York: Manchester UP, 1996. 111–38.

—— *Kipling and 'Orientalism'*. New York: St. Martin's Press, 1986.

Morris, James. *Farewell the Trumpets: An Imperial Retreat*. London: Penguin, 1979.

—— *Heaven's Command: An Imperial Progress*. London: Penguin, 1979.

—— *Pax Britannica: The Climax of an Empire*. London: Penguin, 1979.

Moss, Robert F. *Rudyard Kipling and the Fiction of Adolescence*. New York: St. Martin's Press, 1982.

Mukherjee, Sujit. 'Tigers in Fiction: An Aspect of the Colonial Encounter'. *Kunapipi* 9.1 (1987): 1–13.

Murray, John. 'The Law of *The Jungle Books*'. *Children's Literature* 20. Ed. F. Butler, B. Rosen, and J. Plotz. Roanoke, Va.: Yale UP, 1992. 1–14.

Musgrove, F. *Youth and the Social Order*. London: Routledge & Kegan Paul, 1964.

The Oxford English Dictionary. 2nd edn. 20 vols. Oxford: Clarendon Press, 1989.

Paffard, Mark. *Kipling's Indian Fiction*. Basingstoke: Macmillan, 1989.

Parry, Benita. 'The Contents and Discontents of Kipling's Imperialism'. *New Formations* 6 (1988): 49–63.

Phillips, Richard. *Mapping Men and Empire: A Geography of Adventure*. London and New York: Routledge, 1997.

Plotz, Judith A. 'The Empire of Youth: Crossing and Double-Crossing Cultural Barriers in Kipling's *Kim'*. *Children's Literature* 20. Ed. F. Butler, B. Rosen, and J. Plotz. Roanoke, Va.: Yale UP, 1992. 111–31.

Poovey, Mary. *Uneven Developments: The Ideological Work of Gender in Mid-Victorian England*. Chicago: U of Chicago P, 1988.

Pratt, Mary Louise. *Imperial Eyes: Travel Writing and Transculturation*. London: Routledge, 1992.

Quick, R. H. Introduction. *Some Thoughts Concerning Education*. By John Locke. London: Cambridge UP, 1934.

Quigly, Isabel. *The Heirs of Tom Brown: The English School Story*. London: Chatto & Windus, 1982.

Richards, Jeffrey. Introduction. *Imperialism and Juvenile Literature*. Ed. Jeffrey Richards. Manchester: Manchester UP, 1989. 1–11.

Rose, Jacqueline. *The Case of Peter Pan or The Impossibility of Children's Fiction*. London: Macmillan, 1984.

Rousseau, Jean-Jacques. *Émile*. London: Dent, 1911.

Said, Edward W. *Culture and Imperialism*. New York: Knopf, 1993.

—— *Orientalism*. New York: Vintage, 1979.

Schweinitz, Karl de, Jr. *The Rise and Fall of British India: Imperialism as Inequality*. London: Methuen, 1983.

Scott, Carole. 'Kipling's Combat Zones: Training Grounds in the Mowgli stories, *Captains Courageous*, and *Stalky & Co.*' *Children's Literature* 20. Ed. F. Butler, B. Rosen, and J. Plotz. Roanoke, Va.: Yale UP, 1992. 52–68.

Sharpe, Jenny. *Allegories of Empire: The Figure of Woman in the Colonial Text*. Minneapolis: U of Minnesota P, 1993.

—— 'The Unspeakable Limits of Rape: Colonial Violence and Counter-Insurgency'. *Genders* 10 (Spring 1991): 25–46.

Slemon, Stephen. 'Monuments of Empire: Allegory/Counter-Discourse/Post-Colonial Writing'. *Kunapipi* 9.3 (1987): 1–16.

Sommerville, C. John. *The Rise and Fall of Childhood*. Beverly Hills: Sage, 1982.

Spacks, Patricia Meyer. *The Adolescent Idea: Myths of Youth and the Adult Imagination*. New York, Basic Books, 1981.

Spear, Percival. *A History of India*. Vol. 2. Harmondsworth: Penguin, 1965.

Spivak, Gayatri Chakravorty. 'Can the Subaltern Speak?' *Marxism and the Interpretation of Culture*. Ed. Cary Nelson and Lawrence Grossberg. Urbana: U of Illinois P, 1988. 271–313.

Springhall, John. *Coming of Age: Adolescence in Britain 1860–1960*. Dublin: Gill & Macmillan, 1986.

Stokes, Eric. *The English Utilitarians and India*. Oxford: Clarendon Press, 1959.

—— *The Peasant Armed: The Indian Revolt of 1857*. Ed. C. A. Bayly. Oxford: Clarendon Press, 1986.

Stoler, Ann Laura. *Race and the Education of Desire: Foucault's* History of Sexuality *and the Colonial Order of Things*. Durham, NC, and London: Duke UP, 1995.

Strachey, Sir John. *India*. London: Kegan Paul, 1888.

Suleri, Sara. *The Rhetoric of English India*. Chicago: U of Chicago P, 1992.

Sullivan, Zohreh T. *Narratives of Empire: The Fictions of Rudyard Kipling*. Cambridge: Cambridge UP, 1993.

Turner, Victor. *Dramas, Fields, Metaphors: Symbolic Action in Human Society*. Ithaca: Cornell UP, 1974.

Tyler, Stephen A. 'Post-Modern Ethnography: From the Document of the Occult to the Occult Document'. Clifford and Marcus 122–40.

Viswanathan, Gauri. *Masks of Conquest: Literary Study and British Rule in India*. New York: Columbia UP, 1989.

Watson, Ian. 'Victorian England, Colonialism and the Ideology of *Tom Brown's Schooldays*'. *Zeitschrift für Anglistik und Amerikanistik* 29.2 (1981): 116–29.

Wegner, Phillip E. '"Life as He Would Have It": The Invention of India in Kipling's *Kim*'. *Cultural Critique* (Winter 1993–94): 129–59.

Williams, Patrick. '*Kim* and Orientalism'. *Kipling Considered*. Ed. Phillip Mallet. London: Macmillan, 1989. 33–55.

Wurgaft, Lewis D. *The Imperial Imagination: Magic and Myth in Kipling's India*. Middletown, Conn.: Wesleyan UP, 1983.

Young, Robert J. C. *Colonial Desire: Hybridity in Theory, Culture and Race*. London and New York: Routledge, 1995.

Zipes, Jack. *Fairy Tales and the Art of Subversion: The Classical Genre for Children and the Process of Civilization*. New York: Wildman, 1983.

Žižek, Slavoj. *The Sublime Object of Ideology*. London: Verso, 1989.

Index